It's

In The Script!

A HUMOROUS THRILLER
INVOLVING A PRESENT-DAY TV SOAP OPERA
SET IN THE 18TH CENTURY

By

Simon Holder

BY THE SAME AUTHOR:

THE REVOLUTION OF THE SPECIES – a topical environmental thriller

FOR THE LOVE OF A LIFE – an unusual international love story set in England and China

Simon Holder

CONTENTS

PROLOGUE

The line just would not come. He had spent almost two hours looking at what was intended to be the final page of his current script yet it remained a blank. He twirled the fountain-pen in his fingers, as if waving a magic wand which would induce creativity to flow onto the paper but it just fell out of his grasp and made a covid-shaped mess on the virgin page...

Alun had been writing scripts for this series for over seven years and he was responsible for the plotlines, too; for him, it was easy money and he was fêted in the TV industry for his clever dialogue and convoluted but easily-understood scripts which had ensured a huge following for this ever-so-popular soap opera, *'Jonquil's Journals'*, set in 18th century London, featuring a Justice of the Peace named Bartholomew Jonquil.

He never used a PC until the second draft as relentless staring at a screen gave him migraine; yet even without that hindrance the elusive elicitation of the final dialogue and clever *bon mot* to finish the piece, get his wife to type it up and send it so wonderfully electronically to both him and the open maw of the producer's PC was not just concerning him but actively annoying him. He had had writer's block before, of course – any writer had – but his fertile mind could not understand why today it was not just evasive but stubbornly unavailable. He had had some terse words with his wife that morning, which always put him off balance but she had been particularly acid with one of her barbs and he wondered whether, after over twenty years of marriage, they should call it a day. The problem was that he relied upon her so much; she brought him coffee, endured his rages and script-induced pontifications, typed his longhand draft scripts up... and still found time to do the cooking, tidy up, wash and iron his clothes and generally keep him away from any tedium. Yet they both knew that their marriage was not what it had been; and after he had met his producer's new assistant at a script meeting some weeks ago, the image of her young face and lithe body – enhanced by some concupiscent looks and a carefree laugh – had taunted his thoughts ever since.

Suspecting that this was the reason he could not concentrate, his thoughts went off on a tangent as the frustration this girl induced metamorphosed into a lucid series of torrid situations playing out in his mind as once again he found himself imagining how he could see her again. And then ask her out. But that was actually the most difficult part: she was in London and he was out here in rural Wales. He was also overweight, hairy and flabby; his joints ached and he relied too much on alcohol and cigarettes to spark his imagination, being somewhat wheezy as a result. Exercise and he were also alien concepts to one another so he had reluctantly concluded that, all in all, this goddess, Leini, was a lost cause. And yet…

She had obviously been aware of his name when he first met her, and had said how much she liked his scripts; that could have been an instruction from Jonathan, his script editor and producer, of course, yet he felt it had come from the heart. And when she laughed at his jokes, he had felt even better; his wife, Dilys, never did, usually looking up to heaven with a bored look as if implying he was not the wit he thought he was and that the word would be better prefaced with a 't'.

Alun had spent the whole of the previous day's train journey back to Tref-Y-Clawdd struggling with the competing tasks of developing the general storyline for the next thirty or so episodes and increasingly outlandish options for trying to see Leini again. As a complication to this, he had also found himself more frequently contemplating the uncharitable thought of how he could get rid of Dilys. Yet the domestic day had taken over again after she collected him from the station and he had had to force himself to concentrate on the plotlines. After all, if he did not, then he would never be able to see this paean to perfection again anyway.

So he started using his creative flair to mastermind the perfect murder, which was something that he and Jonathan had discussed as a sub-plot for one of the characters in *Jonquil's Journals* and thus would exercise his mind; and if any slips became apparent in the course of the writing, then he and others – perhaps Leini, too! – would obviously discover those weaknesses and they could be rectified… before he actually perpetrated the deed in reality! Yes, it was a good plan: in addition, as his thoughts of a new life had taken seed, he had chastised himself for becoming so unfit, flabby and ugly so – much to the astonishment of Dilys – had suddenly started going for walks, stopped smoking, curtailed his drinking, administered the occasional shave and generally started to tone up.

To his wife, Dilys, all this was hysterical; to Alun, it was survival.

Dramatis Personae – Jonquil's Journals

Bartholomew Jonquil, a Justice of the Peace....

Hattie Wiggins, Housekeeper to Jonquil, wife of Edmund...

Edmund Wiggins, disgruntled husband to Mrs. Wiggins...

Jonas Orchard, a provider of victuals and likely lad....

Abel Price, a murderous rogue...

Zaccheus, as above....

Sander Montoya, a South American tavern and house of ill repute owner...

Jenny, a whore who works for Sander but has lofty ambitions...

Dulcie, as above, but without the lofty ambitions...

Divers other Justices, servants, low-life, whores and tradesmen...

*

CHAPTER 1

After much duress, the plotlines for the next thirty-six episodes of *Jonquil's Journals* had finally been loosely sketched out with Jonathan; Jonathan was always open to any extra twists, however, and one of the characters had been left rather bereft of a situation, which Alun was expected to provide as the muse struck him. The problem was that the muse had struck him very hard indeed in the shape of Leini and so it became incumbent upon him to cunningly feature her in the story, portrayed as a character in the soap, whose name would be Jenny. The actress playing Jenny was nowhere as attractive as his real-life obsession, but she was pretty enough to be a substitute in his mind as he started to lay his plans. Alun had decided that, as part of his subterfuge, he should buy a small flat in London, not because he liked the place any more since his licentious youth but because it would give him the ability to do unrestricted research without Dilys being any the wiser as to his machinations. And, of course, have a love-nest far from his wife if he could manage it. Miraculously, this intention had at last cleared his writer's block and the dialogue and situations fair fell out onto the page; so much so that, on a number of occasions, when hearing Dilys' calls for lunch, he wilfully ignored them so he would not break his torrent of ideas – or hopes. The dog being the receptacle of his uneaten meals, the former became bulkier and Alun contributed to his goal of losing weight.

"I'm going up to London tomorrow," he stated to Dilys one morning; "I want to see Jonathan and also there's some research I need to do which is not adequately disbursed by Google."

"What sort of research?" Dilys enquired in her sonorous Welsh accent, as her generous cardigan, already liberally covered with hairs, congealed food and bits of this and that, attracted a few more of the edible variety as she embalmed a prodigiously-sized cake with butter icing.

"I need to go and see some estate agents, and I have some ideas for one of the characters which I can only really discuss face to face with Jonathan."

"We have estate agents down here," she replied trenchantly, as she popped a cherry on the top of the iced cake, whilst some extra alien bits continued their brief stop on her cardigan and landed on the confection.

"Yes, but they're not as cut-throat as the London ones – you know, all pushy fast wide-boys with even faster women, flashy cars and, me, me, me, money, money, money…"

"I think some of them are pretty fast… They sold Glynis from Mold's house very quickly, I remember…"

Alun's dear rural wife… he left her with her own interpretation rather than his intended meaning of fast as in 'grasping' and 'licentious' but was grateful for her naivety as the thought of him being in a fast sports car with Leini obliterated all others and he fell silent, staring at the plump cake with its cherry sitting proudly atop.

"You'll be having some of that later, if you want," she stated, as Alun's daydream associated the item with his yearning for being in bed with his muse and hoping that Dilys' statement would prove true. He broke off from his reverie and announced in an unexpected falsetto, "I'll go and ring Jonathan to see if he can make tomorrow, then," and walked out.

Upstairs in his study, he looked out at the rolling hills of Herefordshire in the distance and wondered if he could actually afford a flat in London; yet his career was doing well, there were other writing offers, and the mortgage on Dilys' house, called Broom's End, was mercifully non-existent. He had been the beneficiary when her first husband died, just in time to see the last payment completed. He and Dilys had then constructed a beautiful sunroom from which they could take in the beauties of the area – although not in winter, when the mainly glass structure was perishingly cold and damp. Summer, too – which generally lasted only about a month anyway.

He dialled the number and waited for Jonathan to reply, only being suddenly enchanted by a delightful female voice which chirruped sunlight on every syllable.

"Ah, who's that?" he enquired uncertainly, suspecting it was Leini but wanting to make sure before he said anything untoward.

"Hi, Alun, it's Leini. How are you? Haven't seen you in ages. When are you coming up to see us?"

"Ah, hello… How nice to talk to you… Leini… Yes, er, well, I was thinking of coming up to the Smoke tomorrow, actually, if Jonathan's available."

"Let me see… No, it looks as if he'll be out all day tomorrow, but I'll be here if there's anything I can help you with." Completely dumbfounded by the intoxication of her voice and the invitation, he just did not know what to say next.

"Hello? Alun? Are you still there?"

"Oh, er. Yes… I was just wondering if there were indeed some things I could discuss with you… alone…. I mean, that Jonathan could run past you that you could pass on to me…discuss… perhaps?"

"Yes, there are, actually; we had a script meeting together yesterday and we came up with some changes that I'm sure I could pass on to you… If you're willing to trust me, of course!" This was said with that lovely throwaway lilt in her voice that Alun only at that moment realised was the foundation of her attractiveness.

"Erm, yes, that would be great; why not?" he said a little too earnestly, then added, "I might possibly stay the night in London, actually; a few more things I want to do, exhibitions and plays I want to see… so we could discuss them tomorrow and I'll take a look at them in the evening and then meet Jonathan the day after. That would be tidy, wouldn't it?"

"Great idea. Why not? He should be here all day the day after… So what time can I expect you tomorrow?"

"Ah, well, I'll take the earliest train so I should be at Paddington by around 11 and with you at the studios by 12. How does that sound?"

"Excellent. I'll book a table in the executive dining room so we won't be disturbed by anyone other than TV top nobs."

"Wonderful. Ah, Leini… I wonder if you could just email me the typed-up ideas you and Jonathan had so I can read them on the train and be ready to make my own comments and additions, could you?"

There was a slight hesitation, which surprised him, but then she agreed and said that, although she was busy, she'd do her best to get them to him; then they rang off.

Two days with Leini! No, he mustn't hope for anything… nothing, in fact. This was a business relationship and any wrong move could cause his entire persona to be rubbished, his career finished and also to become the laughing stock of the soap opera world. He could see the headlines in *TV Production Weekly*: 'Top soap writer Alun Loyd gets in a lather with his boss's siren', or 'Soap writer has to come clean over affair with producer's assistant – future down the drain', and so on.

Then, all his worries cast aside, he decided he was too excited to write any more and would continue his get-fit campaign by going for a run and exhausting some of his adrenalinised optimism on the hills of Tref-Y-Clawdd. He quickly changed into his newly-acquired running kit and bounced down the stairs past a surprised-looking Dilys. "You're not going for a run now, are you?" she enquired incredulously.

"Yes," he shouted as his lycra-compressed bulges flashed past her.

"You must be *twp* – it's pouring with rain," she observed.

"No, it's not," he said, disappearing through the side door – "Hasn't been so sunny for ages." And he was gone. *He might have taken the dog*, thought Dilys. Actually, the dog was glad: the rain was torrential.

CHAPTER 2

Alun had a bad night; not only could he not sleep with the excitement of seeing his muse the next day but he had also caught a stinking cold after being drenched from his ill-advised run the day before. Even the dog had looked at him with pity when he returned. Not so Dilys, who reprimanded him incessantly about the stupidity of running in that kind of weather. To make matters worse, Leini had not sent the briefing he had requested of her and thus he felt somewhat miffed at being so obviously snubbed. So when he had risen at 04:30 that morning, he was not in the best of spirits – and not helped either by a surfeit of 'medicinal' whisky macs which had done nothing for his cold and everything to worsen his headache.

The train was twenty-five minutes late, too, so he was even colder after waiting on the station for longer than expected and, when he eventually got onto the train the heating was out of order and there were no seats due to a broken carriage having condensed four cars' worth of humanity into three. Fortunately, he had dosed himself up with cold pills so he spent much of the journey dozing on his feet, propped up between the luggage-rack and a man with the structure of a Sumo wrestler.

When he eventually descended from the train in London, he caught sight of himself in one of its windows and observed that he looked dreadful: pallid complexion, hair sprouting at all angles due to the rain and wind, and he could even discern a slight stubble, occasioned by having had to shave at such an early hour. In short, not the best look for a day he was hoping would change the rest of his life for the better. So he decided to nip into the services area for a quick update of his face to better facilitate his meeting with the lovely Leini. It cost him eight quid, too – which was abetted by the piped music playing, 'Hey, Big Spender'; this annoyed him even more.

*

At that same moment, Leini was primping herself up in a ladies' loo at the Tellurian TV studios, strangely buoyant as she layered her lips with a thick but subtly-coloured rouge and then re-lined her very pretty emerald eyes. She looked good but was slightly bemused by her efforts to make herself so attractive. She had met Alun several times before and always thought he could look so much better if he pampered himself a little and wore nicer, slimmer-fitting clothes. His spongy trainers needed changing too – a nice pair of brogues would make all the difference – and his beer-pot needed attention, although she was aware that most writers, sedentary at a desk all day, had a problem with this. She then reflected on his nasal hairs, which protruded at awkward angles from both within – and upon – his otherwise rather pleasant protuberance (even if a little on the large side) but needed trimming or extraction. If only he didn't smoke too, his teeth having the hue of old-fashioned pub walls discoloured by years of nicotine displacement. He had a good head of hair, mind… yet it was always dishevelled and three days beyond its wash-by date. She suddenly stopped and looked at the vision of her youthful loveliness in the mirror and wondered why on earth she was looking forward to meeting this man and put down her eye-liner with a sigh. Girls had it hard these days – modern men were nearly all scruffy like this… us girls always tried to look our best unless there were gender-political reasons for making a statement not to be, she thought… so why? Well, there *were* reasons… very good ones; he was witty, clever, quite rich, could help her get on in television and had a wicked laugh. Hmm. Work to do but she could bear that, especially as she had seen a picture of his wife, Dilys, whom she had thought looked like the disguised Toad's washerwoman from the *Wind In The Willows*. That would be the easy part, she concluded.

A sudden memory of a previous lover entered her mind: without him, she would not be in TV – but that was in the past. Notwithstanding that, a tear fell from an eye and left a fresh trail of mascara down her newly-rouged cheek; she wiped it away and sighed again, restored the damage, checked her teeth, smiled at herself then left.

*

Back home in Wales, Dilys popped a large casserole dish into the oven, started the breadmaker and settled down to do the crossword. Then she realised the forecast was for heavy rain later and decided to take the dog for a walk while the weather was relatively benign, so ventured into the wild sporting her usual green wellies, yellow waterproof jacket and dayglo red hat.

If she had been somewhat slimmer, a distant observer might have thought she was a set of walking traffic-lights.

CHAPTER 3

Leini had gone back to the office and suddenly realised she had not sent the requested plotline summation to Alun; she was angry with herself as she had been keen to make a good impression but had done the one thing that would spoil it. This was a work meeting, after all. Well, at least, that was what Alun thought: she had been hoping for a call from him for some while. In fact, Jonathan had actually been free that day but after Alun rang she had put a planned wheeze into operation, where the location manager, Archy, would ring up and request Jonathan should go with him to urgently recce an old priory the next day some way out of London. All she had to do was call Archy when she wanted Jonathan out of the way and he would concur. Of course he would, he fancied her. So the plan had been swiftly put into action after her call with Alun. And there was always the day after that Alun could see Jonathan, especially after Alun had said he might stay the night in London… Well, that could be worked on, too. She knew a nice little bistro near her flat in Pimlico which… No, she was getting ahead of herself. Nearly time for Alun to arrive. She checked herself again in her desk mirror, pulled down her thin, skin-tight top to reveal a little more cleavage and waited. Then she once again remembered the plotline summation and was furiously trying to finish it when Alun arrived at reception…

*

Jonathan and his location manager, Archy, a very good-looking man in his early forties with a sharp eye and a prodigious imagination, were in a dilapidated but wonderful old priory near Stevenage, where the brutal ghastliness of the town's nearby modern developments had somehow missed destroying this tiny hidden corner of England's heritage. They were both very excited, as suitable locations for period pieces were difficult to find so close to London; yet it was only a matter of time before the concrete of Stevenage would seep over the hills and obliterate it forever. They would have to spend some budget on it but essentially it could act as a stately home, a workhouse, a prison, a storage area – or even a priory. There was a small lake with follies, too, and a boathouse. It was perfect. Jonathan, a tall, sinewy and dark-bearded man with a thick head of coarse hair, had been looking for a location like this for a while and this would really help his ever-challenged budget, being so close to London. And there was a plush hotel nearby, too, where the stars and important crew could stay and have a libationary 18th century time on 21st century expenses.

Being gay, Jonathan was happy scouting around with Archy, and he enjoyed their occasional journeys into the lesser-known or forgotten corners of the country; they got on well and Archy was always hopeful that Jonathan might put in a good word for him with Leini – as well as hoping for a romantic meal with her or, preferably, much more. Jonathan had always hoped for the same with Archy.

Having met the owners and loosely discussed financial terms and the time when they might wish to start using the location, the two men also decided to recce the nearby hotel and so ensure that the cellar and its menu were up to scratch: in the TV world, these considerations were even more important...

*

Full of guarded anticipation, Leini went to reception but could not see Alun, who, still feeling rotten, had secreted himself around a corner so that his appearance would not put the object of his affection into a state of terror too soon. Suddenly seeing him, she was, indeed, surprised at his appearance – but not for the same reasons as Alun would have thought.

Despite being dosed up with drugs, his hair had been cut short, there were no stray hairs circumnavigating his nose, he was wearing a slim-fitting jacket over a clean, well-ironed shirt and tie, and his trousers were pressed. Amidst the delighted astonishment, she almost forgot to take in the clean, polished shoes, which were brogues – her favourite! And he was slimmer, she surmised; how had he managed this in the three weeks since she had first seen him? Or had he been starring in an amdram production of Worzel Gummidge at that time?

Alun, however, saw the look of disbelief on her face and feared the worst – oh, God, she hated the sight of him! That quick shopping spree and haircut had been a total waste of time! And money! Oh, what had he done?

Leini smiled with joy, which Alun again mistook as her laughing at him and looked even more forlorn; but she went over to him and quite ostentatiously kissed him on the cheek, which lightened his being immediately and he lunged forward to reciprocate, her beautiful and manicured hands eventually having to push him away.

"Alun, you look amazing," she said. "I was expecting you to look like… well, how you did the last time I saw you. Sort of… more rustic… wayward. Not well-dressed like this!"

"Ah, well, thank you; yes, you look wonderful, too – but I expected that, of course; you always do."

With that compliment, Leini found herself subconsciously pulling her cleavage down, then felt stupid and pulled it up again. Awkwardly, she offered to carry his suitcase, but he declined her offer as inside it were his old clothes and various prophylactics, purchased in the remote hope of an intimately joyous evening later on.

They went up in the lift which unusually was not filled with the usual flotsam and jetsam of television production and where her subtle scent started to assail his unblocked nostrils. Her shapely, stockinged legs moved and whispered as the lift lurched noisily in a celestial direction and they looked awkwardly at each other, both astonished at the vision in front of them.

When the lift doors opened, they both seemed uncertain on their legs as the emotion of a mutually unexpected desire made their knees weak; they went down the corridor, narrowly missing the tea-lady with her trolley of savoury buns and, more attractively, sweet delights, which would soon be exchanged – Alun increasingly hoped – by a different type of delight; yet the booked lunch had to be consumed first and after depositing his case in her office and picking up a thick folder, they made their way to the executive dining-room.

Inevitably, it took some time to become seated together as Alun knew most of the people there, many of whom wanted a word with him; either those who had worked with him on previous productions or who wanted some knowledge about the series of productions about to be recorded. Leini became slightly testy as these people descended on their table because she wanted Alun for herself and, after several minutes of interruptions, she turned to the two currently there and said sweetly but firmly to them, "Gentlemen, we're supposed to be having a working lunch and Alun hasn't got much time so could you discuss things with him either later, over the phone or over the internet, please?"

Her disarming smile but steel eyes had the desired effect and the intruders eventually evaporated, leaving the two slightly breathless players to themselves.

Leini opened the folder and plonked the plotlines in front of Alun, apologising for not having sent them to him earlier; but he waved away her excuses and explained he could not have read them anyway due to yesterday's run and his subsequent cold. The plotlines, though, stayed resolutely unread, as magical small talk took the place of fabricated stories – theirs seemed so much more interesting. So when the waitress came to ask if they had decided what they wanted for starter, the answer was quite obvious to both of them.

After the first course and a couple of glasses of wine, however, the conversation did progress to the scripts' plots but only by way of Leini reminding Alun that Jonathan wanted him to insert a bit more lust and intrigue into the stories as the programme was going to be broadcast after the nine o'clock watershed from later in the year – so some more adult themes could be introduced. Also, she divulged, that meant the plots could also be more violent: they had already discussed the possibility of a murder or two, of course, which always raised viewing ratings considerably; yet despite wanting these aspects woven into the text using Alun's fecund imagination, Jonathan was not sure how his writer could realistically implement them into the narrative of an 18th century soap opera.

Alun put his chin on his hands as Leini continued that the plots would have to be as watertight regarding murder and law as any present-day scenarios but as he had studied history at university he would not find that difficult, would he? Alun was flattered by Leini's faith in his abilities – and Jonathan's too, although these were less important to him than the lady staring ravenously at him across the remains of the *pâté de foie gras*.

"Hmmm… an interesting development," he mused. "The 18th century moving into the 21st…"

"Breeches and bosoms, methinks," Leini re-joined after a moment, "the only difference being that people cannot now be hung for murder."

"Yes… but that's great for our programme, isn't it, 'cos it's a way of getting rid of characters we don't want any more."

"And if they're transported to Australia, then there's an excuse for you to write in some extremely exotic locations." She looked at him intently with a twinkle in her eye that said everything but revealed nothing – except the length of her cleavage which had slowly descended as the starter was consumed. Alun began to wonder whether he was actually dreaming, as scenes like this only seemed to happen in the movies – or TV dramas. Like the ones *he* wrote.

And it was this which suddenly gave him an idea, one which would ensure veracity of all the plotlines but also – if he could write it carefully and wittily enough – be a thriller within a whodunnit thriller. He found himself becoming very intense and verbose about the possibilities and advantages of hindsight regarding the era he was writing for… and what a wonderful opportunity it would be to use the past as a very interesting way to criticise the present, rather than the other way around, which currently seemed to be the fashion. After a couple of minutes of pensive but creative waffle, he looked up to see Leini's emerald eyes boring into his with wide-open rapt attention, a playful smile on her lips and a shoeless stockinged foot in the nave of his lap.

CHAPTER 4

On leaving the priory, Archy told Jonathan that he had also found another location which might be of interest, stuck in a tiny hamlet; he knew they always needed old buildings which looked as dilapidated and poverty-stricken as they might have been in the 18th century and he had found just such a tumbledown cottage which could be useful if he was willing to take a slight detour. Jonathan was delighted and concurred immediately – but secretly hoped it would not delay savouring the highlight of the day which was the lunch at the Olde Rectory Hotel... with Archy... whose infectious exuberance propelled the car faster down the country lanes. Soon they arrived at a hamlet, where they turned off the road down a bumpy farm track, at the end of which they eventually stopped at what looked like the perfect TV location. The stones from which the house was constructed were rough-hewn and there was definitely a paucity of mortar holding them together; the windows were all of differing sizes, unpainted and small. The front door had an old stone porch with the legend '1786' carved into it and the bald space in front was reminiscent of an old farmyard – indeed, it was easy to imagine ducks, chickens, geese and dogs running around even though the place seemed empty. Yet as the car pulled up, the front door opened and a wizened old lady, wrapped in a shawl which looked as if it had been knitted at the time of the building, came unsteadily out. She recognised Archy and shook Jonathan's hand as Archy made the introductions. The two executives concluded that it would, indeed, be perfect and when Archy told her how much they were willing to pay her for its use, the lady was visibly delighted. "Oh, sir... that would be a huge help, thank you, sir..." she said in an accent which would generally be assumed to have disappeared in that part of the Home Counties a hundred years ago. Jonathan went around and looked inside and admitted it was worth the detour as Archy explained all the contract details to the lady, which he would put in a letter to her, after which he would be in touch with filming dates when they had been firmed up.

Jonathan joined him and, as they left, Archy said, "I hope you don't mind, Jonathan, but she's got hardly any money so I agreed to give her some in advance if that's OK with you."

"Of course," Jonathan said, now more intensively looking forward to his expensive hotel lunch, whilst pondering that perhaps the 18th and 21st centuries were not so different as often imagined…

*

Whilst Jonathan and Archy, Alun and Leini were severally enjoying their respective lunches from different perspectives, Dilys was mending Alun's socks and doing the washing-up. She quite enjoyed her days without him as she could get on with things – even if they were still mostly to do with looking after him. She had given up on herself years ago and the result was so obvious that she had become used to ignoring her image in the mirror and pretended it was someone else. Yet she still had a spirit… it was just submerged under a sea of abandoned aspirations. She had once been pretty, although never made the most of her potential as she had never possessed any clue how to dress; every colour and pattern contradicted the other and an iron had been an alien concept until she had met Alun. Since then, Alun's own attention to dress had fallen by the wayside too, but she had reluctantly swiped his shirts with a modicum of steaming intent so he would look no more scruffy than most of the other people who worked with him in television. Living mostly at home, he had not needed to bother too much anyway… The rub, however, was a sudden – indeed, *very* sudden – regimen to lose weight, shave occasionally and, when he went out (even to the village) to obviously try and look his best. Yet even now this was not up to much, she caustically noted; but this observation was nonetheless constantly troubled by the omnipresent question: why?

She decided to enjoy the solitude and picked up her copy of *The Guardian* in order to keep abreast of what she was supposed to think in this complex 'woke' age and complemented it with a cup of coffee, much of which was soon contributing to the other random designs on her woolly top.

She had just become comfortable in front of the Aga when the phone rang in the hall, the surprise of which made her jump, spilling the remains of her cup onto the same garment. She managed to get there before the caller hung up and found it was her husband, Alun.

"Hello, dear; everything all right?" he asked mechanically without waiting for an answer, as he carried on with the news that he had decided to stay in town that night as there was unfinished business with Jonathan to discuss.

"You told me that you might," she snapped; "you made me spill my coffee."

"Ah, sorry, dear. Well, look after yourself and I'll see you tomorrow evening sometime. Got to see some estate agents, too, for research…"

"You told me that, too."

"Ah, yes… well, just keeping you informed, as a good husband should."

"Say hello to Jonathan for me…"

"I will when I see him, of course…"

"I thought you were with him now…"

"Ah, well, something came up…" She was sure she heard a stifled giggle at the other end but thought it must have been a noise on the line as Alun quickly continued, "… so I'll pass on your best wishes when I see him later."

"All right. Bye." She put the phone down, shuffled back to her spot in front of the Aga and sat down. She brushed the spilled coffee off her clothing and then suddenly became alert as she wondered if Alun was having a relationship. Overnight… estate agents… no Jonathan today… and the keep-fit regime! It all suddenly fell into place. It wasn't as if she cared very much, actually; two could play at that game. She went to her computer and typed in 'dating sites', then perused the results. There were some nice-looking men there, she admitted, and went off into a trance as she imagined herself with a square-jawed, dark-haired stud rippling with muscles who would transport her from the cooker to a jet set life of sex, fun and plenty. Then she caught sight of herself in the mirror and realised she was being ridiculous.

*

Alun switched off his mobile and looked at Leini's form in front of him. The plotlines were between them with various notes, question-marks, crossings-out, arrows and the like, exposing a good afternoon's work. The pieces of paper strewn around the bed could not, though, cover up the fact that both he and Leini were somewhat exposed, too. In fact, they were both stark naked. Yet they had not had sex – much to Alun's discomfiture – because she professed to be an old-fashioned girl and would only do so if they were married, which was somewhat putting the cart before the horse as far as Alun was concerned. She had obviously presumed that there would be little chance of him not submitting to her intense allure but this was a business deal to her rather than a romantic one and she had to be sure that the dreaded, dour Dilys was out of the way before there was any chance of a commitment, whereupon she could become the spouse of a well-known writer who was very successful. The age gap troubled her somewhat but that could be overcome – it was only nineteen years; that was a mere trifle these days in the fast-moving world of TV.

So the seed had been sown – or not, in his case – but the promise was good enough. All he had to do was to ensure he could jettison Dilys without too much fuss or expenditure; and, as a writer, he could manipulate his very own plotline by researching and testing the subterfuges and legalities and putting the resulting processes into his scripts. It was a wonderful idea, to which Leini had readily contributed – helped create, even, doubtless inspired by his imaginative embellishments: a sort of telly whodunnit which would play out as his marriage ended and their affair blossomed. The audience would be transfixed, as he was, too – but more by Leini's anatomy and sense of inventive, wicked fun. And it would be their secret – notwithstanding the three million viewers of *Jonquil's Journals* – who would be in the dark regarding his and Leini's sinister intentions but be swept along anyway in what would actually be a true story, playing out at the same time as the show was being broadcast; best of all, the audience would be thrown off the scent by the fact it was set in the 18th century, when life was so different that there could be few similarities…

Could there…?

CHAPTER 5

Dilys had downed a couple of remedial gin and tonics and subsequently found herself even more inclined to try a computer dating site; she had done some research a few months earlier when Alun was away and found that there were those where one could search for permanent partners and others where overtly subterfugal affairs were the order. She decided the latter was a better option and found one that was cheaper than the others; she filled in the preliminary details and found a picture of herself some twenty years before when she was definitely prettier and slimmer than now. Going for a month's free trial to assess any incumbent possibilities, she uploaded her picture, filled in her details and when it pinged back saying 'Welcome to Clandestine Clients', she investigated some of the men on offer but was not readily attracted to anyone... until she came to a page with the heading, 'Still Available...'. These men were generally older than the mainstream ones and had obviously been craving success for a longer while, yet one or two were characters who she felt she'd be more comfortable with: one did, indeed, stand out and, she felt, might even find her attractive. There was something familiar about him which drew her towards him, too, as he looked almost as scruffy as she was. She hated men who over-preened themselves and at least it might be something they had in common. So, she opened his profile to have a better look. What she discovered both surprised and angered her: for, in the second photo, the man had obviously been with another woman when the photo was taken as his arm stretched off the frame and a hint of skirt was just visible at the bottom edge. There was something familiar about the skirt, too... she looked back at the man's face – and observed that his clothes style did not match the present fashions, so it must have been a photo taken several years ago. The cheat! Women could do that, but not men! And then the penny dropped: it was a photo of her and Alun taken on their honeymoon in Llandudno twenty years ago! He was *definitely* having an affair! What infuriated her most, though, was that she'd been lopped off the photograph... She was also much miffed by the fact he was in the 'Still Available...' section: Alun was better than that! Surely *someone* would have wanted him? Yet the biggest slight was that he must have been on the site for rather a long time... and possibly ever since their marriage. The fiend...

She instantly withdrew her trial offer, cancelled her credit card details and poured another gin and tonic – a significantly larger one than the two which had preceded it...

*

Alun admired the shapely form of Leini as she got off the bed and walked sveltely to the adjoining bathroom. She was magnificent to look at: every part of her body was in perfect proportion to the others; her bottom was rounded without being too pronounced, she had a flat stomach – he still had some work to do on his own in that area – and she had a waist! In fact, he had not seen any woman as beautiful since he was a teenager, when he had not had the benefit of many conquests to compare her with. Her legs were slender but shapely and her mound of Venus would have defeated even Rubens or Goya. Her blonde hair fell just short of her plump but wide-based breasts, which ensured that age would be kind to them and they would not droop until her fifties, if even then. And her face! Well, that was what had attracted him to her first, of course, before he started imagining what other delights would be revealed if he had ever been offered the chance: and now he was living it. He also noted that her smooth, tight skin was slightly olivey, which offset her other natural colours to perfection, as well as her minor enhancements, such as her beautifully manicured nails, which were painted in a subtle pink and completed her perfectly formed hands and feet; these were straight, slender, soft and sexy. In short, she truly was the goddess he had anticipated her to be and if he had seen her on a porn site would have imagined that every shot had been digitally enhanced. Oh, Leini... even her name was mystical; Dutch, she had said.

He eyed his own flaccid body and was glad of the new clothes to cover it up; the haircut had helped, too, as well as his recent fitness regime which had so swiftly yielded this result. He managed to tear his eyes away for a moment to find his notebook, then started scribbling down some plot ideas and a couple of lines she had come up with after kissing; he did not want to forget anything she had said and ideas for future episodes were bouncing around in his head: that's what a muse did for a man, and why he had had writers' block so much more frequently recently. Dilys was a non-starter in that department… and the thought of his wife made his manhood dwindle in an instant. Yes, *Jonquil's Journals* was about to become more intriguing, saucier and wittier: he could feel it within him.

As for Leini, she was quietly pleased with stage one of her plan. He was so much better than she had imagined and was ripe for development. And with her background help, promising but withholding, teasing but resisting, the task of getting Alun rid of dowdy Dilys suddenly seemed a lot easier than she had first imagined.

CHAPTER 6

Jonathan returned to the office from his travels with Archy late in the afternoon. He had expected to see Alun and Leini in the boardroom, papers strewn about, bursting with multitudinous ideas and twists for the upcoming storylines. On arrival, however, it was obvious the room had not been used and he was told by one of the secretaries that Leini and Alun had last been seen leaving the executive restaurant some hours before. Instinctively, Jonathan felt snubbed – and had been looking forward to being in Alun's presence again, with his great sense of humour and friendly demeanour, as well as the promise of more stories and inspiring debates about their direction. Archy was a good man and a very excellent location manager but his conversation was limited and they each viewed the programme from different artistic perspectives.

He decided to ring Alun on his mobile – but was surprised to find it switched off, as was Leini's. So he sent them each a text, suggesting they meet up for a quick drink before going home to prepare for their morning meeting tomorrow. He hung around for a while, pottering with general ideas, one of which had been inspired by the location that afternoon, where he felt their hero, Bartholomew Jonquil, could suddenly find himself thrown into prison on some obscure 18th century legal pretext.

Then, just as he was about to give up and leave, his phone burst into life: it was Alun.

"Ah, Alun; where are you? I was hoping to see you for a drink to set the scene for our meeting… Did Leini look after you OK?"

"Yes, thanks; splendidly. We've seen quite a lot of each other this afternoon, actually…" He smirked at Leini, who was opposite him.

"Ah – good. Did you get any ideas?"

"Plenty." It was Leini's turn to silently laugh.

"Excellent. Where are you now? Are you up for a drink?"

"To be honest, Jonathan, I'm rather tired after the early start and we had a very good session which has left me somewhat exhausted. I also want to develop some more ideas over the evening and sleep on them, if that's OK."

"Of course. Whereabouts are you?" There was a slight pause before Alun answered, as he looked at Leini for inspiration. 'Putney', she mouthed.

"Er, Putney-ish. Got a good deal on a B&B," he embellished.

"Putney? I think Leini lives around those parts. Did she tell you?"

"No, no. We split around 5:30. But if I can stay awake there are a few positions I've thought of that I'd like to bed in before we meet at the studios tomorrow: is that OK?"

"Of course. Putney's a bit off my beaten track anyway – I was hoping you were nearer the studios. Sounds as if you've uncovered quite a lot of potential today, though."

"Indeed."

"Well done. So, looking forward to seeing the results tomorrow, then. 10 o'clock, my office?"

"Yes, as originally planned. See you then."

They both rang off. Jonathan wondered if Alun sounded a little awkward but went to the bar opposite the studios – affectionately known as 'Studio Six' – and downed a couple of pints before returning to his empty bachelor flat in Clerkenwell. As for Alun, he and Leini – who was giggling profusely and sexily about the conversation – were about to go to a local restaurant to discuss just about anything other than *Jonquil's Journals*.

*

At the script meeting the next morning, it was apparent to Jonathan that both Alun and Leini were somewhat tired but strangely did not draw any conclusions; Alun, particularly, seemed to be lacking his usual mine of suggestions, although the idea that there should be an

18th century paid assassin, who could be bubbling under the plots over several weeks – eventually leading to the murder of one of the main characters' wives – found favour as it would create many extra options, ongoing intrigue… and a relentless frisson as the viewers wondered who might be next. From Jonathan's perspective, too, there was the character of Mrs Wiggins, an irascible, curmudgeonly, heavily-upholstered and smugly vindictive housekeeper whose TV personality was totally based on the actress's own real-life persona; he had wanted to get rid of this obstructively rebellious woman for ages, who diligently appropriated all the latest social media fads and virtue-signalling standpoints without any thought of balance or discussion… consequently, this development might present a plethora of possibilities to finally bump her off. The only problem was that she was one of the main stars of the show and very popular with viewers; when he had tried to remove her a few years before, the intent had been leaked by another scriptwriter and a campaign to keep her was successfully launched. From then on, the actress, Lottie Brace, had been mutinously on her guard and treated Jonathan with a pernicious contempt. This, of course, made him even more determined to have her removed, by fair means or foul – and preferably the latter: the scriptwriter had been summarily dismissed at the time for betraying the plotline to her, but then quickly reinstated when Lottie angrily told Jonathan that the man was her partner; so it was going to take discretion, subterfuge and propriety to keep the news of her pending demise secret – and at precisely the same time as her 18th century life was terminated by a 21st century termination of her contract. To quell the inevitable viewer revolt, Alun's earlier introduction of an attractive, rag-clothed girl – a whore – would become involved with Bartholomew Jonquil himself after her trial for importuning; she would subsequently try to use her association with him to become lady of his house. Along with her knowing some other whores in a tavern frequented by the low-life of the time, this could then engender a lot of sex and nudity, which would raise viewer numbers in direct correlation to those lost by the disappearance of Mrs Wiggins.

After three hours of discussion, they were all aching for lunch;

Leini decided to stay behind for a few minutes to type up what had been discussed so they could hit the ground running again in the afternoon; she also wanted to book a couple of viewings of a flat for Alun that evening, which were suitably close to her but not so near that people might talk or see them together too easily.

The appointments made, she found that the men had eschewed the sterile pleasures of the canteen for the more lubricating confines of Studio Six and a Scotch egg apiece; on arrival, she ordered a Pinot Grigio and a packet of crisps. As she had walked in, Alun was struck once more by her beauty and could not believe his luck at having bedded – if not yet been pleasured by – this pulchritudinous princess of a woman and wondered how and why he had managed to squander so many years of his life with the desuetudinous Dilys. Indeed, how on Earth had he even married her in the first place…? Then he remembered: at the time, he had been skint, and the lure of an easy life in rural Wales, away from city distractions, and with a woman who took up far less space at that time, seemed a reasonable motivation. The added clincher had been that the first husband had left her with a beautiful 17th century stone farmhouse and a lot of money when he died, the latter which he had made as the leader of the regional Labour Party and all its attendant opportunities for making discreet but illegal pots of cash through patronage, backhanders and extortion. In fact, his bloody comeuppance by a number of aggrieved bigwigs – who had made absolutely certain of his death without leaving any evidence to commit any of them to justice – had given Alun the idea for Mrs Wiggins' end. An added frisson now was that whilst Dilys *might* have eventually viewed *Jonquil's Journals* and discerned the series of events leading up to Mrs Wiggins' removal – her parallel character in Alun's plotline – she would by then have been removed from this life by the same means… At that juncture, though, he would be living in blissful and licentious harmony with the angel now standing before him. At least, that was the plan. Suddenly, life was looking good.

CHAPTER 7

Dilys received the call at just before five o'clock, not long before she was thinking that Alun would want a meal when he arrived home and was contemplating what to make him. His call, though, alerted her to the news that he would not actually be home that night as the plots had hit a snag and he needed to stay in London another night; also, due to these delays, he would have to see some estate agents regarding property law tomorrow, which he could then use in a backdated 18th century context with the benefit of a little more general knowledge. He would try to be back tomorrow but even that might have to be postponed if things were not resolved. She suddenly wondered what was wrong with the telephone and modern technology but he was adamant his meetings had to be face to face and rang off in a slightly peremptory manner, which upset her. She did still like Alun actually… perhaps it was time to start showing it: if it wasn't too late.

The sun broke through the usually leaden, light-smothering clouds, causing weak shafts of light to illuminate the flagstones, the inglenook fireplace and various crannies normally clothed in perpetual gloom; this dispelled some of her annoyance and she decided more firmly that it was time to make an effort. Yes, she must clean up, use some make-up, wear nicer clothes and especially lose some weight – quite a lot, actually – so she could tempt Alun to stay. It would be a hard task but he had started to look after himself more recently – looking a lot better for it, too, she had to admit – and realised that this woman, whoever she was, must have been the reason. Well, two could play at that game: perhaps she should join a dating site after all… not that she was really interested, of course; it was just time to rekindle the spark and use the experience to hone her sex appeal whilst burnishing her chat-up skills as she tried to lose some bulk. Perhaps she could book in for some cosmetic surgery in Rhyl, she pondered: a friend had done so and looked better for it…

She had had a tummy-tuck, love handles removed and her arm 'wings' reduced. Yet time was of the issue – and she despondently realised that if she did the same then it would be weeks before she could put her plan into action; and even if she took away the same bits as her friend, there would still be far too much of her left to make much difference. So she would have to present herself as she was and hope for the best. After all, she had a lot to offer – well, that was the problem, of course. Still, she had a lovely farmhouse with land, enough money and could cook. So there was no reason why someone might not be interested and so she would bite the bullet and see if a clandestine affair were possible. With renewed determination, she went back to her computer and looked at another dating site. This one, called Rural Romances, seemed to hit the spot and appeared to sport the type of rustic ruins she might appeal to; she signed up and was soon engaging online with a tractor-driving farmer from Rhayader and had soon made an arrangement to meet him at a midway point for a lunchtime drink tomorrow. After shutting down on this ruddy, jovial agriculturalist, she went up to the loft and searched for her lycra gym clothes which she had last worn thirty years before. Finding them buried behind a number of steel boxes left by her late husband, she went downstairs to the bedroom and put her dirty clothes in the laundry basket, then stretched the skin-tight garments to breaking-point as she pulled them over the layers of flab which had accumulated since they were last worn.

She looked at herself in the mirror and wondered that it did not tear into a thousand pieces as she did so: she looked like a relief map of the Himalayas, with Mount Everest the most prominent feature located around her midriff, and K2 taking up the rear. She looked awful, as she then noticed a tiny rip slowly lengthening up one thigh as the strain on the perished lycra took its toll.

She burst into tears, then dried them and, in a bid to beat the advancing total destruction of her once-pristine gym kit, put on the also-perished trainers and went out for a short stumble around the kitchen garden.

She was soon back in the kitchen, panting, aching and faint but at least it had not killed her. Sadly, her unexpected exercise *had* killed the dog, although she had not yet realised this, assuming it had had enough and run off – but she was too exhausted to go after it: despite her stumble being only five minutes... But it was a start.

The dog's end, however, had come after the first few moments, having been the recipient of too many treats, cakes and unfinished dinners over the years: trying to keep up with even this slow, stumbling woman after no exercise in years, it had expired after a couple of minutes and crawled to a pleasant place to die underneath a grim old reaping scythe in the barn...

*

Alun and Leini entered the estate agents and asked for Tobias Whimple, the man who would guide them around the two properties they were going to view. They had purposely asked for an older member of the agency who might even be aware of any 18th century practices that had still been prevalent in the 20th, but when he shuffled in, they wondered if, in fact, he actually had been present at that time as he was very old, thin, and had a well-worn dark, old-fashioned suit, upon which lay the remains of some of his wispy white hair. An ostentatious fob-watch completed the caricature. Indeed, he was completely unlike any of the more dashing, thrusting young lads roundabout – and an even further cry from the eager, smilingly vacuous but very attractive ladies who embellished the remaining desks.

On introduction to Mr Whimple, however, there was a steel and knowledge about him which surprised them and, getting out his fob watch to regard the time, he did seem very much of the last century, even if closer to its beginning than its end.

"Here are the details of the two flats we think you may like," he wheezed, as he proffered the highly-coloured sheets of paper – in stark contrast to his monochrome bony fingers. "The first is a new-build and highly desirable," he continued, and has the benefit of underfloor heating and underground parking; there's a ten percent discount if you buy this month, as they're off-plan but it will be built within six months; the rest are already taken. The other is a charming conversion, constructed in the 18th century, a lovely garden flat with total and exclusive access to aforesaid garden. Part of a mansion. Built by a local justice of the time, a Mr Theodore Blankitt, a copy of whose autobiography is included in the deeds, laid down in law to be passed onto new owners in perpetuity ever since the house was built in 1797. As it's now flats, of course, it is the garden flat property to which this quirk appertains." He turned to Alun and said, "I think you might like the flat for that reason alone," as his face creaked into a wider smile.

"Indeed," said Alun. "How pertinent of you to have thought of that."

"At your service," he answered, with a slight bow of the head, then continued: "Multiple period features, including stained-glass door-panels, a preponderance of dado rails, some splendid plaster ceilings and a Victorian-style bathroom — although not the original one, I hasten to add," said with a hint of a smile as if to prove he really was alive.

Then he turned to Leini and said, "But I suspect you'll be more comfortable with the new-build, Madam?"

Leini was unsure what to say as she had never bought a flat before: her father had bought hers. Yet the warmth factor and the thought of a safe place to park her anticipated sports car after she had snared Alun were certainly not far from the truth.

"Well, it's my partner's flat, really," she replied uncertainly, looking at Alun. "He's the one who will finally decide." As that was said, Alun felt a frisson of pleasure shoot up his body, emanating from his nether regions: with Dilys, it was always what *she* wanted and stuff his opinion because she had the money. But now the boot was on the other foot and it was he who was in charge and had the money, not Dilys. And Leini instinctively knew she had scored another clutch of valuable points.

"Well, I'd like to go and see them both," he ventured, as Leini agreed.

"Then, I shall drive you there," Mr Whimple said, rising with a speed that surprised both him and his two clients as he grabbed the desk to steady himself. "I shall get my car out and meet you at the front in a minute or two." He disappeared through a back door, which revealed a small room festooned with brightly-tagged keys on hooks – and also the office loo behind, in which cubicle was also the tea-making equipment, its dirty and brown-stained mugs matching the general tone of the area, the squalor and filth of which was in sharp contrast to the clean, bright and tidy office.

The door mercifully closed and they turned to go out of the front, both wondering if a hansom cab and horses might pull up to take them to their destination; but no, a spotless, leather-upholstered metallic black limousine arrived, into which they disappeared.

*

Dilys had eventually discovered her dead dog in the barn, tripping over it in the dark whilst putting the rubbish out. This somewhat annoyed her – she was always tripping over it even when it was alive – so having fallen over it one final time, she tossed it into the silage heap with the disdain she normally reserved for her husband. Realising there would now be nothing to eat the leftovers, (neither the husband nor the dog) she decided to lose weight by *not* eating the chicken pie with puff-pastry in the freezer she had previously set her eyes upon: instead, she opted for three slices of ham, chips, triple boiled eggs and a few slices of bread. If she felt hungry later, she could always pop down in the night for a cup of Horlicks and a packet of digestive biscuits. Yet all the while, the thought of Alun, having it off with some other woman, was playing on her mind – and so certain was she of this that she decided there and then that, whether farmer Nathan Grubb was ugly or not, she would try to seduce him. Why not? She and Alun had abstained from sex fairly soon after the ignominy of the first attempt and, as she never felt much bothered about it either way, it would not matter any more or less with this man either. At least she would be getting her own back. And some good rumpy-pumpy might help her lose weight, which would make her more attractive to Alun. Then she wondered if she was making the point before witnessing the fact. Yet if only she had known that Leini's resolute proposal was no sex with Alun before commitment, Dilys would actually have been proud of her...

*

Leini and Alun, along with Mr Whimple, left the second flat – the new-build – with the lingering smell of sawdust, damp cement and plaster in their nostrils; it was, indeed, a beautiful apartment and had everything. But the period flat they had seen first had entranced Alun, especially as the property had its own garage, which had been the carriage-house; Leini could put her new car in there too, she schemed, as it was quite deep and could probably hide two cars. Better still, above this was a substantial room that Mr Whimple said had been a small ballroom, which would make a wonderful study for Alun. This building, which was detached from the main house, also had an underground passage connecting the two. It was perfect – especially if, at some stage, he might have to make a quick escape from the anger of a deranged Dilys.

For Leini, it was perfect, too – and ready to move into, bar a few improvements. And she had always wanted to have a garden, denied her by the relatively impecunious state she was in now... But that was all about to change...

CHAPTER 8

Two days later, Alun finally started making it back to Wales and his distant Dilys. He, Jonathan, Leini, various budget controllers and heads of diverse television departments had all been appraised of the slight shift in tone of the programme, which they all agreed to, with the overarching feeling that the series needed freshening up. Buoyed by this, and his plotlines well sketched out and generally approved by the top brass, Alun's happiness had prompted him into taking a somewhat lubricated lunch on his way back on the train as a celebration of joy at his appropriation of Leini – and a need for Dutch courage on meeting the soon-to-be-deleted Dilys. So much so, that after changing at Shrewsbury, he had fallen asleep and missed his stop at Welshpool, much to the fury of his wife who was then forced to drive another thirty drunken miles to pick him up from Newtown. Yet Dilys' inebriation had also been applied for the same reasons as Alun's, for her escapade with the ruddy farmer had turned out rather well and, his having ploughed a rather lonely furrow for some years since his wife died and the cat left, had been very grateful for Dilys' openness. In fact, so open that she was actually in the lead regarding the number of times her furrow had been ploughed; significantly so, in fact, compared with Alun and Leini.

So, when she finally caught up with him in Newtown, they were both in much the same anguished and irritable mood, which defused much that was on their separate minds. The fact that Alun had put a deposit on the garden flat and Dilys had wondered how she could keep her sex-obsessed sodbuster at arms' length were topics that preoccupied both their minds from different viewpoints as the car's headlights cut through the dark of deepest Wales. Wherever he peered in the gloom, all he saw was the beautiful form of the girl he wished he was still with now, whereas for Dilys, all she could think of was her new man on a tractor with a very impressive set of tools.

On arriving home, they were too tired for anything but going to bed to sleep, which was rudely awakened at eight the next morning by the phone ringing downstairs in the hall.

Alun bounded down the cold stairwell into the hall and answered the phone in the nick of time before Leini hung up.

"Your mobile's off," she grunted disappointedly.

"It doesn't work down here," he whispered.

"Oh. Is there really somewhere without a mobile signal in this country?" she responded with surprise.

"Yes. Have you ever rung me on my mobile down here before?"

"No – but that was before... well, you know. I just thought that was for professional reasons..."

"Yes, but no," he hoarsely replied, his flimsy dressing-gown and worn holed slippers no match for the encroaching chill of the flagstone floor and a lack of underwear in a house with zero central heating in rural Wales at eight in the morning. There was a pause, and then she said, "I miss you." Instantly, he felt warm again, as his delight at hearing her soft voice say something affectionate caused a parting of the two sides of his gown just as Dilys appeared at the top of the stairs.

"Who's that at this time of the morning?" she snapped.

Alun had to think fast: "Ah, it's a farmer... he says he's stuck in a ditch at the end of our drive."

It was then Dilys' turn to be terrified and she ran back to the bedroom to don some warm clothes; in seconds she bounced down the stairs with the car keys, attired only in a ski-suit which was again far too small for her; then she was out of the door and revving up the Land Rover.

Alun was somewhat bemused by her concern and actions as he quickly said goodbye to Leini whilst wondering what he had said to make Dilys react so strangely.

*

After Leini finished her call with Alun, she felt a little depressed and empty; she realised with surprise that, actually, she really was beginning to feel something for him — well, far more than she had originally intended... or expected. There was this hole in her stomach which, she realised, meant some sort of emotional vacuum that she could not suppress. She thought hard about what it was that was particularly attractive about Alun and focussed on every aspect of his persona and body. He was obviously up for improving the latter, and she admired him for that sense of determined purpose, which was obviously due to meeting her, even if it had never been said. And his scruffy attire when she first had dealings with him had definitely not been a turn-on but he was addressing that, too. Yet while these improvements helped, she knew they were not the main reason: it was something more tangible, immediate. His mind! Yes, again, that helped... and his sharp wit, knowledge and repartee were hugely attractive, too, as was his sense of humour — he could make a joke out of almost anything. That was very disarming, as she had been laughing at something he said when she had suddenly found herself hanging off his shoulder with her face in his neck... which suddenly moved upwards and sideways where his receptive and indulgent kiss was first experienced. His tongue had had a sweetness about it which she had not anticipated — he had smoked when she first met him but surmised he must have given it up: was that for her, too? Probably, as his taste could have been testament to a toothpaste commercial. Becoming increasingly concerned at the things she liked about him, she reflected on her original plan, initially eyeing him up as a successful writer whom she could woo, clean out and then divorce, so inheriting his fortune, as many of her friends had done to others. There was another reason, too, but that was a business irrelevance now, and she dismissed it. So she had found herself being ashamed of this brazen exploitation. She chided herself: in television, men and women were more equal than in many other professions and she suddenly realised her actions were maliciously sexist. She admonished herself as she imagined him sadly ticking her off for her deceit in that silky, deep but strangely gravelly resonance, laced with an omnipresent sadness, only tempered by his humour and wit. And then it struck her — it was his voice. Yes, that was it: she could just sit and listen to its cadences and nuances forever, as if a vocal representation of a Mozart symphony; it just 'spoke' to her — as voices do, of course; but this was different...

Having realised his USP, or Unique Selling Point, she felt released that she knew what the key was... and then found herself wondering how much longer she could resist having sex with him... which would, in one big bang, destroy her own USP — the perennial promise of lust without fulfilment! This depressed her once more; after all, it would be some time before she saw him again as he had to write the scripts and, until the judge's flat was purchased, he could not do so in her tiny one. Alun had told the estate agent to get in touch with her first so that there would be no awkward situations with Dilys; in fact, he had not even given Mr Whimple anything but the basic necessities to obviate the very chance of that...

*

After his call with Leini, Alun went back upstairs to put on his clothes; he could be in writer mode today: slovenly. He was used to that. He wondered if — when living with Leini — she would expect him always to be as well-dressed with her as he had recently been and whether, if he felt strait-jacketed in nice clothes and being shaven, it would affect his imagination. Most writers were scruffs, he mused, and almost all 19th century greats like Tolstoy, Hardy, Carlyle and Trollope had hair sprouting from almost every inch of skin and orifice; some of the women sported similar tendencies as well. Yet, despite ablutionary deprivations, they were all impeccably dressed, according to the mores of the time — something he now felt he, too, could perhaps aspire to with aplomb. After all, if he was writing in the ballroom then she would be at work anyway, so he could be in slovenly mode all day and then a quick wash, re-dress and brush-up would restore him to being the Adonis she expected before arriving home... to be greeted with a loving kiss, a mutual gin and tonic and a promise of much slap and tickle later on. Well, he could hope...

His reveries were suddenly blasted away by the sound of an obviously very angry Dilys doing an emergency stop on the gravel and slamming the front door with the shouted observation, "There was no-one stuck at the end of our bloody drive... What do you take me for? An idiot?"

"Well, you *went*..." Alun shouted back ungenerously. "That's what the voice said. If you weren't so jumpy about something or other then you might have walked down to check it out first."

"Who was it?" she demanded, her menacing rolling gait putting him in mind of a tanker in a heavy sea as she mounted the stairs.

"Well, you just said it was no-one," Alun answered with a smile on his face.

"Don't try and be smart, Alun; you know what I mean. Who were *you* talking to?"

"Oh, Jonathan's assistant."

"At eight in the morning? Give over."

"It was important – they didn't want me to write a scene today that they would almost certainly have to change. It needed a different angle."

"I'll give you a different angle," she riposted with the fire of the dragon she worshipped on her nation's flag. "You don't normally talk to Jonathan in that hushed way."

"I didn't want to wake you."

"It was a woman, wasn't it?"

"Well, Jonathan's assistant *is* a woman, yes..."

"What's her name?"

Alun did not want to divulge the appellation of his inamorata as a whole host of inappropriate monikers appeared before him in a whirlwind of creative possibility: Cuddles, – no, unbelievable; Phoebe – no, too last generation; Gladys – no, too grandmotherly; Doris – too common; Clarissa – too aristocratic; Anoushka – too sexy... "Anna," he blurted before the microsecond extended further and became a proof of guilt. "Yes, Anna."

Dilys stared at him with the venom of a serial killer, then said, "Well, I hope you're not having an affair with her." She turned and stomped down a couple of stairs and then turned back to spit: "But I am."

This caused total confusion in Alun's mind: Anna? Who was Anna? And had Dilys become a lesbian? It might explain a few things...

"You're having an affair with Anna?" he enquired incredulously.

"No, you *fel rhech mewn pot jam*. With a man – a *real* man; a farmer. Not a pansy writer."

Suddenly, it all fell into place; his innocent bluff about someone having ditched a tractor at the end of their drive had exposed a truth which had been completely unexpected. His wife was cuckolding him! The cheek! Here was he, trying to conceal an affair with someone whom he hoped would be the love of his life so as not to upset his wife – no; correction – did not want to experience the wrath of a fire-breathing scorned woman – and had been upstaged in the process. What peeved him most was the obvious fact that she had acquired nirvana before he had. "Ah," he breathed limply.

So when she asked again if he was having an affair with this 'Anna', he could honestly say: "No, I am not having an affair with Anna."

"Ah," said Dilys, in much the same feeble tone as his. Then: "Well, the cat's out the bag now. His name's Nathan and he's got a huge – "

"I don't want to know."

"– farm," she concluded. "With a thousand acres, outbuildings and workshops. Near Dolau."

"Ah, that makes all the difference," he said cheekily. Inside, though, he felt relieved: now he could leave Dilys and live in Elysium forever more with Anna. Leini. But he was not going to let the farm go without a fight: he had put a lot into this house and relationship over the years and had been – until now, at least – a very good and faithful husband. Now, though, was the moment to turn the screw: "But I won't divorce you," he proclaimed, feeling that he now had the moral high ground. He would, of course he would – he couldn't wait...

"Why not?" Dilys enquired warily.

Alun had already started his tirade, perfected on the train the night before: "Well, because it's an equal society now and as a man who has put a lot into this - " and he waved his hand vaguely at the surroundings – "I want to have a share of what's mine. Women do it all the time – now, as a man, it's my turn. And being a 'pansy writer' as you call me, you will see the full weight of my intellect bearing down on acquiring the fairness of an inclusive society which I thought your previous husband inculcated into you."

"Don't you bring the standards of my previous husband into this, Alun; he was a fine man who died before his time."

"No, he was a corrupt, hypocritical tyrant who used his political views as a front to cover everything he was not expected to countenance but did – and made a lot of money in the process."

Dilys fumed, reddening the while, as she tried to construct a riposte. But the moment evaporated and she just went redder still, then turned back down the stairs and slammed the kitchen door so hard that a picture fell off the wall, smashing the glass. A second later, she reopened the door and looked up at Alun, saying, "And you don't need to smash the house up just because you don't like what I've told you," and slammed the door again, whereupon the second shockwave rendered the sister painting to the previous one ending up in the same condition.

Then the door opened again and she stood in the opening – a framed representation of the tragic Muse Melpomene – jabbing her finger and saying: "You were quite happy to use the money my husband made for your own use." Before she could slam the door again, Alun just calmly explained: "We vowed to share everything, in sickness and in health, as part of our marriage vows. Corrupt or not, that was the deal you offered when we wedded." The door slammed shut again and Alun heard a selection of pans crash to the floor in the kitchen.

Well! What a turn-up! The road to Shangri-La had been discovered! He went up to his study and wrote one of his best ever scenes in rapid time – Jonathan would love it. Yet his mood soured when he realised that it would make the connection with fact and fiction even more difficult to write: there was now a motive to murder his wife rather than she him – and that could incriminate him: the plot would now be influenced by a jealous lover and a wife who wanted her husband gone: so perhaps the television murder of Mrs Wiggins – his wife's *alter ego* in real life – was now too close to the truth he was intending to mirror? This blending of fact and fiction, which had started as a mentally gymnastic exercise was now causing him a headache. But he was determined to persist...

In the kitchen, Dilys made herself a strong coffee and followed it with half a bottle of Merlot. She wanted to see Nathan again, who had sowed some very fertile seeds – quite literally, she felt. And it meant that her fitness regime could be jettisoned as well, for he seemed to like her the way she was – cuddly, domestic and a creator of wonderful meals, cakes and puddings – the perfect wife. How lucky she was to have found him... even though she knew she looked like something between a punctured barrage balloon and a charity shop sale item which was bursting at the seams.

Upstairs in his study, Alun pondered his unintended comment made in the heat of the moment about not divorcing Dilys and wondered why he had said it. Of course he wanted to divorce her – he couldn't be with Leini if he didn't. Yet, in one sense he was right: he wanted to ensure that at least a half of her first husband's ill-gotten gains were transferred to him and he would only get those if she was dead and he was the only beneficiary. So of course he wouldn't divorce her unless the settlement was right and legally agreed; yes, and he had been correct to bring up that very modern and 'inclusive' point: what was good for the goose was good for the gander in these strange new 'all-must-have-prizes' and gender-equal times. He had said the right thing – how instinctively attuned he had obviously become since he met Leini!

And he continued writing with a renewed passion of purpose...

CHAPTER 9

EPISODE 138. Sc. 6. WIGGINS' PARLOUR. INT. DAY.

MRS WIGGINS: Edmund? You lazy shabbaroon! Get down here and help me. I'm exhausted. What with cooking for you, washing your hose, gaiters and spatterdashes after that rainstorm and then mending your frock-coat; I'm true flummoxed. And attendin' to the master, an' all every hour God give us... Come here!

EDMUND: (COMING INTO THE PARLOUR). Stop whining, you corny-faced fussock. I do a day's toil for him, too, you know... Just 'cos you're 'ousekeeper 'ere working in this grand 'ouse for that just-ass don't make you the mistress o'me. Silence yersel' or I'll stop up yer gob for good.

MRS WIGGINS: At least I'm no beard-splitter... Going off with that feisty little bob-tail Arabella, the little hedge-whore! I know what you're up to!

EDMUND: I haven't touched her! She's betrothed to Samuel Lowings, the cheese-maker, anyway; I wouldn't finger her after that gundiguts.

MRS WIGGINS: So he's splitted her too, has he? The little witch. Now, 'nuff of this dawdlin' and help me lift this cauldron off the fire or neither you nor the master'll get no supper.

EDMUND: Thou'll have ter do it yersel'; I have to go and fetch some wood fer his fire or he'll be in a mood wi'you too as well as mesel'. You're stronger'n me anyhows...

MRS WIGGINS: You shag-bag! (HE EXITS).

Alun looked back over what he had written and smiled with pleasure. Yes, the Wigginses were definitely falling out with each other, he mused, as were he and Dilys; another few episodes – around number 152, he felt – and they would really be at each other's throats… at just about the time he aimed to be moving in with Leini. Then the fictitious dam could burst and the murder could be perpetrated. Then he could sell the house in Wales and live happily ever after on the proceeds of Dilys' first husband's ill-gotten gains. He looked back at his writing: the name Arabella he liked, too: it was a good substitute for his real-life Leini – two names totally different in century and sensation. But he had a name for her already in the series – Jenny. But *'Tis pity she's a whore'*, he thought – which Leini certainly was not. But Arabella could be the substitute name for his supposed flirtation, Anna, should he need it as a parallel character. Yes, that was a good one to have up his sleeve…. He was beginning to rather enjoy this dual subterfuge – real life and fiction coming together in such a fecund way. It was giving him renewed creativity…

It was then that he realised that Dilys would not be able to type up his first draft scripts anymore or she would twig what was going on. Despite her other drawbacks, she was not stupid. He sighed… still, perhaps Leini would do it for him. Either way, the odd migraine acquired looking at a computer in order to jettison his wife and gain his paramour was a splendid bargain, he felt.

Feeling pleased with himself, he decided to go for a run before it got dark and ignored his wife as he raced past her cooking at the Aga: cooking in both senses, in fact – not just her bottled anger but because she was very hot indeed and a rime of perspiration encircled her eyes like a miniature barrier reef…

Immediately after Alun's departure, Dilys went out to the hallway and called her farmer…

*

Dilys' new lover, Nathan Grubb, sat on his tractor cab, trying to make out what Dilys was saying as he held the mobile to his ear, the words as diffuse as the fine drizzle which was enveloping the magnificent landscape he was such a tiny part of. She was either angry, hysterical or dying – he was not sure which: perhaps it was all three. He was a kindly man, though, and wondered how he could help, so tried to calm her and confirmed he would ring her on the landline when he got back to his farmhouse.

Alun was getting good at his running and had lost a lot of weight, much to Leini's approval, and his new 'get smart' regimen had ensured the disappearance of much wayward hair and quite a lot of his waistline; and as he splashed through the mud he imagined what would be happening this time tomorrow… He was off to London but had not yet told Dilys: what was the point? Sudden script meetings were par for the course. His pace quickened again…

An hour later, the phone rang in Dilys' hallway: she rushed to answer it and was just about to pour out her spleen about Alun not understanding her (as a pretext to implying that Nathan obviously did) when Alun raced back, cheekily asking what was for supper on the way past her and up the stairs. When Alun was in the shower, poor Nathan got the full tirade. Had he done the wrong thing, meeting this ample woman, he wondered?

*

The next morning, Leini picked up a package from the post office, stuffed it into her bag and went on to work. Once there, she opened her computer and whilst it booted up, opened the parcel – which contained a letter written in all sorts of legalese pertaining to the purchase of the flat. She shuddered with excitement – this was really it! She and Alun were making a move together – in more ways than one! Also in the package was the Justice's book, a result of her using her charms on Mr Whimple to ask a favour of the solicitor – helpfully, a friend of his – who had agreed to loan it to her for a couple of days, which she could photocopy any interesting parts of but then return prior to completion, when it had to be presented to Alun and Leini with the deeds. She dipped into it and found it so fascinating that she found she was late seeing Jonathan to organise the chores for the day.

She still had not seen Alun since the last meeting and was becoming anxious as to whether she would still like him when she saw him again. That was in hand, though: he was coming up today and would spend quite a few days with her.

She texted him, hoping he'd actually receive it before she saw him, saying that the legal documents had been received. She and Alun had agreed not to tell Jonathan anything – about them, the flat, the book... nothing. It was their secret. And, eventually, of course, that of the whole viewing public as well. Although even she knew nothing of the extent of Alun's subterfuge: if she had, she would have known how he planned to raise the money for the flat.

For Alun, it was all in the script...

CHAPTER 10

Dilys awoke to find no sign of Alun. She looked all over the house, her humour improving with every room she found he was not in. His running-kit was in the laundry basket and his study was ordered and shut down. So where was he? Glad of the solitude but angry that he had not told her, she then found a scrawled note in the kitchen saying he had had a call the night before and needed to attend a script meeting in the morning, so had taken the Fiat runabout at five in the morning and was driving to London. The runabout? That car was so clapped-out it might not make it to the end of the drive! Still, why should she cocoa? He would probably be gone a day or two and so she could now indulge herself with Nathan... he could leave his cabbages and sprouts for a bit and give some attention instead to her very own brassicas; she made a cup of tea, slapped a couple of rashers of bacon and an egg into the frying pan and went to the phone in the hall.

Nathan was not expecting her call and was driving his tractor to the organic produce shop he owned, with half a ton of ripe produce in the trailer behind him. But on hearing Dilys' plea for company, he said he would drop it off and continue on the tractor so as to avoid returning back to his farm so he could see her earlier. Dilys wondered whether he might not arrive for much longer than she had hoped but was pleased he was keen to put himself out for her. They rang off and she decided to make him a lovely lunch, washed down with some homemade beer. Having finished her breakfast, she prepared the lunch and then went up for a long, hot, relaxing bath...

What Dilys did not know, however, was that Alun had opened her computer in the early morning and found out everything there was to know about Nathan Grubb. He was very rich. And he had a classic Porsche, too – Leini would like that...

Things were getting ever better and faster – nought to sixty in three seconds, in fact.

*

Alun's car had somehow made it to the outskirts of London, but its slowness had meant he was now stuck in a monumental traffic jam on the M4 and he would not make the meeting on time. He cursed himself for not taking the train but had wanted a car to drive Leini around London in. He hoped it would not put her off him as it was, like himself, well past its prime; but he would part-exchange it in London and get something more appropriate to match his new, svelte and very dashing image. He had brought the documentation with him for that purpose and smiled as he thought again of appropriating Nathan Grubb's Porsche – it looked in superb condition – which he would then give to Leini as compensation for Nathan seed-drilling his wife.

Leini was becoming somewhat privately agitated when Alun failed to appear for the ten o'clock meeting and hoped he had not decided to stay away because of her… *Wife found out, met someone else, gone off her, doesn't want to share a flat with me, doesn't fancy me anymore*, and so on: the occasional paranoias of young women who know what they want but still don't quite know whether they want it. She listened as Jonathan spoke to the wardrobe and make-up designers, the set dresser and the senior lighting cameraman; the only person not present – apart from Alun – was the designer, Archy which was causing some consternation as he had phoned in earlier saying he had a bit of a problem to solve but would be there as soon as he could. Without him, there was a lull, and so Leini stopped making the appropriate notes and offered to go and get some coffees to calm her nerves, whilst hoping she might bump into Alun outside for a sort of sneak preview. It was soon to be production time; the series was shot eight at a time over eight days in studio, with usually another four for exterior filming: they had many in the can already but any delay would find them running out of days as it was shown four nights a week. She hoped Alun was all right…

At that same moment, Nathan Grubb was navigating his tractor across the potholes in Dilys' drive and parked right outside her front door. She rushed out and flung herself into his arms, knocking a bunch of flowers he was holding into the air and into the mud. She kissed his weather-beaten face apologetically as he tried to retrieve them, and found she was holding his belt, so pulling him over, whereupon he fell onto the flowers in the dirt and crushed them completely.

"Oh, I'm so sorry, Nathan," she spluttered, as she grabbed his belt again, pulling him up. "I'm so clumsy… it's just I've been looking forward to seeing you so much…" and she kissed the somewhat discombobulated grower whilst pulling him inside and into the kitchen. "I've got some lunch for you here," she beamed: "Would you like it now or… you know, a bit later, after… you know?"

"I think later will do nicely," he opined, and allowed her to drag him up the stairs – whereupon much bumping, rusty springs and sighing could soon be heard. In the oven, the roast was just coming to a turn – as was Nathan.

*

Leini returned to the office and her knees nearly gave way as she saw Alun had arrived; the relief and joy was palpable as she offered to go and retrieve a coffee for him, too. He consented and opened his briefcase, whereupon the new scripts and storylines were soon being scrutinised in minute detail. Which is what Leini found herself doing to Alun.

They started discussing the next shooting schedule but could not get finally started until Archy the designer arrived; this he suddenly did – in somewhat of a lather with some distressing news… although he also had a smile about his lips which intrigued them all. He had, he said, just been to check over the cottage location with some construction staff to get it ready for shooting the week after next; however, the crews had found the location difficult to find from the description and photos he had taken some weeks before. When, to his horror, he had arrived to join them, he realised that they *were* all in the right location – but it had changed beyond recognition from that described, redolent of the Georgian period in all its squalor: now, there were new, modern plastic windows in place of the old decrepit

Georgian ones, a sunburst glass front door, frilly multi-coloured curtains and gnomes around the garden, which now sported embedded plastic flowers. Finding the owners – and beside himself with anger and disbelief – he asked what they had done to their house and why. The answer had been that they had spent their location money, 'making the house look nice for the telly'. The room erupted with disbelieving laughter, with the exception of Jonathan, who now realised that the delay would now blow a hole in his already-exceeded budget… and would have to spend more money putting the location back to how it had been before. And, as Alun reminded him, he would also have to re-write some scripts to change the narrative order of the story or the filming would get behind.

Not that he minded: he had an even stronger excuse to stay in town, now… as Leini's beaming eyes betrayed, too. And also, it had just given him another twist to add to the plot…

*

The lunch and frolicking over, Dilys and Nathan decided to walk around her estate; it transpired that Nathan had known her deceased husband vaguely, and his stiffness on acquiring that knowledge worried her somewhat: he suddenly became detached and monosyllabic. He eventually softened a little, but Dilys was aware that he suddenly had an urge to leave as he had to mend some fences and fix his distributor head, whatever that was. So he left somewhat abruptly and left Dilys wondering what it was that had been said to cause this change…

As he drove his tractor in a somewhat hazy line along the narrow byways of Wales, the reasons for his sudden concern about this relationship with Dilys crowded in on him. Yes, it was *her first husband* who had fiddled him out of several thousand pounds some years ago and then – as if to compound his sin – had ensured that a contract for millions of cabbages and assorted veg over the years had been taken away from him and almost certainly given to a colleague of that ruthlessly bent council leader. He felt smug about having managed to plunder his wife's anatomy but mused that this was unimportant now as any sense of revenge was lost, the man being dead. But if he could get her farm as part of any agreement, that would at least leave things somewhat settled. Perhaps he had been too influenced by what he had found out and should have kept his feelings to himself ... but the germ of revenge and appropriation of her assets – in more ways than one – were suddenly his most urgent task. And woe to anyone who tried to stop him – including her current husband. Should be no problem: he was a 'pansy writer' as Dilys termed him, whereas he was a strong, robust rural specimen. He smiled. It was game, set and match – after he had made it up to Dilys, of course...

*

It was ten days later and Leini had taken advantage of the hiatus caused by the filming delay to sort out the flat they had just moved into the morning before. It was a pleasant day and, after finding homes for various bits and pieces removed from her own flat – Alun's stuff would complement hers later on when things had progressed further – she decided to find out more about the man who had built their new home, Justice Theodore Blankitt. So she again opened the autobiography – included as part of the flat purchase – written by this august-looking gentleman and started reading some passages in more detail than those she had photocopied as being of interest earlier; what had then caught her eye were some of the 18th century trials that had been judged by him. Although neither had really had more than a cursory look at the photocopies due to the whirlwind of events – emotional and professional – which had engulfed them, seeing that it would be a few hours before Alun came home, she made herself a cup of tea, snuggled up in the living-room, facing the garden where the sun was shining, and started reading.

It became apparent that most 18th century murders had been one of three types: poisoning, stabbing or smashing in someone's skull, with the odd duel quite prevalent as well; she had, by now, been advised of Alun's schemes regarding the duality of Dilys and Mrs Wiggins and she had accepted them gleefully without hesitation; yet in the context of what she and Alun were looking for scriptwise, this would make the plots trickier as there were more 21st century murder methods. Justice Blankitt had, it transpired, sent many people to the gallows and – whilst this was fine for the plots of *Jonquil's Journals*, it was trickier if one were trying to ascribe both the crime and the sentencing in a 21st century context…

And then a trial caught her eye…

A young girl – a maid at a house in Putney – heavens, it may even have been this one! – had been taken on by the widowed master and he had eventually seduced her; this had not gone down well with the housekeeper, who – despite a hefty surfeit of years over the other one – had hoped for the position of lady of the house herself. In a jealous rage, she had confronted her master – a successful gunsmith with two shops in Spitalfields – and said she would leave his employ if he did not eject the 'little hussy' from the premises. Inevitably, he refused and threatened to send *her* packing instead. The young girl, though, had a young, good-looking brother and, in trying to get him appointed in the same house as she, introduced him to the housekeeper as a purveyor of victuals with the full support of the master – the employment proviso being that he would give the spinster a 'goodly time' so that she would stay, her plum puddings, beef roasts and game pies being the talk of the immediate neighbourhood and also the master's ample waistline.

This happened and the housekeeper was placated, but she had a suitor of more advanced years who became jealous and decided to rid her of this pesky young intruder – despite her rather enjoying the terms of employment with him that he had been subjected to by the master's plot. So the older man was out to get the boy – but without being suspected. So he employed an ingenious way of doing so… but Leini was just about to read what the manner of his crime was when Alun returned, and the deed and punishment stayed unexposed for the time being.

But it would soon be appropriated with a few minor differences…

CHAPTER 11

A lun's plot twist due to the delay engendered by the couple's prettying up of their cottage for television involved the programme's hero, Bartholomew Jonquil, finding himself accused of a sexual misdemeanour – not unusual in Georgian England. It was also the first opportunity to spice up the series with some sex, agreed at a previous meeting but now brought forward by necessity of this new situation. The character of the girl was supposed to be a destitute waif from Shropshire, who had apparently importuned Jonquil on London Bridge at midnight. Jonquil himself had denied the charges, but the air was thick with doubt, and backed up by two witnesses who had been sworn in as 'honourable people of the realm', being in trade as a baker and seamstress, named Dick Hoult and Lisa Sparrow, respectively. The scene Alun was writing – in their newly-occupied flat – meant that Jonquil, a Justice of the Peace, was in the unusual position of being in the dock rather than presiding on the bench. The scene involved flashbacks to his supposed misdemeanour and the witnessing of this by the two characters.

The poor harlot, Jenny Ludlow, was being played by a sweet young actress called Beth, whose first TV role this was; but terrified by what her parents and grandmother would say when they saw her exposing her charms to the televisual nation, she had caused a disruption with Jonathan which was only resolved when her fee had been heavily increased as a result. Needless to say, the press coverage of the event ensured that far more people would view her naked beauty than would have done so before – which was good for Jonathan but neither Beth's modesty nor her parents' despair. The delay, while it was discussed whether to get a different actress or bribe Beth until she consented, was such that the haste needed to get these scenes written and then filmed had left very little time for Alun: when writing quickly, it was also more likely there might be glaring storyline errors to come back and haunt him in future episodes. Consequently, he was somewhat flustered, not helped by having to do extra research into the legalities of the time to ensure all was historically correct. Leini, though, had offered to do this research to provide the detail while he created the outlines and scripts – and which left them very much together for the writing of the relevant scenes…

JONQUIL'S JOURNALS:

EPISODE 140. Sc 17: JONQUIL'S COURTROOM. INT. DAY.

LORD PAISLEY: This is a hearing before full trial to decide whether the Justice of the Peace, Bartholomew Jonquil, of Spitalfields town and usual Chief Justice of the Peace in this very building is innocent or not with the importuning of Miss Jenny Ludlow, harlot, who is also up for the same offence with the aforesaid Justice at around midnight on Saturday, 18th January, 1793. If ultimately found guilty, he will be stripped of his office. Call Jenny Ludlow.

MUCH MUTTERING FROM THE COURTROOM AS SHE TAKES HER PLACE IN THE DOCK. A BEWIGGED FACTOTUM OFFERS HER A BIBLE ON WHICH TO SWEAR BUT PAISLEY WAVES HIM AWAY.

LORD PAISLEY: Never mind about the oath; the lass has already gone too far for a Bible to have any influence on the poor girl. (LOOKING DOWN TO HER). Just admit it – you're guilty, aren't you?

JENNY: No, my Lord Justice. I am innocent of the charge.

LORD PAISLEY: But you were seen with Justice Bartholomew

	Jonquil giving him pleasure on London Bridge! How much did he pay you?
JENNY:	He did not pay me, Sir, as I did no such thing. We just talked for a few moments.
LORD PAISLEY:	To discuss the price? (SHE STAYS SILENT AS THE CROWD LAUGHS). If you do not answer, little lady, then I will bring in the two witnesses to prove it.
JENNY:	(CHEEKILY). May I ask <u>you</u> a question, Sir?
LORD PAISLEY:	Er… well, yes, I suppose so…
JENNY:	Why are you doing this to me, Sir? I admit I spoke to the Justice Bartholomew Jonquil on the bridge, but we were discussing some business – (GENERAL LAUGHTER). No, not that sort of business! It was to discuss whether I could become a maid for his wife and so take me away from the temptations of a squalid life which might be my only other choice.
LORD PAISLEY:	At midnight on London Bridge?!
JENNY:	I had nowhere to go, Sir. I asked him for a penny or two to help me – there was no 'doings' discussed. He's a Justice of the Peace as you are, and a good man; I think you are using me to try and besmirch *his* name, Sir. (GENERAL UPROAR). I never touched him.
LORD PAISLEY:	Silence in the court! This is a gross calumny! (WE CUTAWAY TO JONQUIL WHO IS SITTING SMUGLY, A SMILE ON HIS FACE).
JENNY:	And I think you're trying to frame me for this so's *you'll* get his position here. (MORE UPROAR).

LORD PAISLEY:	'Pon my soul, the girl is a witch! How dare she say that! Indeed, how much has Mr. Jonquil offered for your testimony in complete contradiction of the good witnesses sitting over there?
JENNY:	None, my lord.
LORD PAISLEY:	So you still deny the charge?
JENNY:	I do, my lord.
LORD PAISLEY:	And you had no 'doings', as you say, with Justice Jonquil?
JENNY:	I did not.
LORD PAISLEY:	(AFTER A PAUSE). The court is adjourned for one hour. Little Missy, I wish to question you for a few moments in my chambers… to hopefully save your character without going into all the details in front of the court and all these people – if it's not too late, of course. (TO THE USHER). Sir, bring the little lady to me…
	THE COURT RISES AS HE DISAPPEARS INTO A SIDE ROOM AND JENNY IS ESCORTED TO THE ROOM AFTER HIM. WE CUTAWAY TO JONQUIL LOOKING AT WHAT LOOKS LIKE A LAWYER ON THE BENCHES; THEY NOD SURREPTITIOUSLY TO ONE ANOTHER AND THE LAWYER DISAPPEARS.

JONQUIL'S JOURNALS:

EPISODE 140. Sc. 18. SIDE ROOM, BJ'S CHAMBERS, INT. DAY.

THE JUSTICE IS SEATING HIMSELF ON A LOW CHAIR AS JENNY IS BROUGHT

IN. HE WAVES THE USHER AWAY AND
THE DOOR CLOSES BEHIND HIM.

LORD PAISLEY: My dear – come here, don't be shy… Now, you're a pretty little thing but I am willing to help you to clear your name, so come closer and we'll discuss the truth of the matter…

JENNY: How so, Sir?

LORD PAISLEY: Well, we all know that you *are* a harlot. Nobody would stand on London Bridge at midnight unless they were… um… 'looking' for something…

JENNY: No, Sir, it's true – I had nowhere to go, and it's easier to escape off a bridge rather than down the dark alleyways of London town.

LORD PAISLEY: Well, come here and we'll discuss it. Come, come; we don't have too long…

Alun stopped writing and looked away from the PC to observe Leini behind him, her bare feet up on the edge of the sofa and a sheaf of documents in her hand, which she was reading; facing his back with her legs apart, her open skirt allowed a direct view of her tight underwear…

"Leini?"

"Mm?" She looked up.

"How long would it take in the 18th century, d'you think, to get through all that clothing and achieve penetration quickly without causing too much noise and rolling about?"

"What a question! I thought you'd know more about that than I do!" They laughed. Alun looked at her acutely and said, "Is that a reference to my age or your supposition of my sexual experience?"

"A bit of both, I think!"

They laughed again and just looked at each other. In that instant, the bond of their mutual emotions became firmer. She gave him one of her wry looks, which then turned into a coy smile; her heart was racing. She had wanted to cast aside her restraining mental preconditions for a few days now and had been waiting for the perfect opportunity to express her lust for Alun without it seeming cheap, irrational or capitulation; and now was that moment.

"Why don't we find out? If we each put on a few more togs – the bigger and heavier the better, we could then time it with a stopwatch."

Alun looked at her with an expression of disbelieving astonishment: had all conditional resistance suddenly dissipated in a whispered breath of insouciance? Her smiling face would imply that it had: "What a wonderful idea. Go and get some of your baggiest clothes and I'll fetch another pair of trousers to put over these and then we'll find out."

Leini was already heading for the bedroom.

JONQUIL'S JOURNALS:

EPISODE 140. Sc. 20. SIDE ROOM, BJ'S CHAMBERS, INT. DAY.

	LORD PAISLEY IS IN A STATE OF HURRIED FLAGRANTE DELICTO AS JENNY SITS ASTRIDE HIM, HER SKIRTS PARTED AND HER BREASTS EXPOSED AS SHE PUMPS HIM HARD. AT THE POINT OF RELEASE, THE DOOR OPENS AND THERE STAND BARTHOLOMEW JONQUIL, THE TWO WITNESSES AND THE USHER TRYING TO HOLD THEM BACK.
USHER:	No, no – you can't go in without permission!
LORD PAISLEY:	Curses! It's a set-up – I am undone!
JONQUIL:	(LOOKING AT HIS STATE OF UNDRESS). You most certainly are, Sir!

LORD PAISLEY:	And to think I paid you handsomely for this, you scheming little wench!
JONQUIL:	Witnesses – there you have the truth! He was paying her off to ensure she testified against me!
JENNY:	(CRYING). I didn't want to! It was because he paid me, I had to let him have his way with me!
JONQUIL:	Sir – you are as corrupt and licentious as you say I am! And in my room in my chambers, too! A pox on you, Sir! You sent this good lady and these two witnesses to follow me and cause a meeting as I crossed London Bridge after an evening at the theatre in Southwark. But what you did not know was that I knew you had been trying to oust me as you're jealous of my worth as a Justice of the Peace, which you have been trying to become for many months. So, Sir, this trial will never go to the Old Bailey and I shall see to it that you be struck off the judicial system for bribery and corruption, as all these players knew your plot. It's over, Sir! And now, I will acquit these people and return to my very own bench. Good afternoon, Sir! (THEY ALL EXIT, LEAVING LORD PAISLEY ON HIS OWN IN DISTRESS).

*

Leini had started the stopwatch but the desire to caress and give pleasure, despite the encumbrances of their voluminous clothing, had meant that it was several minutes before all the garments were discarded and the first act of love had been acquired. Instinctively, neither had wished to rush this first sublime acceptance of each other and even Alun had not desired to make it look hurried rather than consensual; and it had worked beautifully. They lay in each other's arms for many minutes after the first explosion of passion – and then did it three times more before tiredness and dusk enveloped them. Yet the reasoning that it must have taken far longer at that time to make love quickly meant that some tweaking of the script was necessary – there needed at least to be a longer interim scene. For the moment, though, any tweaking would be administered upon the somnolent form of Leini. But the 18th century reasons for impeded 21st century intercourse would all go in the script. Tomorrow.

CHAPTER 12

Nathan Grubb was driving his tractor whilst talking to Dilys on his mobile, spreading muck the while from a tank being pulled behind him. He was apologising for his sudden exit and offering to take her out for a treat in his vintage Porsche, despite not really wanting to overdo the sense of appearing rich. But a Porsche swayed emotions, particularly his bright yellow one... Dilys was ecstatic and replied effusively in the affirmative; *Step one achieved,* he thought – *now for the next phase.* He had been weighing things up and deviously realised he should stick with Dilys as he had a very good plan for carefully compromising her and grasping her assets; his farm was doing well but some extra land, with its ability to expand his vegetative volumes, was a big attraction. And her house was bigger and nicer than his – and closer to civilisation and his organic farm shop, too, which would help with administrative chores. He smiled to himself: Dilys was the perfect ticket in so many ways, even if there was rather more of her than he would have liked. And if he became bored, he could just push off back to his own farm, having snaffled the money and the land. With the first husband mercifully out of the way, things would be easier: not a man to cross in life, as he knew to his disadvantage; but in death, that was another matter. And if her current husband really was on the way out, too – either by his own design or hers – it would give him a clean run at appropriating her, the farm, and her money... Yet what Nathan had not thus far anticipated was Alun's desire for much the same result – at least half the proceeds of the house and estate – as well as that Porsche of Grubb's which he wanted for Leini. In fact, Nathan Grubb did not know what was about to hit him. But then, neither did Alun.

Dilys, though, whilst relishing Nathan's undimmed lust for her body and cooking, was not aware of his greater lust for her belongings. So she told him that she thought there was 'a floozy' in Alun's life in London, which she stated would help grounds for a divorce, which gratified Grubb further. Yet this was just a ruse for her to keep Grubb interested: she had a secret of her own, too…

*

Two days later, the block of scripts was finished — only delayed somewhat by frequent breaks for sex. What had started out as a flirtatious but delayed desire (on Leini's part) had soon become a carnal necessity for both of them: their wish to ensure that the scripts were accurate, along with Jonathan's request for more libidinous content, had become not just personal desire but also agreed as mandatory by the need for its proof. Jonathan was aware that Leini seemed to be taking much more time 'helping Alun with his research' than before and was subsequently away from his office for much of the time, which he found odd and annoying; yet he put the extra time needed down to the re-structuring of the scripts and storylines on account of the interrupted filming schedule. Yet when he had offered to come round to help clear what he perceived to be a case of writers' block, this was firmly resisted. Alun had told Jonathan about the flat but had not revealed anything about Leini living with him — he wanted Dilys to be the supposed partner for as long as possible. In addition, Alun and Leini still had not given any time to putting away — hide, even — all their effects until some wardrobes and drawers could arrive from Wales, which might be a long time hence. Jonathan would obviously have recognised many of Leini's clothes, too, which had been randomly hung around the apartment — and would readily be realised as hers rather than the dowdy Dilys's; Leini's dress sense was somewhat younger, sexier and more revealing than that of Alun's wife, too — and certainly more petite. He was curious, though, as to why Alun had told him in no uncertain terms not to mention the flat to Dilys, his pretext being that she would accuse him of squandering what was essentially her inheritance from the bent former husband. It was all very odd…

Now that the people who had 'prettied up their house for the telly' had had their home returned to its 18th century condition — much to their annoyance, but handsomely paid for the inconvenience — shooting at that location was possible; and what with the Priory also on stream, a huge number of extra filming venues had become available. Alun was on his way to the shoot cottage at that moment and Leini had carefully arranged to be in Jonathan's office early that morning so she could go with him to meet Alun at the location: the subterfuge had to be continued – they could still not be seen as an 'item'.

Alun was there by the time they arrived, the director, sparks, location manager, designer, grips, master carpenter and lighting director already scurrying around taking pictures and checking angles to get the most out of the location as possible. The owners had been given a luxury house nearby for the duration of the shoot, into which they would also be shunted whenever scenes needed for their home were on the filming schedule – although no-one had told them that yet.

After the meeting, the TV folk repaired to the local restaurant, whose coffers had been swelled by the arrival of the film crew. Leini and Alun always kept as wide a berth as possible during these meetings, the propensity for astute eyes around television circles in sussing out relationships being legendary. It was all about attention to detail and any quick glance or hand-touch would betray them immediately. If suspected, it would be around the network within minutes. And that would do Alun's dastardly plans no good at all.

With the next few scripts written, the easier part was to develop the storylines and then – in TV parlance – 'word them in'. This creation of future script directions entailed Jonathan and Alun being together more, and therefore Leini was always there, rather than 'helping Alun' away from the office. However, inevitability always arrives at some point and it was on one such day that Jonathan suddenly put two and two together, and, one afternoon, after a canteen lunch, he suddenly asked the question.

"Are you two having an affair?" he enquired, his eyes peering at them over his half-moon glasses.

"No."

"Certainly not!" they each proclaimed together – with such

firmness that it made Jonathan realise without a doubt that they were. *Methinks they protest too much*, he thought as he observed: "You seem to look at each other a lot."

"She gives me inspiration," Alun parried lightly with a laugh, as if trying to feign embarrassment for Leini's sake.

"I don't think it would be a good idea," Leini said quickly, flushing slightly; and then, so as not to risk hurting Alun, added, "even if it is a nice idea in principle."

The quick glances between them made Jonathan ever more certain that his postulation was correct but any further delving was curtailed instantly by Alun, who, eager to move on, murmured, "Anyway… Talking of affairs… You remember we talked a few weeks ago about getting rid of Jonquil's Mrs Wiggins?"

"I do," confirmed Jonathan.

"Well, I think we could advance that as it's nearer the end of Lottie Brace's contract now. So could she have an affair with a farmer who has a grudge against her husband and wants his money and position in the Jonquil household? If so, then he could – after many more twists and turns over several episodes – turn out to be in league with a couple of assassins… It would be a marvellous part for Pat Duffy… Then he could find himself in a tricky situation with her current husband who's also cuckolding *her*. So does he arrange to get rid of him, too? What d'you think?"

Jonathan looked away and thought about it; "Might have some mileage," he concurred, "and it would mean some rural shooting, which would save some money. We're well over-budget, thanks to those idiots prettying up their house. What with that chaos affecting the filming schedule and having to compensate with new studio sets as well, it could claw back some unexpected costs."

"And we could get some more sex in," Leini added, much to the surprise of both.

"With Mrs Wiggins?" Jonathan laughed. "We'll lose our ratings."

They all rocked with laughter, as much as to defuse the

awkwardness of the suggestion as the thought of the voluminous Mrs Wiggins *in flagrante delicto* with a hirsute rural farmer, straw, knickerbockers, petticoats and smocks flying around in grand disarray…

Alun and Leini thought to themselves how they might play out the very same scene at home for veracity as Jonathan then observed: "Lottie wouldn't do it."

"Then you could fire her. She'd be in breach of contract – I'm sure there's no clause stipulating no nudity because no-one would ever ask." They all fell about again as Leini went into her office and dug out the relevant contract, returning shaking her head as she plonked it on the desk, saying, "No – no exclusions at all."

"Well, I never thought this would be the way to get rid of that bloody actress," Jonathan stated with some feeling. "I'm surprised I never had the idea before."

'You didn't,' the two others thought – 'We did,' as they fleetingly exchanged a glance.

"I like it," Jonathan confirmed, his eyes deep in his notes. "I shall enjoy telling her she's doing a nude scene; it'll be in all the papers and our ratings will go up. Not because they'll see much, but the public love her as much as we hate her, and they'll be wanting to see the 21st century court case in parallel with the 18th century one. Pure genius."

Leini then injected a note of caution into the proceedings. "If she wins her real case, though – not the fictitious one – with the real public today on her side, we could be in for severe damage costs."

"And we might have to write her back in, like Arthur Conan Doyle magically bringing Sherlock Holmes back after his plummet down the Reichenbach Falls," added Alun.

"I can live with that," Jonathan replied, "As far as I'm concerned, it's win-win either way. Either no Mrs Wiggins and a quieter life; or more Mrs Wiggins with an even bigger ego who will raise the programme's ratings and advertising revenue. As I say, pure genius. Go off and write it."

*

As expected, the actress playing Mrs Wiggins, Lottie Brace, was apoplectic as she faced Jonathan and Alun in the former's office. For once, Leini had decided to listen from her desk through the partition, where she could get on with her work and listen to the warfare without getting involved. The partition was very thin, but did not need to be – the exchange was very loud indeed.

CHAPTER 13

Like the lull between a mild storm before a second of hurricane proportions, the office went quiet and then an explosion of invective from Lottie was heard as she crashed out of Jonathan's office, threatening lawsuits, revenge, public opprobrium on social media and many other disasters of biblical proportions. She swept past Leini with a glance of doom and could be heard flinging fire doors open as she disappeared down the corridor, their swinging noises gradually returning to calm after the tornado had passed.

Jonathan poked his head around the door and asked Leini: "Has she really gone, or is she hiding behind the filing cupboard to ambush me?"

"No, but she left a trail of destruction down the corridor."

"Fine. Well, Alun will be pushing ahead with writing the script for her removal so we can expect even more invective and requests for why we're axing her. I suspect you might be busier from now on..."

He was right. Within a couple of hours, social media was alight with protestations for and against Mrs Wiggins' removal. Yet the anger was met with some glee, too, for whilst some saw her as an interfering old bag, others defended her with the 'woke' angles such as that the decision was 'fattist', 'uglist', 'cookist' and 'revengist'. The current vindictive world had met the courteous 18th century one head on – and with a vengeance... In anticipation, Tellurian TV discreetly raised its advertising rates for the programme.

*

JONQUIL'S JOURNALS:

EPISODE 146, SCENE 33. WIGGINS' PARLOUR.

> MRS WIGGINS IS COOKING AT THE
> KITCHEN TABLE, HER SLEEVES
> ROLLED UP AND VARIOUS BITS OF

PRODUCE STICKING TO HER AMPLE
FORM AND MUSCULAR ARMS.
THROUGH THE BASEMENT WINDOW,
SHE SUDDENLY OBSERVES A SET OF
LEGS COMING DOWN THE AREA STEPS
AND THEN THERE IS A KNOCK AT THE
SERVANTS' DOOR.

WIGGINS: (TO HERSELF). Now, who can that be...?
(SHOUTS).

Enter!

A GOOD-LOOKING, IF SLIGHTLY
ROUGH, FARMER TYPE IN HIS MID-
THIRTIES APPEARS, BEARING IN A
LARGE CLOTH-COVERED PANNIER
TWO RABBITS, SOME VEGETABLES, A
BRACE OF PHEASANTS, A COUPLE OF
FRESH FISH AND A LEG OF MUTTON.

ORCHARD: Good day, madam. Do I have the pleasure of
addressing the housekeeper and cook to Sir
Bartholomew Jonquil, Mrs Wiggins?

WIGGINS: That's me. I'm busy, so state your purpose.

ORCHARD: No scullery-maid to assist you, milady? (AS HE
STARTS TO UNCOVER HIS WARES).

WIGGINS: Huh! My master's too mean to employ a
scullery-maid. I have to do everything mesel'.
Work, work, work... And me husband's no
help, either... Anyway, what's your name, you
scallywag?

ORCHARD: Jonas Orchard at your service, milady. Purveyor
of fresh meats to the gentry only.

WIGGINS: Orchard? You should be selling fruit, not meat!

ORCHARD: That's what most gentlewomen say! But I heard
on the street that you're very circumspect about

	your meats and I'm here to replenish your stocks at times to suit you with the best victuals available…
WIGGINS:	I see… and where are you from? And your victuals, too, sir…?
ORCHARD:	I'm from Islington, madam, where the countryside meets the town… open fields, streams and woods to replenish the needs of the gentry.
WIGGINS:	On whose land do you scavenge? Are you a poacher? If you are, we'll all be for the Trine!
ORCHARD:	You wound me deeply, madam.
WIGGINS:	A prigger of cackling cheats, then?
RCHARD:	Madam, I am no stealer; I have some land. So I rear or catch produce on my own small estate left to me by my father.
WIGGINS:	Well, you're no Malkintrash, I grant you. Show me your wares, then…
ORCHARD:	There, madam. And I tell you again, Mrs Wiggins – I do not steal. I also provide for the Earl of Haringey, if you wish to know.
WIGGINS:	Do you have some mutton, perhaps, then?
ORCHARD:	On occasion, yes – but it's not a good time of year for mutton.
WIGGINS:	So what's that, then?
ORCHARD:	Mutton.
WIGGINS:	Looks fresh and wholesome…
ORCHARD:	My apologies, madam, but I cannot sell that. It's reserved for my next patron.
WIGGINS:	My master enjoys a good roast of mutton and that looks a fine piece to me…

ORCHARD:	Well… as I say, it's for another gentleman… (SHE GLARES AT HIM). But for the right price…?
WIGGINS:	You turncoat! What about your next customer, then?
ORCHARD:	I can get some more…
WIGGINS:	So you're a napper of naps, then?
ORCHARD:	No! I steal nothing!
WIGGINS:	Hmm… Well you seem like a well-bred young man. I'll have the rabbits and the mutton – if you'll sell them to me… If not, I'll have nowt.
ORCHARD:	You drive a hard bargain, madam. But if I can return…?
WIGGINS:	You have a good demeanour and a nice smile, young sir, so I'll accept your return as long as you give me what I want for a fair price now.
ORCHARD:	Two shillings.
WIGGINS:	Daylight robbery! One shilling and sixpence!
ORCHARD:	All right, madam…
WIGGINS:	And then you can come back whenever you want – but don't expect me to buy your wares every time, young man.
ORCHARD:	You do me a great service, madam, and thank ye. (SHE GIVES HIM THE MONEY). Thank you. I shall return in due course.
	SUDDENLY, HER HUSBAND EDMUND ENTERS.
EDMUND:	Who's this rapscallion, then?
ORCHARD:	I am no rapscallion, sir, but a purveyor of high-quality peck.
EDMUND:	(LOOKING AT THEM). Hm… better be.

	Mmm, looks all right. Buy it. Now off with you, or I'll call the guard. This is a respectable house and the lord's a high-up queer cuffin so watch yourself. (HE LEAVES).
WIGGINS:	Pay no attention to that old badshag, even if he is my husband. In fact, come whenever you can and I might just be able to offer you a bit more… (SAID WITH A GLINT IN HER EYE).
ORCHARD:	Thank you, madam, I shall return with pleasure. (HE LEAVES.)
WIGGINS:	(TO HERSELF AFTER HIS EXIT). Or <u>for</u> pleasure, if you wish it, young man… very handsome! And a real mutton-monger I'd wager, with those lovely eyes! He can take a slice with me if he wants, as long as he's no shitten-prick, that is…

*

The writing was going well and the storm over Mrs Wiggins' being written out was the main topic of TV gossip and was all over social media. Jonathan felt vindicated, but Alun had to come up with a means of her disposal. Which he had already decided upon, but not in the manner he had planned.

Out of respect rather than desire, he had rung Dilys to say he would be coming down for a night or two soon but could not say when. To her, that usually meant in a week or more's time, so she was not troubled by the fact that she had invited Nathan over for some company the next evening.

The proverbial manure was about to hit the fan – and that would be relevant to the next few weeks and the fans rooting for Mrs Wiggins' retention in the soap, too. It would be an unholy mess on all counts…

CHAPTER 14

Alun needed a break and so, after an early evening of carnal delight with Leini, followed by a meagre supper, he got into his car and left the flat for Wales. Being a long journey, he stopped for a coffee at a service station on the M4 and then continued up the M5 and cut across through Tewkesbury, arriving at Tref-Y-Clawdd just after midnight. He was surprised to see what looked like the back of a classic car of some sort parked just inside the adjoining barn but, being tired, thought little of its relevance until he entered the kitchen and observed the remains of a *repas à deux* on the table – which had seemingly been deserted in a hurry. It was not like Dilys to leave a mess: she was very fastidious about washing-up and leaving all pristine and well-ordered for the morning. Suddenly, like a fog clearing, he knew what was going on. A smile crept across his lips as he then heard unfamiliar gruntings and bed squeaks coming from the bedroom. Then the relevance of the car he had spied kicked in – it was her farmer's Porsche! He now had proof she was cuckolding him and realised this would also make things easier with Leini! Now he could probably get the Porsche as part of a settlement and would not have to pay for it! His mind was suddenly crystal clear and alert again but, the long journey having bludgeoned his oratorical powers, he tiptoed up the stairs – deftly missing the squeaky ones – and went to sleep on the sofa in his study.

The next morning, he arose early, only to find that whoever was in the bedroom with his wife had arisen even earlier and was again in the midst of a carnal exploitation of his wife's nether regions. So he picked up the laptop he had borrowed from the office, quietly descended the stairs, made himself a cup of tea, then cleared the table and re-laid it for breakfast. That all accomplished, he sat back to wait.

*

JONQUIL'S JOURNALS:

EPISODE 149, SCENE 17. A DARK ALLEWAY IN LONDON. NIGHT.

MRS WIGGINS COMES INTO VIEW, HOLDING A BASKET FULL OF VARIOUS COMESTIBLES, SUCH AS VEG AND EGGS, A LARGE JOINT OF MEAT, A PIE OR TWO, ETC. A ROUGH, SWARTHY TYPE APPEARS BEHIND HER AND STARTS TO FOLLOW HER AND, OUT OF SHOT, WE HEAR SCREAMS AND CRIES OF RESTRAINT, HITTING AND SO ON, ENDING WITH A LOUD 'OUCH' FROM THE MAN – AND SUDDENLY HE IS RUNNING BACK FROM WHENCE HE CAME, BLOOD POURING OUT THE BACK OF HIS HEAD, FOLLOWED BY AN IRATE AND SLIGHTLY DISSHEVELLED MRS WIGGINS, BRANDISHING A LARGE BUT BONY LEG OF MUTTON, WITH WHICH SHE HAS OBVIOUSLY HIT HIM.

MRS WIGGINS: (CALLING AFTER HER ASSAILANT). I'll swaddle you with a real cudgel and much harder next time you try to snavel me, you girt damber!

*

Alun had just finished writing this when the kitchen door opened and a tired-looking Nathan Grubb entered and then froze as he saw Alun sitting there. Alun just smiled and watched the embarrassment ooze from the stranger's being, as Grubb then turned and shouted up the stairs, "Dilys, you've got a visitor… down 'ere in the kitchen, look you."

There was some sudden movement from upstairs and after a

minute or two a lanken-haired, barefoot and equally disarrayed Dilys entered, her unsupported breasts swinging heavily from side to side under her nightshirt and her face wearing the expression of a disbelieving, dismayed delinquent.

"What are you doing here?" she snapped.

"I live here," replied Alun, a smile playing across his face. "And I could ask the same of this gentleman..."

"He's a friend."

"Obviously."

"He's been helping me planting things – he's a farmer."

Alun gave a wry look to both. "Where?"

"Round and about... Anyway, I wasn't expecting you until at least tonight. You never come immediately."

"Does this man?" said Alun, laughing. Nathan looked discomfited but out of his depth in such a situation and just watched the combatants as if observing a tennis match.

"Well... more often than you ever did..."

"I see. And does your seed-planter have a name?"

Suddenly, Nathan sprang into life, proffered a gnarled, rustic hand and, with a stifled tremor in his voice said, "Nathan Grubb at your service, sir."

"Well, my wife's, anyway," Alun retorted. "Never mind, the breakfast's all but ready and if you both make yourselves more presentable then we can discuss things afterwards." And he stood up, reached for the bread knife and cut himself a large slice of bread which had the hue and texture of Portland stone. *Don't care much for this farmer's grain,* he thought.

The two lovers sheepishly left the room and he could hear the sounds of a fierce discussion going on upstairs. By the time they came down again, Alun had formulated the next *Jonquil's Journals* scene.

He couldn't wait to tell Leini what had happened...

CHAPTER 15

Soon after the scene in the kitchen, Nathan had been dismissed by an embarrassed Dilys and a smug husband. Alun noted the fine sound of the Porsche as it receded down the drive and imagined Leini sitting in the driving-seat, her hand on some part of his anatomy as they sped roofless through the Marche in Italy, buoyed by summer breezes and large doses of Chianti.

Then his mind switched from its reverie when Dilys snapped tartly, "You should have told me you were coming back last night. Now look what you've done."

"Look what *I've* done? I wasn't caught in bed with your grubby farmer!"

"Don't take the mickey out of his name – that's cheap."

"I can't even remember his name, except the Nathan bit."

"Grubb. It's Grrrrrub," she rolled the R's expressively, for no reason Alun could comprehend.

"Well, he's acting up to his name, I think." She glowered at him. "Look, Dilys, I knew you were up to something so it's no great shock. We'll get a divorce and I'll have half the money when we sell the farm. Plus a few other things, which I can extract from your new lover. If his farm is worth as much as you suspect it is, I'll find your settlement money quite handy, thank you. I've bought a flat in London so I can live there; I suppose you'll go and move in with him?"

"No!" she spat out, making Alun wince as a tiny tad of toast sailed into his eye. "This is *my* farm, *my* house and *my* money. And you're having none of it, you spongeing bastard."

"It's equal rights these days, Dilys… We've been married several years and you're cuckolding me. In law, that means you're the guilty party."

"But I'm a woman – we have different rights."

"Not anymore."

There was a stunned silence as Dilys took this in. Then: "Well, you've got a floozy, haven't you...?"

"No," he lied. That subject was for a later moment when – now knowing he would get a large settlement – he could afford to buy the London flat outright and keep Leini out of the equation. Just in case she tried to wrest it from him later on, for whatever reason. One had to be careful these days.

"You're not getting a penny of this house," she stated. "It's been in my family for centuries."

"I think you'll find that Mr Grrrubb, as you call him, has more interest in this house than I have."

"What d'you mean? He's got his own house and land."

"Precisely. As far as land is concerned, the more the better. Economies of scale... And this is such a lovely historic house, with a big barn, land for crops or pasture, not *too* far from the motorway... he'd get a good deal, marrying you."

"I haven't agreed to marry him and neither has he asked."

"Might be a good idea," Alun teased. *I* won't ask for much – and certainly far less than he's likely to want from you."

There was another silence.

"Why did you buy a flat in London?" she asked suspiciously after a few moments.

"I need to be there. Part of the mix. Jonathan's delighted as I'll be on hand – not stuck down here on the end of a phone line, no mobile signal and a dodgy internet connection."

"I know you. I bet you've got a floozy."

"Well, even if I had, I'd do better than allow you to find me in bed with her. Discretion in all things, you know..." Alun could feel the arrogance of her demeanour becoming punctured like a flawed balloon; slow, flatulent, irreparable. She seemed to have visibly slumped before him.

"Well, I was going to stay with you for a day or two, for old times' sake but now... *now*... I think I'll go back to London and plan my future."

He climbed the stairs, walked straight through the bedroom, disregarding the turbulent state of his bed – *his* bed! – took a shower, picked up his things and a few other keepsakes which might be useful, and put them in his car, leaving a deflated Dilys sitting in her cavernous kitchen, an ever-smaller figure in a seemingly enlarging room.

"'Bye, Dilys," he called airily as he firmly shut the front door, in his mind thinking of Miss Havisham's house in *Great Expectations* collapsing under the weight of its shortcomings and a conceit for the lady's similar collapse. As he got into his crummy car, he looked back at the house to check it had not, in fact, subsided, and soon after, he was cruising back to the Smoke with a carefree demeanour, the spring air filling his nostrils and the entrancing thought of an earlier than expected meet-up with his floozy.

When he got into an area with a mobile signal, he pulled into a pub car park, where the building was just opening. He entered and ordered a pint, got his phone out and called Leini. "Hello, darling," he said, "I'm on my way home."

*

Nathan Grubb's mood, travelling in the opposite direction, was somewhat different... He cursed himself for joining the dating site and meeting this strange woman, yet knew he wanted her farm with its lovely house and unused acreage. Dilys' acreage was substantial, too, and at least he liked that: he preferred 'something to get hold of' in the parlance of a doughty friend and she was not lacking in that particular. But now the damn husband was involved. That would knock thousands off his great financial expectations... But he still wanted revenge on the first husband who had deprived him of similar amounts.

No such malice appertained to his feelings about Alun, who seemed much nicer than Dilys had painted him: what a pity that he would be the one who got hurt in the process…

CHAPTER 16

Alun arrived back at the flat to find Leini in overalls painting a wall which he had filled and smoothed a few days before. Her hair was bound up in a jazzily-coloured scarf, which gave her a Bohemian look. An hour later, the wall was still unfinished...

They lay on the sofa, naked but for a blanket, whilst Alun regaled her of his experience with Nathan Grubb shafting his wife. She was delighted: this news was a welcome catalyst in her plan to appropriate Alun; indeed, as he became slimmer, fitter and richer, so she became more and more determined this would end up how she wanted.

After a while, she went back to painting the wall and Alun went back to his script; the scene he had written in Wales in which Mrs Wiggins had been attacked – just before he first found himself exposed to Nathan Grubb – was foremost in his mind but, due to this recent experience, he was contemplating a new twist. He had intentionally not given any clue as to who the assailant of Mrs Wiggins in the alleyway might have been for the simple reason that he was as yet unsure. Then he wondered whether it should be the young farmer, Jonas Orchard – not the character he had originally intended – who realised that he would be found out if she saw his head was injured, so he would have to get rid of her in case... That was the tricky bit: or perhaps he could make something more of it...?

He pondered further: so what if this young farmer, Jonas Orchard, was, indeed – contrary to what the character had proclaimed – a 'napper of naps' and stole produce from farmers, shopkeepers or wherever he could appropriate it? If he had attacked Mrs Wiggins less out of malice but – almost having been caught stealing by a shopkeeper close to Mrs Wiggins' residence – felt that if the proximity of the two would risk a meeting, his cover could be blown. If so, the Tyburn gallows would be his next destination... would that work better? Yet as both resolutions would offer the same fate, he decided to write that Orchard *would indeed* see Mrs Wiggins again – with the fake news that it was one of his 'suppliers' who was stealing the produce so she could be implicated as a receiver if it came out. Then she would have to keep quiet about what she knew or he would have to silence her... Alun decided to follow that course – which then gave him the idea for a surprising and innovative new direction.

When he ran the idea past Leini, she thought it was perfect – she had been thinking about it too as she painted the wall and was going to suggest the same thing, she said – which slightly surprised Alun: were even their creative juices, too, becoming perfectly aligned? Nonetheless, pleased that he had found a motive that Leini agreed with, he started writing the scene. Yes, Jonas Orchard would definitely be Nathan Grubb's parallel character: what a pity that he would be the one who got hurt in the process...

*

Nathan had arrived home in a thunderous rainstorm and so decided to forget any farming that day and catch up with paperwork – much of which was to do with Dilys. He had already looked her up on Google, which had not rendered much information beyond what he had found out before – that her ex was obviously the man who had diddled him out of many opportunities and humungous amounts of money. Yet he had found some more information about her farm and confirmation that she was indeed married to the man he had just crossed swords with – Alun Loyd. This confirmation was not only infuriating but highly embarrassing; it would also complicate his objectives hugely. It was all right for him to know what Alun looked like but not the other way around. Dilys had told him that Alun wrote for 'a silly TV show' called *Jonquil's Journals*, which held no interest for her, being set in a century far removed from today, despite living in a house built at that time which she loved. And so did he – but for pecuniary rather than nostalgic reasons. Dilys had, apparently, watched the first couple of episodes then given it a miss. He decided it was time to start watching it, as it might give him some insights into Alun's character: writers always betrayed their true thoughts, however deeply covered by the minutiae of the stories.

It would be a good decision.

*

EPISODE 149:

SCENE 29. WIGGINS' PARLOUR. DAY.

> MRS WIGGINS, HUMMING, IS – AS USUAL
> – PREPARING FOOD AT THE KITCHEN
> TABLE, A LARGE LEG OF MUTTON ON IT
> – THE SAME AS WAS SEEN IN THE
> ALLEWAY! THERE IS MOVEMENT
> OUTSIDE AS JONAS ORCHARD SKIPS
> DOWN THE STEPS AND KNOCKS ON
> THE DOOR. HIS HEAD IS COVERED BY A
> LARGE, WOOLLY HAT.

WIGGINS: Who's there?

ORCHARD: Jonas Orchard – your purveyor of fresh produce.

WIGGINS: Again? I only saw you a day or two ago! What do you want now, you little varlet! (AS SHE LETS HIM IN). And why are you wearing that silly hat?

ORCHARD: Oh, Mrs Wiggins; I have a tale of woe…! You know I told you I got all my victuals from the most honest and noteworthy sources, as well as my own little farm…?

WIGGINS: (CAUTIOUSLY). Ye-es…

ORCHARD: Well, I found that one of them was a napper and I was buying from him without knowing!

WIGGINS: (DISBELIEVING). Well, I never…!

ORCHARD: Trouble is, I told him I'd have to tell my clients and he got angry… and he threatened to kill me if I told anyone who he was, 'cos he'd be for the gallows… and me. (SHE STARES AT HIM, AS IF NOT BELIEVING HIS STORY). Worse… and you.

WIGGINS:	(AGHAST). ME?! Why me?
ORCHARD:	'Cos you'd be taking in stolen goods, see?
WIGGINS:	But I didn't know!
ORCHARD:	Yes, but the justices don't know that – and they love a good hanging; the more the better to keep the streets clear of riff-raff… Not you, of course, Mrs Wiggins, but you did say that your master was a Justice… What if he had to try you? You'd be out on yer ear…
	(WIGGINS LOOKS TROUBLED. THEN A REALISATION CROSSES HER FACE.)
WIGGINS:	Come here, you little gagger. (HE HESITATES, SO SHE LUNGES AT HIM AND WHIPS OFF HIS HAT).
ORCHARD:	Hey – what you doing? (SHE LOOKS CLOSELY AT THE GASH ON HIS HEAD). That's what he done to me – to keep me quiet.
WIGGINS:	(PICKING UP THE LEG OF LAMB AND SIZING UP ITS DIMENSIONS WITH THE GASH ON HIS HEAD). Looks more like what you did to me to keep _me_ quiet!
ORCHARD:	No! I never!
WIGGINS:	What's his name, then?
ORCHARD:	I can't tell ye – if he finds out I've told you, he'll kill me!
WIGGINS:	I think it was you. Same height and build… And I could see your lovely eyes despite the mask, Mr Orchard. It was you who attacked me.
ORCHARD:	Me? No, never. I wouldn't hurt you, Mrs Wiggins. You're a good client and, and… a nice person. I wouldn't, honest.

WIGGINS: I don't believe you. You stole this from an honest shopkeeper, I'll wager, and he nearly caught you – probably close to me here. So you tried to kill me in case I recognised you in front of him – too close for comfort, I'd say, to here. And the leg of lamb fits that gash nicely…

ORCHARD: But that's what I sold you a couple of days ago! It can't be the same one!

WIGGINS: Well, it is as it happens, it is, 'cos my sister in St Giles's was poorly and I took this with me when I went to see her to make her a nice mutton stew… but she didn't need it so I brought it back – and that's when you tried to do me in!

ORCHARD: (REALISING HE'S LOSING THE ARGUMENT). I was only trying to scare you into not recognising me… and I had to try to save my neck – and yours.

WIGGINS: My neck's fine, young lad – it's yours that's half in with the roper. But there's a way out of this, I think…

ORCHARD: What's that?

WIGGINS: If I keep quiet about you, would you keep quiet about me?

ORCHARD: I don't understand…

WIGGINS: (LOOKING SHIFTILY AT THE STAIRCASE AND DROPPING HER VOICE SO NO-ONE CAN HEAR). My husband's an old curmudgeon, as you saw… and although he doesn't like sex no more, I do. So if you furnish _me_ with the occasional mutton, I'll allow you into my _woman's_ mutton, if you get my meaning…

ORCHARD: But… what about your husband?

WIGGINS: He's not invited!

ORCHARD: No. I can't! I don't do horn work!

WIGGINS: Then it's the gallows for you instead, my little foyst... Stolen food, a shopkeeper on your tail and assailing an innocent woman... you'd be drawn and quartered as well as hanged with all that evidence...

ORCHARD: All right, all right! I accept. But when?

WIGGINS: I think about now for a quick rantipole would do for a confirmation of our agreement, don't you? The house is empty as my Edmund's away and the master's at the assizes ... so let's pop into the pantry and see what we can find, shall we? Bread and butter fashion might be nice...

               (RELUCTANTLY, JONAS FOLLOWS HER THROUGH THE PANTRY DOOR SHE HAS JUST OPENED...)

Alun sat back with satisfaction. All was back on track. And as for Nathan Grubb, he'd had a few more ideas for him, too...

*

Nathan rang Dilys, who immediately burst into floods of tears, apologising for the unexpected return of her husband, much to the embarrassment of all. Nathan tried to calm her as best he could and eventually she became quieter, when he could then push his own agenda better, which was to ensure that Dilys started divorce proceedings before Alun, making out that it was he who had strayed first and so she was only paying him back. Then, if they won their case, it would be Alun's loss and she would be free to marry him with few financial or legal obligations.

"But my husband's due at least half the house and its value," she sobbed.

"I've thought of that," Grubb answered archly. Then: "I've thought of a few ways around most of that, too."

"You have?"

"Trust me. I'm doing this for you. We're going to be very happy together."

"Are we? Oh, Nathan, thank you for supporting me; what would I do without you?"

"Not half as much as I could do without you," he replied cryptically, then made all the necessary right noises before ringing off. He stroked his stubble and smiled to himself... perhaps the meeting with Alun had worked a treat.

As for Dilys, she was delighted to be needed by such a fine man... but she was still unsure how she could get around her secret. *But one thing at a time*, she thought; *snare the man good and proper first then work around the problem afterwards.* But, she then realised, that *was* the problem...

CHAPTER 17

The perfect cottage location that Jonathan and his designer had waxed lyrical about - before the intrusion of unwanted 21st century modifications by its owners so then re-dilapidated - had worked well and several scenes had been filmed there; but the owners' annoyance at the reversion to its original state now extended further: they were now tired of living in the property nearby and wanted to move back into their own house *now* in the condition they had rendered it previously. But Jonathan was a shrewd producer and realised that the comparative costs of re-refurbishment, any further delay whilst searching for other ideal locations close to London and the attendant re-writes and re-scheduling of actors' and crews' availability were extremely prohibitive; in fact, now the location had been returned to its original squalor, it was even better than it had been before, and various additions had also been made – such as a gallows at the back of the lot, which the owners worried had been constructed as a threat to them. Time was of the essence – they could not lose this location now. Added to that, ratings had started to pick up, helped by the social media buzz surrounding the expected demise of Mrs Wiggins, as no-one knew when and how it was going to happen. That was a genius stroke from Jonathan by not divulging anything, and also by Alun for teasing an outcome without yet actually delivering it – or even knowing what that would be.

As a result, it became financially imperative to offer the inhabitants of the house their dream home, wherever they wanted it – preferably as far away as possible, like Australia – to shut them up and so keep the TV company's prized location for several years for as long as the series progressed.

The couple, both thin, straggly and poorly-clothed despite their windfall, were now entering the offices of Jonathan and Leini, with Alun in attendance. A lavish buffet had been laid on for them by the catering department, with precociously-placed lashings of alcohol in abundance. As another incentive to accept their prospective offer, Jonathan had invited the actor who played Jonquil to the proceedings – an old-fashioned thespian named Charlton Horthorne – to help them win over Mr and Mrs Decrepit (as they had been charmingly dubbed).

Charlton, who knew from long experience in the business that there would indeed be fathoms of libation to consume, had arrived early and was already in a state of jovial insouciance at his prime role in the subterfuge.

The Decrepits came into the office and were welcomed by the ensemble; Mrs Decrepit – the livelier and more friendly of the two – was targeted first as they realised the male Decrepit would need more persuasion and take quite a few drinks to loosen up before he could ever be introduced to their scheme. Sadly, however, he refused any drink at all – he was teetotal. So the attack was engaged purely on his wife, Rose, who imbibed gleefully and was soon open to almost anything, while her husband, Dave, looked on in morose indignation.

Realising that Rose was 'in the bag' but Dave would not desist in his refusal to drink anything, they had no choice but to resort to ever more devious methods: this task was initiated by Jonathan, who then left the persuasion to Charlton... who had by now completely forgotten what he was there for. Realising this, Leini tactfully prised him away and proffered another Scotch and ginger to him before introducing him to Rose and going in for the kill with the husband, Dave. It was hard work even getting him to smile, but every time she looked away, she unbuttoned her blouse a little more, so soon his eyes were fixed on her cleavage and he started to sweat; it was then that she offered him a beer, to which he finally consented – as long as it was non-alcoholic.

"Of course," she said, "I'll get catering to come up with one. Back in a jiffy!" She discreetly picked up two beer bottles – one with a strong alcoholic content and the other 0% – and went into her adjoining cubicle, taking a glass on the way. Once there, she opened both bottles, donated the 0% one to the cactus in the window, then poured the alcoholic one into the glass. She then took the full glass and the empty 0% bottle back to Dave and presented them to him, ensuring the 0% label was facing him. He downed it in one. "Another?" she asked perkily. Dave nodded.

By the end of the afternoon, Dave and Rose would soon be the proud owners of a four-bedroom villa in Spain with a swimming-pool. All expenses paid. And the location would soon be the property of Tellurian TV… and worth millions… So the deal was alive. Sadly, Leini's cactus was not…

*

Now that Alun had professed to leaving Wales and Dilys for good, things became easier for Nathan to take stock of his ambitious takeover of her farm without concern about any sudden presence of the husband. Yet he *was* now becoming concerned about his takeover of Dilys, whose company was beginning to grate – despite the rumpy-pump and profusion of pies and puddings she gave him; in short, his doubts were expanding in step with his waistline.

Yet his avarice and quest for revenge over the hapless Dilys' first husband was totally lost on the woman, who still looked forward to his arrival like an 18th century sailor's wife would stare out to sea for the return of her beloved.

As it happened, this displacement of the two centuries was having a more pertinent appeal to Alun's writing than Nathan Grubb's acquisitive vengeance…

JONQUIL'S JOURNALS:
EPISODE 149. SCENE 71. WIGGINS' PARLOUR. DAY.

MRS WIGGINS IS SURREPTITIOUSLY OPENING THE DOOR TO ORCHARD. THEY SPEAK FURTIVELY, QUIETLY…

WIGGINS: Hello, my lover…!

ORCHARD: Hello, dearest Hattie!

WIGGINS:	What have you brought me today, my little apple?
ORCHARD:	A large sausage from Smithfield!
WIGGINS:	Ooh! That'll go down nicely! Shall I take delivery now, just to test the quality?
ORCHARD:	I think it should go straight into the pantry!
	THEY GO FURTIVELY INTO THE PANTRY, ORCHARD OBVIOUSLY ENJOYING THE SITUATION AS MUCH AS THE MUCH OLDER AND LARGER MRS WIGGINS IS.

EPISODE 149:

SCENE 72. INT. WIGGINS' PANTRY. DAY – BUT DARK.

	THEY ENTER THE PANTRY; IN IT ARE HAMS, VEGETABLES, PHEASANTS, CHICKENS AND SO ON, WHICH WE SEE AS THE DOOR OPENS; THEN IT IS SHUT AND WE CAN ONLY JUST OBSERVE THEM IN THE ONLY LIGHT FROM A TINY WINDOW NEAR THE CEILING. MUCH GIGGLING AND RUSTLING OF CLOTHING.
WIGGINS:	Mind, Jonas! You're disturbing me leeks.
ORCHARD:	Better than peas!
WIGGINS:	Oh, you little rapscallion, you! Ooh! That sausage is special…!
ORCHARD:	I just knew you'd like it – and very fresh…
	MORE GIGGLING AND RUSTLING.

JONQUIL'S JOURNALS:

EPISODE 149. SCENE 73. WIGGINS' PARLOUR. DAY.

	WE HEAR FOOTSTEPS ON THE STONE STAIRS LEADING DOWN TO THE PARLOUR AND MRS WIGGINS' HUSBAND, EDMUND, COMES DOWN THEM.
EDMUND:	Hattie? (NO ANSWER). Hattie, you girt trollope. Where are you, woman? HATTIE! Where are you shooling…? Oh, must be in the dining-room with the master…
	HE TURNS TO GO BACK UP THE STAIRS WHEN HE HEARS SOMETHING SOFTLY DROPPING IN THE PANTRY AND SOME MOVEMENT – THEN SILENCE. HE LOOKS BACK, THEN REALISES THAT THE NOISE HAS COME FROM THE PANTRY… AND QUIETLY GOES OVER TO IT, LISTENING AT THE DOOR. SUDDENLY SUSPECTING, HE THROWS IT OPEN…

ROLL CREDITS AND TITLE MUSIC:

END OF EPISODE 149.

Alun sat back, enjoying the scene he was writing as he visualised it, and then started to wonder how Edmund would respond in the next episode. Actually, he already knew the answer to that.

CHAPTER 18

Dilys was sitting in Nathan's Porsche, enjoying a sunny break with the roof down, a rare pleasure in the mountains of Wales.

Nathan had decided that he needed to show his softer side in order to prove to her that he was capable of warmth and affection, rather than what he knew himself to be, which was gruff and grasping. He had never re-married but he knew he had scared off a few women since his wife's demise due to his abrasive manner. His favourite, Edna, had stayed with him in mounting despair for three years; then, when he took her to Benidorm to patch things up in the sunshine, she had run off with a Spanish deck-chair attendant. As far as he knew, she was still there, stacking the chairs and loungers, opening parasols and wallets: her chirpy sexiness and fulsome bust had that effect on the transitory clientele. Her other job was to permanently clean up fag-ends and litter from the beach, lubricating her tonsils the while with sangria and *pina coladas*. He hoped she was happy... but then a brooding and somewhat violent resentment erupted on occasion when the memory of that distant but unexpected wrench surfaced. He had had one of those a few days ago when he drove away from Dilys' farm after the confrontation with Alun, but at least had used the angst to good effect by scheming what to do next...

As the car glided towards Aberystwyth, Dilys noted that he seemed more jocular, accessible and humorous than she had previously experienced in their limited, if intense, relationship. She liked that – especially as it reminded her of someone... then realised that particular someone was Alun – as he used to be. She sighed for a moment, asking herself if she should be making more of an effort to keep him, rather than continue with this rustic... then she felt indignant at the fact he obviously had a floozy in that septic den of iniquity, London, and instead focussed on looking out of the windows and at the blue sky, as her hair matted in the turbulent, whimsical breeze, the car gracing corners with a throaty roar as wonderful vistas opened up at every turn.

Nathan was thinking, too – or scheming, anyway. How could he get rid of this woman after he had married her and inherited her farm, wealth and land? Then a pang of compassion enveloped him: it wasn't her fault her first husband fleeced him, so should he be taking it out on her? She knew nothing about that episode and it was best that it never came out as it would point directly at his dastardly scheme.

As they pulled into Aberystwyth, the sun broke through more strongly, which had a conciliatory effect on his persona; he still wished she would lose some weight… although he, too, had porked out somewhat on Dilys' delicious pies, despite the violently rampant exercising of his genitalia… Well, as they parked the car and walked along the front, he decided he would try and like her more for who she was rather than what she possessed – although that was, of course, far more important – and it was not just revenge on her previous husband… the bastard.

*

Alun had received an e-mail from Dilys the night before explaining that she and Nathan were getting on well but that she would not divorce Alun as she felt she could trust him more than her acquisitive agrarian; she had already surmised Nathan's overtures were more to do with what she could provide (in every sense) and not who she was. This troubled her; yes, the sex was good, the conversation lively but unremarkable, and she enjoyed investing her love of cooking into the man without any resentment from Alun who had all but stopped eating her creations ever since he got the fitness bug. And then she remembered once again that the catalyst for that must have been that damn floozy… she filled with resentment again and resolved to stand her ground; it was time for her to have the few benefits of this awkward situation – and she knew the best way to do this was to humour Nathan, resist Alun and deny them both.

For Alun, though, he wanted out – and Grubb's Porsche, too, as part of the settlement. Half the proceeds of the house, farm and estate – if he could get that – would only just cover the cost of the flat, and the Porsche was both a revenge on The Grubb, as he had taken to calling him, and satisfying Leini. In fact, it was the icing on the cake. So Dilys had to go, full stop.

*

The next morning, Leini, fully dressed, made-up and breakfasted, drew back the curtains of their garden flat and watched Alun groan as the sunlight hit his unshaven face; he turned away, burying his head under the pillow. "Come on, sleepyhead," she cajoled, "It's a lovely day and I've got to get to work. Added to which, you have to come up with the next finished script by tomorrow so I can take it in to Jonathan – and you've hardly started it yet. I've just got time to make you a cuppa, then I'm off and you've got to work out what happens on your own. I've left you one idea, though, which I had in the night after reading one of Blankitt's cases, but whether you like it or not is up to you. It's by your computer." She kissed him and then, as she reached the door, said: "Oh, another thing: you know we're trying to get some more sex and international characters into the series, to make it more relevant to today?" Alun nodded with a yawn and she continued: "Why don't Edmund and Jonas Orchard meet in the pub unexpectedly – a bit of aggro – ... and we could introduce a South American or Spanish type into the plot. There were quite a few in London at that time, descended from those shipwrecked after the Spanish Armada in 1588 in the south-west. Like today, many eventually made for London, so why not the pub landlord? We've seen the pub before, but not who runs it... and we could elaborate on that in any way we like... Tobacco, for a start. And piracy. And we haven't had anyone, sort of, romantic from different climes before. Might be an idea?"

He sleepily consented without really thinking about it and she soon left: having downed the tea she had left him, Alun got up and, in his dressing gown, found himself moving rather like a hovercraft with no pilot towards his desk. As he came to, he wondered why

Leini had suddenly suggested this twist to the plot out of the blue but, being in a hurry and glad of something to write, opened the computer and looked at the flickering page... After a few moments, his brain kicked in – but found himself first having to address the next scene with Mrs Wiggins and Jonas Orchard, which had put him in a quandary: suddenly, it was more important to start leading up to the process of dispensing with Mrs Wiggins, wasn't it? He had initially thought so, but now wondered whether the deed could be strung out somewhat longer, which would be good for ratings. But not for too long, of course, or the viewers would lose interest. In his head, he already had the first scene of the episode after Edmund's discovery of his wife, Hattie Wiggins, *in flagrante delicto*, with Jonas Orchard, which would motivate him; he would then write a scene finding Jonquil in bed with Jenny, the whore from London Bridge, whom he has acquitted and befriended after the court case; Alun then saw Leini's note she had alluded to, which suggested that a young maid was taken on, who could be a distraction for Jonas as he tries to avoid being killed by Edmund. *Brilliant*, thought Alun – in fact, Jenny could now become the maid, whom Jonquil would employ as such in his house, so she would 'always be on hand'. However, Jonas – still secretly seeing Mrs Wiggins and providing her with supplies – would become infatuated with this new maid, who decides to use blackmail to take over the house and become Lady Jonquil: and, perhaps, Jonas would become Lord of the house, too. Which would be another reason for Edmund to get rid of his wife, Mrs Wiggins... and Jonas to get rid of Edmund, should he not get to him first. He started writing... Yet Leini's suggestions kept creeping into his mind and as the morning progressed he engineered a way of detailing the plot further, and realised her idea would work very well a little later on. Soon, the fact that he had been niggled when she had suggested the proposal decreased in prominence as the plot developed.

It would, though, become very obvious at a somewhat later date...

*

JONQUIL'S JOURNALS:

EPISODE 150. SCENE 1. WIGGINS' PARLOUR. DAY.

EDMUND HAS JUST LOOKED INSIDE THE PANTRY DOOR.

EDMUND: Hattie – what are you doing with that in the dark? My goodness me! I've heard of 'in the hams' but what are you doing, you dirty young scape-grace twiddle-poop – get out of that pantry – and my bitch-booby of a wife! You rammish wench! (TO ORCHARD). And if you've given her Venus' curse, that'll be the end of *you*!

*

On her way to work, Leini was feeling confused. The idea for how Mrs Wiggins could be dispensed with was, indeed, based on a case that Blankitt had written about – but the other one was a pure confection… based on fact and a conflict of loyalties which were becoming ever more pressuring: they would soon need resolution one way or the other. But not yet; a lot could happen between what she had to do now and how it would all pan out later. But it was concerning her deeply.

*

At home, Alun was 'wording in' the episodes which had been agreed upon at the last production meeting with Jonathan:

*

JONQUIL'S JOURNALS:

EPISODE 150. SCENE 2. JONQUIL'S BEDCHAMBER. DAY.

JONQUIL IS IN BED IN HIS NIGHTGOWN, SITTING UP AND LOOKING RATHER PLEASED WITH HIMSELF. IT APPEARS HE IS ALONE AS HE STARTS SPEAKING.

<u>JONQUIL:</u>	That was most pleasurable, my young lady. What a wonderful disposition you have, besides all the rest…
	SUDDENLY, THE BEDCLOTHES MOVE AND THE HEAD OF JENNY, THE WHORE FROM LONDON BRIDGE WHOM HE ACQUITTED, SITS UP BESIDE HIM AND GIVES HIM A PECK ON THE MOUTH.
<u>JENNY:</u>	Glad to be of service, sir!
	(AND SHE DISAPPEARS UNDER THE BEDCLOTHES AGAIN).
<u>JONQUIL:</u>	Ooh! 'Pon my soul, that is *most* pleasurable, my dear… And – ooh! – talking of 'service', my housekeeper has told me she's – ooh! – in need of a new maid… The other one, Doris… Ooh! How would you like to join us here as her maid? And that way, you could always be on hand – ooh! – so to speak…
<u>JENNY:</u>	That would be most desirable, my lord – thank you!
<u>JONQUIL:</u>	Capital! Let's go downstairs to the parlour now and I can tell her the good news that *she* has a maid and *I* have… well, that's not so easy to explain, but… Well, anyway… Come, come… let's go down now…
	(THEY START TO GET OUT OF BED).

<u>**JONQUIL'S JOURNALS:**</u>

<u>**EPISODE 150. SCENE 3. WIGGINS' PARLOUR. DAY.**</u>

EDMUND IS STILL TRYING TO GET ORCHARD OUT OF THE PANTRY,

WITH MRS WIGGINS TRYING TO KEEP HIM IN TO PROTECT HIM.

EDMUND: Be off with you, before I break yer neck – or perhaps I shall, anyway!

ORCHARD: Let me alone, you Butcher's dog!

THE SCUFFLE CONTINUES AS ORCHARD, SOMEWHAT HAMPERED BY HIS BREECHES AROUND HIS ANKLES, MANAGES TO BREAK FREE OF MRS WIGGINS AND THE PANTRY, TRYING TO ESCAPE, AND BREAKS CLEAR OF EDMUND AS MRS WIGGINS RESTRAINS HIM FROM HITTING THE MAN WITH THE SAME LEG OF MUTTON WITH WHICH HE ASSAILED HER.

MRS WIGGINS: Edmund, stop it – he was only trying to help me –

EDMUND: Out of your clothes, by the looks of it. I never liked that young man – a hobbledehoy if ever I saw one. And as for you, you brazen hussy…

HE TURNS TO HIS WIFE, THREATENINGLY, AS ORCHARD BREAKS FREE, THEN GOES AFTER EDMUND IN HOT PURSUIT, WAVING THE MUTTON LEG AROUND AS ORCHARD DODGES A BLOW BY DUCKING UNDER THE TABLE. THIS HAPPENS A COUPLE OF TIMES, WHEN FINALLY, ORCHARD ESCAPES UP THE SERVANTS' STEPS AND AWAY, STILL ADDRESSING HIS ATTIRE AS HE GOES.

> EDMUND RETURNS TO HIS WIFE AND IS ABOUT TO HIT HER WHEN WE CUT AWAY TO SEE BARTHOLOMEW JONQUIL AT THE TOP OF THE STAIRS, OBSERVING THE PROCEEDINGS, WITH JENNY AT HIS SIDE AND BOTH IN THEIR NIGHTWARE.

JONQUIL: (SHOUTING). 'Pon my soul, Edmund – what the devil's going on. 'Tis like a madhouse in here! Leave your poor wife alone. Come and see me upstairs in a few minutes but for now, be gone with you!

> EDMUND GLOWERS AT MRS WIGGINS, THUMPS THE LEG OF MUTTON ONTO THE TABLE, GOES UP THE STAIRS TOWARDS THEM – LOOKING A FRIGHTENED JENNY UP AND DOWN APPRECIATIVELY AS HE PASSES – AND DISAPPEARS. JONQUIL TURNS TO MRS WIGGINS AND SMILES.

JONQUIL: Mrs Wiggins – I have some good news for you.

WIGGINS: Oh, thank you sir – I could do with some of that at the moment!

JONQUIL: It would appear so… Anyway, you have a new maid. This is Jenny. She will also be able to keep an eye on your husband – whilst also keeping an eye on me. (THEY GIGGLE TOGETHER). She's starting now.

WIGGINS: But she's in her nightclothes!

JONQUIL: Ah, well, yes… Er, she's been learning how to put the bedchamber in order… and fold her clothes as a lady would, don't you know… (FLOUNDERING). She –

JENNY:	(HELPING HIM OUT). But the commotion…
JONQUIL:	Ah, yes…! (QUIETLY TO HER). Thank you, me dear… (NORMAL). …Yes, but the commotion here… yes, that's what brought us down… Erm, yes… but she can go and change and then come back to learn what to do…
JENNY:	His lordship has taught me a lot already, Mrs Wiggins… (WIGGINS SHOOTS HER A LOOK, AS IF TO SAY, 'I BET HE HAS'). I'll be back down in a trice. (SHE CURTSEYS AND GOES, SWIFTLY FOLLOWED BY JONQUIL).
WIGGINS:	(SOTTO VOCE). She'll be in his bed more than my kitchen, I'll wager!

*

It was at this moment that Alun received an unexpected call from Leini in the office, who informed him that Lottie, the actress playing Mrs Wiggins, was up in arms about her portrayal as a woman of loose morals in the pantry; Leini feared it was the start of her fightback against being written out of the series as the previous set of confirmed storylines had recently been sent to her and she had clearly seen the writing on the wall, if not yet the actual script. Alun was not surprised – her wrath had been burnished and fed by the Twitterstorm that she had started and now the venom was propelling her like a tanker in a force nine gale towards a resentful cadre of TV executives who would not baulk at her demise. She had to go – it was all in the script, they would say: if only she would go quietly, whilst also being pleased that the furore was giving the programme welcome extra publicity. Alun and Leini laughed at her unwitting support of their strategy – adding that it was already giving him extra momentum to perhaps write this objectionable woman out of the series somewhat sooner than planned.

*

99

JONQUIL'S JOURNALS:

EPISODE 150. SCENE 4. JONQUIL'S DRAWING ROOM. INT. DAY.

EDMUND WIGGINS IS SEETHING. HE LOOKS AT A BEAUTIFUL DECANTER AND SHERRY GLASSES ON THE EXQUISITE SIDEBOARD AS IF WISHING TO SMASH THEM BUT DESISTS AS HE HEARS JONQUIL PASSING OUTSIDE IN THE HALL, FOLLOWING JENNY ON HIS WAY BACK TO THE BEDROOM.

EDMUND: (TO HIMSELF). Me – cuckolded! How dare the wench! I'll be no catsfoot to her, the bunter! Time to be out of the parson's mousetrap! Time to join giblets wi' someone else…

HE STORMS OUT AND NOISILY CLIMBS THE STAIRS AFTER THEM.

As if to complement the direction of the storyline, some several hours later Alun received a voicemail message from Dilys which annoyed him: she was obviously three sheets to the wind, telling him she had just come back home from a nice day with The Grubb in Aberystwyth and, although she wanted to stay with the man for 'fun and games' as she put it, she was just explicitly reiterating that she would not divorce Alun under any circumstances – she had too much to lose. Alun wondered whether The Grubb had been pressing his suit and his demands a little too fervently… Yet that angered him too: he wanted to be rid of Dilys in the flesh as much as Mrs Wiggins in the TV series…

So, having caught up with his scripting and not a little tired as a result, he decided to finish for the day, poured himself a large scotch and watched a mindless quiz show as he awaited his inamorata's return home... Yet his decision to stop had given his brain some time to catch up and he suddenly found he was having a eureka moment – and perhaps the scotch had a hand in it, too: some answer to a question on the moronic quiz-show had given birth to a better way of getting rid of Mrs Wiggins. The answer to the question had been Lord Byron, concerning a duel between him and William Chaworth. It also had parallels with Leini reading one of the trials explained by Justice Theodore Blankitt. The two were similar and could be elided – and seemed to offer a more factual direction for the continuation of the plot – and the final demise of Mrs Wiggins...

CHAPTER 19

Nathan Grubb was annoyed. Not only was his seed-driller playing up but Dilys was becoming stubbornly uncooperative in the marriage department; did she not realise he might go off her and she would lose him forever? He only wanted her farm, money, house... and revenge on the former husband. Was that such an unfair exchange? It wasn't as if he had nothing to offer, was it? Another farm, house – if rather dilapidated, as hers was – land, machinery, loads of lucre, a good business and a thriving farm shop. And the Porsche, too, which she really liked. A real puller, that, whatever his age. She did take up more space in it than his other conquests but there were compensations, like her farm, money, house and revenge on the former husband... which kept going around his head like a noisy merry-go-round at Llandudno fair. Except there was nothing fair about this: he wanted what she had. Full stop. No, nothing fair in that... Not in Dilys, either... she was well past her prime. As was his recalcitrant tractor.

He sowed another row as the driller coughed this way and that behind the infernal machine and then looked back at the wavy lines it had seeded as it swayed around; damn, he had missed a few inches of ground here and there but this had been over-compensated by drilling several furrows across each other. That made him even angrier: now the automatic pea-picker would get confused at harvest-time and that would need re-calibrating, too. Just like Dilys. Ah, there he went again... the woman had somehow obsessed him, though whether for honourable reasons or not he was absolutely sure.

Yet one thing about Nathan was that he was stubborn. Very stubborn. A true Taurean – except for disliking a tidy home. That was unimportant to him: as long as he had a clean bed and somewhere reasonably presentable to relax or watch TV during the cold winter evenings in front of a blazing fire, he was happy. But with more money and wealth he could afford to have someone in to clean a bit – though not too much, of course. If Dilys wasn't there. But he still wanted her farm.

Then he contemplated an idea...

*

Alun had gone back to his computer and made some notes and changes. But as if to add purpose to his thoughts of getting rid of Mrs Wiggins, he unexpectedly received an e-mail from Nathan Grubb. It read:

Dear Alun Loyd,

It would appear that I wish to appropriate Dilys as much as you wish to leave her, but she seems reluctant to do so for emotional reasons. Perhaps we could come to some mutual arrangement together – without Dilys knowing? I'm sure we could find a way to make her more mutually disposed. I have a number of assets I could throw into an agreement to make it more worth your while. Could we talk?

Yours,

Nathan Grubb.

The word '*disposed*' struck him as strange; it could mean a number of things. But The Grubb was obviously hell-bent on having her for himself and, as Dilys would be entitled to a greater share of her own property and financial spoils than he, Alun, would, wondered what the farmer had in mind. 'Assets...' well, the Porsche would be a good starter for ten... Leini would be delighted. And perhaps Grubb's house could be extracted, too – but not the land. No, Grubb could have that. The deal would double or triple his acreage, Alun surmised; good for both of them. And whether the house was nice or not – which he doubted – he could flog it, whatever its state. It would help to pay off his flat, if nothing else. And Dilys could keep her farm and live there with her rustic Romeo in bliss. He would discuss it with Leini and then write back.

What Alun had still not fully comprehended was the degree of revenge contained in the Grubb's potential suggestion. He soon would – although the word 'disposed' kept troubling him. That was *his* plan, not the Grubb's ...

*

JONQUIL'S JOURNALS:

EPISODE 150. SCENE 43. A NOISY TAVERN. DAY.

EDMUND SITS DISCONSOLATELY AT A TABLE, HIS THOUGHTS DROWNING IN THE PINT OF ALE IN FRONT OF HIM. HIS BACK IS TO THE TAVERN DOOR.

EDMUND: (MUTTERING). Damn wench... Nasty little Trollope... After all I managed to get for the hussy, too, in Master Jonquil's residence. She was nothing 'afore she met me...

(THE LANDLORD, A SWARTHY, HIRSUTE LATINO TYPE WITH A PIRATICAL EAR-RING AND A NASTY SCAR ON HIS FACE, COMES OVER TO EDMUND. HIS NAME IS SANDER: HE SPEAKS WITH A THICK SPANISH-LIKE ACCENT).

SANDER: Ah, Mr Edmund... You look depressed, my friend; are you worry-ee-ing about something?

EDMUND: None of your business, Sander.

SANDER: Something a-wrong weeth the missus again?

EDMUND: You could say that...

SANDER: Well, your leetle favourite, Dulce, will be free in a while. Shall I tell her you're a-waiting for her?

EDMUND: Don't tempt me. If it had been Arabella, I might have consented — but not since she went off with that Sam...

SANDER: All-a right... (SV) Then how about a leetle bit of my best snuff stuff?

EDMUND: Snuff's for toffs. I am not a toff.

SANDER: No, no, no, This ees better than that. Much a-stronger. From a ship we found from South America…

EDMUND: (SUSPICIOUSLY). Found?

SANDER: Well, you know… Was floating in the sea so we took it!

EDMUND: You bloody pirate!

SANDER: Ees a-business. Will make you feel happy, I know.

EDMUND: No. I'm not touching any more of your stuff. I felt ill for ages after that last lot you gave me…

SANDER: All right, my-a friend… But if you change your mind…

HE SMILES BROADLY, EXPOSING A GOLD TOOTH, THEN RETURNS TO THE BACK OF THE TAVERN. EDMUND LOOKS FORLORN AND TAKES A SWIG OF HIS PINT.

BEHIND HIM, THE TAVERN DOOR OPENS AND JONAS ORCHARD ENTERS, WHO DOES NOT RECOGNISE EDMUND FROM THE BACK. WE SEE HIM ORDER A PINT BEHIND EDMUND AT THE BAR, THEN HE COMES FORWARD TO LOOK FOR SOMEWHERE TO SIT. SPYING A SPACE IN FRONT OF EDMUND, HE COMES ALONGSIDE HIM.

ORCHARD: Kind sir, might I sit opposite you at this table, pray?

(EDMUND NODS, WITHOUT LOOKING UP. ORCHARD SITS AND SUDDENLY RECOGNISES EDMUND AND STANDS UP AGAIN). Ah, sorry…! (AND HE GETS UP, WHICH DISTRACTS EDMUND'S REVERIE – WHO SUDDENLY RECOGNISES ORCHARD AND STANDS UP).

EDMUND: You little bastard! (AND GRABS HIM BY THE

THROAT). *You're* the one cuckolding me!

ORCHARD: I'm so sorry sir – but I didn't want to do it, neither!

EDMUND: Didn't want to? Why? What's wrong with my wife?!

ORCHARD: She forced, me sir; if I hadn't done it then she'd have reported me to the Watch! (EDMUND SHAKES HIM AND GROWLS, RE-ATTRACTING THE ATTENTION OF SANDER, WHO COMES OVER TO WREST ORCHARD FROM EDMUND'S GRASP).

SANDER: Ho, Mr Wiggins, that's enough! This is a respectable establishment!

EDMUND: He's been shagging my wife!

SANDER: What – a-your Hattie?

HEARING THIS, THERE IS SOME RAUCOUS LAUGHTER FROM A GROUP OF DRINKERS BEHIND.

EDMUND: Yes – my Hattie!

SANDER: (LAUGHING). No disrespect, Mr Wiggins... but you should be glad. Now you can have Dulce as I said ... or my Maisie or Dolly – as you so often do – without any worry!

THE TWO WHORES WINK AND WAVE AT EDMUND FROM BEHIND. EDMUND GLOWERS AT ORCHARD.

ORCHARD: (SEIZING THE MOMENT – TO EDMUND). Honestly, sir – she tricked me into it or she'd betray me to the Watch! (TO SANDER, REFERRING TO EDMUND). And she don't get nothin' sexual from *him*, you buttock-broker!

(SANDER LAUGHS AND GOES. ORCHARD AND EDMUND GLARE AT EACH OTHER).

ORCHARD: Please, sir, believe me... I sold her some victuals which I didn't know had been stolen and so she's blackmailing me for sex or she'll tell the Watch and I'll hang at Tyburn.

EDMUND: Well... Well – we can't have that.

ORCHARD: Thank you, sir.

EDMUND: No, not that – it's just that your mutton was the best I'd tasted in ages! And the master liked it, too. A bit bloody around the knuckle, though, for some reason... Where'd you get it?

ORCHARD: (RUBBING HIS HEAD IN MEMORY OF THE BLOW). I can't say – but I can get you some more!

EDMUND: Let's talk about it... Oh, forget Hattie – it's good she's getting some attention, shall we say – she don't get any from me! In fact, you're doing me a favour – stops her pestering me...

THERE IS A PAUSE AS THEY EYE EACH OTHER.

ORCHARD: I can get you some good cod and eels, too...!

THEY START TO TALK...

*

Alun stopped writing, now calm in the knowledge that he knew where he was going with the script – and Hattie Wiggins' demise would not only be conclusively final but have a comedic touch to it to boot. He subsequently enjoyed a very relaxed meal with Leini, where no thought of avoiding any physical relationships would ever enter his mind...

*

Dilys looked at her kitchen and the amount of food she had on the table, as if wondering how soon her Nathan could devour it. She had been to his farm shop to buy it in the hope that she would see him, but he was out in the fields somewhere, tilling. Her journey back, then, was a somewhat gloomy affair and even her ancient cassette player regurgitating 80's golden hits had done little to lift her spirits. She started to feel lonely; Alun was gone and, although she would not consent to a divorce under any conditions, she realised he had been a better husband than she ever gave him credit for and wondered again whether Nathan would continue to provide the 'fun and games' she aspired to after a few years together. And Nathan had recently taken a deep interest in her first husband's affairs which had begun to trouble her; he had muttered something once that there were 'reparations' to be made but she had no idea what he was talking about. Yet as Norris had been leader of the council at the time of his death, many supposedly suppressed stories, whispered in hushed tones, had been evident in the aftermath, and his loyal henchman, Iwan Daffydd, had fuelled increased speculation by mysteriously disappearing to a small island off the coast of Peru with suspicions of dirty money and a stripper called Rosita who hailed from those warmer, drier regions but whom he had met at a fundraiser in Merthyr Tydfil.

Still, Dilys ruminated, that was nothing to do with her. At least Norris had left her a nice house and a huge stash of what he had called 'emergency money', which was accruing nicely in an offshore account. And neither Nathan nor Alun knew anything about it. At least, she hoped not.

*

Alun pressed 'Enter' and the e-mail sped its way to the depths of Wales. He had discussed the missive received from The Grubb with Leini and together they had come up with a response. It read:

Hi, Nathan,

I am in receipt of your e-mail and find your proposal interesting, although we will have to put more flesh on the bones. You are correct in your assumptions so a discussion under less embarrassing conditions than at our initial meeting might achieve a beneficial mutual execution. I would ask you that we keep this correspondence private so that we cause my wife — and your intended — no further pain or rancour. Perhaps we could meet sometime soon at a venue somewhere off the M4 equidistant from both of us. If you could bring your Porsche, then — if we agree terms — there may be the opportunity to conclude the first part of any arrangement by both travelling in the directions we wish to proceed by.

I look forward to your swift and more revelatory response.

With best wishes,

Alun Loyd.

CHAPTER 20

Jonathan read the storyline with glee, as Lottie Brace's contract had already expired and she had only agreed to the extra episodes leading up to her removal from the series by demanding a ridiculous salary for each extra one, which was making serious dents into Jonathan's programme budget. Fortunately, the social media storm had caused the ratings to continue their heavenly ascent, which at least made the company happy…

Nathan read Alun's e-mail with interest, concurring that a meeting on neutral ground might be a better starting-point and so suggested a pub near Chipping Sodbury which he felt would inconvenience each of them equally. Alun, still much intrigued, agreed, and the meeting was set for a week's time…

Meanwhile, Dilys – despite her insistence that she would not divorce Alun – found herself becoming ever keener on Nathan… in direct comparison to the latter increasingly losing interest in her corporeal endowments but gaining a more voracious interest in her financial ones…

*

Alun drove his heap of a car with care to the Chipping Sodbury pub and, having arrived early, entered the bar for a swift pint to calm his nerves before the meeting – only to find that Nathan was already there and at least two ahead of him. There was an awkward moment as the two men eyed each other up, both fearful of accosting the wrong man after their embarrassing and fleeting first meeting; yet Alun's memory of a swarthy rustic in clothes too small for him due to their longevity – bulging due to his expanded girth since they were purchased in the 80s – and Nathan's of Alun as being a slim, slightly pansy-looking man in clothes which matched perfectly and fitted even better, confirmed their mutual prejudices and they hesitantly shook hands.

"Dilys doesn't know I'm seeing you," Nathan blurted out awkwardly.

"No – she doesn't know I'm seeing *you*, either."

There was another pause, and then Nathan sat down as he told Alun there was a drinks tab he could use. Alun grunted appreciation, went to the bar and ordered a pint, then came back to sit uneasily with his contestant at the table.

"I like your wife and I want to marry her," Nathan said flatly, coming straight to the point.

"And I don't like her so much now and want to divorce her."

"But she won't, she says," Nathan added.

"So it seems," Alun replied, taking a large slug of his delicious English ale.

"Why not?" enquired Nathan, with a slight twist of disdain on his lips.

Alun paused a moment, wondering how much he should divulge. Then: "She thinks I have a 'floozy', as she calls her and is jealous."

"And do you?"

"That's *my* business."

Nathan smiled a knowing smile and a glimmer of male understanding cast a dew of composure over the proceedings, each realising on the moment that the other might not be so bad after all.

Alun, feeling a little calmer as a result, decided to expand the reasons, perhaps unwisely, but he wanted a result today if possible, so was happy to push the boundaries a little. "I think there are also reasons to do with her first husband," he opined. Nathan nodded, a little too knowingly, Alun thought, but he continued anyway. "I think when she married me it was on the rebound of her husband dying and there were some financial improprieties he had which, by quickly marrying me, would get covered up sooner."

Nathan was beginning to like Alun's candour, so felt bold enough to open up himself a tad, too. "Indeed. And I was, shall we say, 'influenced' by that…"

"So it's revenge as well as love," Alun retorted bluntly.

Nathan looked surprised at Alun's perspicacity, then said guardedly, "One of those is more relevant than the other."

"So which is it?"

"That's *my* business."

The resentment at the mutual lack of full disclosure weighed heavily on them both for a few seconds, and then they found themselves smiling at each other with a sense of a deepening understanding.

Alun took a deep breath and continued: "I think that there was – still is, probably – a lot of money tied up in Dilys' farm which I think must have been paid for by underhand means – sort of money-laundering, if you like. I don't know if Dilys knew about it – I suspect not – and neither did I when I married her after the husband died."

Nathan agreed. "Yes, I think Dilys was probably innocent of his crimes at the time she married him, but I think she was soon availed of them after the ring was on the finger. Sort of bridal blackmail…"

Alun reflected for a moment. Then a penny seemed to drop. "Yes, actually… you're probably right – soon after we were married there were always strange people turning up uninvited and asking for money – and one of them was supposedly a tax inspector."

He suddenly felt he had said enough – too much, perhaps – but it had troubled him at the time too until, after several years, he neither cared nor bothered as the people never came back again. He told Nathan this.

"Hmm. Well, I heard about some of those rumours too at about that time, and I felt they were true because I was being ripped off by council authorisations, extra taxes, fees for planning permissions, licences for things I should never have had to pay for and much more. I decided to stay clear because it was obvious that Norris Griffiths was a bent council leader – it was so blatant. Flash cars, foreign holidays, backhanders, the two minders… and I certainly didn't want to get on the wrong side of *them*... Vicious-looking bastards, they were – Fist and Knuckle, I called them. But after a 'friendly' visit, as they called it – when I complained about some exorbitant charges – I knew to stay well clear." He looked into his beer glass, reflecting on what he was saying, then realised it was empty and rose to get another.

"You, too?" he enquired.

Alun nodded: he needed a moment to think and was glad that Nathan left the table. A blaze of thoughts went through his mind: he had never known Norris but Dilys always talked of him guardedly and in hushed tones, as if the walls of the farm were listening. And it was true that the people who visited never came again. Were they paid off? Disposed of? That word suddenly seemed relevant again – did Norris Griffiths either pay people off he had wronged or, perish the thought, dispose of them literally if they didn't comply? Was that the real reason Dilys didn't want to divorce him, Alun, as all these nefarious goings-on would arise in the course of the divorce?

Nathan returned with two foaming pints and sat down heavily, as if weighed down by the burden of his own dilemmas. Alun finished his first pint and, putting the empty glass to one side, leaned forward and looked more closely at Nathan, his hands under his chin. "So what are we going to do?"

"I was going to ask *you* that," Nathan replied. Then: "But I do have a few ideas."

"Such as?"

"Well, as I said in my e-mail: I really want to marry her, despite the possible repercussions of finding out about her past."

"I think you mean *because* of the possible repercussions of the past." A wry smile crossed Nathan's face. They were beginning to really form a male bond now and suddenly the mutual enemy was Dilys, not either of them.

Nathan leaned forward too and said quietly: "You see, as the husband, I'd have a legal right to delve into her past and get the money back I was swindled out of by her bastard husband, Norris bloody Griffiths." The name was spat out with venom.

"Which is – as I said – something I neither knew a lot about nor cared much about either," added Alun, "especially now."

"Indeed." There was a pause, then Nathan leaned even closer to Alun and whispered: "I'm willing to seal the deal with a financial offer, if you like. It's worth it for me."

Alun gazed at the weather-beaten eyes, crowned by rugged eyebrows – more like hedgerows – which were tinged through the grey with the ginger remnants of his Celtic heritage.

"How about the Porsche for starters?" he said, with a glint in his eye.

"I think I could run to that," Nathan replied. "It's outside." *He must be really desperate*, thought Alun; that man Norris had really got to him. He continued: "Well, whatever we decide to do, we still have to force Dilys to divorce me somehow…"

"Tell her you want to marry the floozy."

"Ye-es… But she doesn't know about her for sure as I've never admitted it. But if she *did* know for sure then she'll be jealous and would dig her heels in further. She's like that – a stubborn woman, as you've found out already. Anyway, it's the fact that she won't divorce *me* that's the sticking-point, not anything else."

"True. But as well as either or both of us finding out about Norris's misdemeanours, I think she's just as worried about you going for too much money in the divorce that's motivating her rather than not wanting to leave you, if you don't mind me saying so. *And the fact that the exposure could destroy her financially and reputationally. So…*" his eyes narrowed and he spoke in such hushed tones that Alun had to lean even closer to hear him, "… if I made you an offer you couldn't refuse with *my* money – so you didn't need so much, if any, of *hers* – then I think she'd play ball. As we said, it's what might come to light during divorce proceedings she's more worried about than having any idea of what *I* really want out of her, I think." There was a pause, then he looked intently at Alun and said: "I think she's more terrified she'll lose the farm and the 'buried millions', if you get my drift, and paying for the sins of Norris Griffiths, than anything else."

"Wait a minute – then I get nothing from her and I need the money to pay for the flat."

"I haven't finished yet! As I've just said, we can get over this using *my* money, not hers. I'll put a large sum into escrow for you – we'll do it all legally – and when the divorce is finalised, then you get the money. I'll discreetly tell her that there'll be no delving into her past – why should there be, as you and I will have settled amicably. Then I can marry her, as she'll know that I've made you a good offer which is independent of her... And all that bollocks about my loving her so much that it's worth it, of course."

"But your plan *is* still to delve into her past?"

"Of course! But I wouldn't tell her that! I just want retribution for what that man did to me – and others, I'm sure."

Alun pondered for a moment. "But what happens if it all goes wrong and she finds out? She'll then know we're in cahoots and I don't get the divorce – or my floozy – and she gets what she wants, but *we* don't."

"Then we'll have to think of something else."

"Such as?"

"I live with her for a couple of years and we become common law husband and wife – you'll be living with your lady by then – and then I acquire legal rights as long as you don't contest them."

"Which I wouldn't."

"Exactly."

"How much would you offer me?"

"250,000."

Alun was aghast – but delighted. "£500,000."

"Done." Stunned, he asked, "Is it really worth that much to you?"

"Yes. Norris Griffiths swindled me out of land and property worth £2.5 million. With Dilys' help, I can get it back – although she doesn't know that yet."

"Nor ever must," Alun added firmly.

"Indeed," Nathan confirmed.

Alun took all this in. No wonder he had a grievance – and Dilys had just happened to pop up at the right moment, as had his relationship with Leini. "I'm in," he said simply.

A gnarled hand swung in front of his face and Alun grasped it warmly. "But if nothing budges her, then what?"

"We dispose of her. Then, as her husband, you just sign the house, farm and land over to me and we haggle over the bits and pieces. We can easily make it look like an honest transaction."

"And the idea of having to dispose of Dilys, as you so eloquently describe it, doesn't bother you?"

"Well, a little… But thousands of acres, ponds, farm machinery, outhouses, cellars, wells… there are hundreds of ways of disposing of unwanted things…" The word 'things' chafed in Alun's ear but the offer was too good to refuse. And he'd get Leini, the Porsche, loads of money – and perhaps quite a lot more. Nathan could see he was deliberating, so went in for the kill – but not literally, at this moment, at least.

"How about a down payment to show I mean it? You take the Porsche now – I'll swap it for yours – and I'll tell Dilys it's been stolen, broken down, whatever. She really likes the Porsche, so she'll be well annoyed. I'm not going back to hers tonight, so I can get rid of your car on my farm – and then say when we're married – and *only* when we're married – I'll get her another Porsche – or an even nicer car. I think that should persuade her."

"So do I," added Alun, a wild notion suddenly crossing his mind, inspired by the thought of Leini driving a Porsche, the association in his mind thus leading to his idea for the removal of the offensive Mrs

Wiggins in his television script. "And if she doesn't, I've got an idea, too."

After another few drinks and a splendid meal – all paid for by Nathan – two very happy men went into the car park, exchanged details and car keys, and drove their swapped cars away in opposite directions – even Alun's former heap having a zip due to the elation of Nathan, its new owner.

*

The phone rang in the hall and Dilys answered it. She was glad to find it was Nathan, who seemed somewhat more jovial than of late, despite his 'bloody Porsche' having broken down and so could she come to him tonight as he had been compelled to ring the AA to bring him home after an otherwise successful business meeting near Chipping Sodbury, so he said...? She wondered if he was a little inebriated – especially as he seemed little perturbed by his treasured car's demise, but was intrigued and happy that she would be seeing him soon. Perhaps one of her splendid game pies might be on offer, please, he enquired? She concurred and replaced the receiver, wondering what sort of meeting it was which could make him so much more accessible and light-hearted...

She would soon find out.

Leini, meanwhile – waiting in their flat – was surprised to suddenly see a vintage yellow Porsche pull up outside and wondered who it could be. Curious, she went out and saw it was Alun, who climbed out awkwardly with a beaming face as she appeared, a bouquet of roses from a motorway service station in his arms, complemented by a bottle of expensive champagne.

"What's all this?" she enquired with a puzzled smile. "Have you gone mad?"

"Not at all, my darling, not at all. This, my love, is for you!"

"But... how on earth did you come by it?" Not waiting for an answer, she walked around the vehicle and then sat in the driver's seat, only wincing at the muddy carpets and plethora of sweet wrappers in the passenger footwell. "Whose car is it, then?" she asked as she got out. It needs a wash and vacuum…"

"It's a down payment on a deal to improve our lives together," Alun replied mystically and evasively. "Let's go inside, consume the champagne, make love and as we do so I'll tell you."

CHAPTER 21

Dilys refused point blank: she would not leave Alun. There was too much baggage to sort out, she said, and there was no point. As well as things she did not wish to admit to Alun or divulge to Nathan. Which, of course, made them even more sure that she was hiding something. But she agreed to let Nathan move in.

So it was time for plan B – Alun's idea.

*

JONQUIL'S JOURNALS:

EPISODE 151. SCENE 6. WIGGINS' PARLOUR. DAY.

	EDMUND AND ORCHARD ARE SITTING BESIDE EACH OTHER AT THE KITCHEN TABLE IN THE MIDDLE OF A QUIET DISCUSSION. MRS WIGGINS IS NOWHERE TO BE SEEN.
ORCHARD:	But, Mr Wiggins – Edmund, sir – as I told you, I had no choice but to do what your wife said, or she'd report me to the Watch! And I have a farm in Islington – a small one with a stream – where I rear a few cows and pigs and chickens and catch the odd trout or pike, which I sell to people like you.
EDMUND:	And what about the mutton?
ORCHARD:	That's one of the things I have to acquire from elsewhere. My farm's not big enough for sheep, too.
EDMUND:	So you stole it? (RELUCTANTLY, ORCHARD NODS). I see. Well, as I said in the tavern yesterday, I bear you no ill-will, really – my wife needs a good seeing-to sometimes and you're saving me the bother. I prefer that young Dulce at

the tavern.

ORCHARD: So would I!

EDMUND: Don't you touch her! That's enough of that… Well, Hattie won't leave me 'cos it would cost her position with the lordship here – and mine, too, probably. That scheming little whore who's stolen the master's heart – or another part of his body, I wager! – will soon be running things here, I believe – and they like a married couple in service. So that puts us at odds. But if I could marry Dulce…

ORCHARD: But what about Hattie?

EDMUND: What about Hattie indeed, sir?!

ORCHARD: You mean…? (HE DRAWS HIS HAND ACROSS HIS THROAT AS IF IMPLYING SLITTING HERS. EDMUND NODS AND SMILES EVILLY).

ORCHARD: I see. And how are we going to do that?

EDMUND: I have a plan…

*

Alun paused to think where the next scene should be to take the plot forward but was pleased it was now progressing well and that he could keep up the mystique as to Hattie Wiggins' demise, which everyone knew would happen due to the social media interest in the actress's being written out. His plot with Nathan would soon be enacted, too, and there was a synergy between the real characters in life and the fictitious ones in his screenplay. In fact, that was what was driving both the professional and personal sides of his life – and they were converging beautifully.

He had also just had details of the £500,000 in escrow from Nathan's solicitors. And the change of Porsche ownership. All seemed to be going well. Too well – and that worried him…

*

Leini was admiring the Porsche at a car valeting garage, the machine gleaming in front of her, its yellow paint and metallic wheels now deeper and more resplendent for being bereft of mud. The short time she had been the new owner of this lovely motor though, she had been unsure as to how on earth she had come by it as Alun would categorically not tell her, always having a sardonic look in his eye as if he were toying with her and would use it to lever favours from her at awkward moments, albeit in a playful and loving manner.

She got into the driving-seat and breathed in the smell of the rich, newly-polished leather; she knew it had belonged to Dilys' 'toy-boy', as Alun wickedly called him, but the reason for the exchange was a mystery to her — and she felt would be for some time. The throaty roar of the engine gave her a thrill, which also made her feel very sexy as the engine's vibrations complemented her joy at attracting a lot of attention when she stopped at lights or received a smile when letting someone through a restricted space. But her love for Alun was growing: how many men would do a deal which involved a vintage Porsche and not want it for himself? She pressed the accelerator a little further — she could not wait to get back to him...

In Wales, though, Nathan was cursing the exchange: Alun's former car would not start, so he would now have to tow it to the garage by his tractor, only hoping that Dilys would not surprise him with one of her unannounced visits as he pulled it down his long drive to the main road...

*

In the latter course of Alun and Nathan's conversation — which they dubbed the *'Sodbury Chronicles'* — they had discussed the means of Dilys' demise should she not avail herself of divorcing Alun under normal terms, to which Nathan had agreed. It ran thus:

Alun would tell Dilys that he was coming down to see her 'to sort a few things out' before he left her — despite no divorce — so that Nathan had the freedom — and vacated space — to move in. He would hire a van and drive his most important belongings back to London. In the course of the day, Nathan would 'unexpectedly' turn up and a contrived, filthy row would evolve between them. Nathan would be so angry that he would go for the shotgun in his tractor and Alun would ensure that Dilys' shotgun, too, was in its usual place in the porch – which she kept for shooting moles, crows, squirrels, whatever – and readily loaded. They would find themselves in a stand-off, pointing the guns at each other, with Dilys pleading with them to stop – which they were both sure she would (hopefully) – and the guns would go off. Plan B was live. But Dilys might soon not be…

CHAPTER 22

With the date of Lottie Brace's removal from *Jonquil's Journals* now firmly set in the schedules, a certain tension took hold in the show's production office; no-one but the top echelon of staff were told the transmission date and all were placed under strict instructions to keep it absolutely secret. Social media was watched relentlessly for the slightest leak so that any speculation might be quashed immediately – until nearer the day when selected leaks would be sent from the office to ensure the biggest possible TV audience. Indeed, the advertising fees had already climbed episode by episode as audiences increased, each waiting for Mrs Wiggins' impending demise.

As if to underline the production team's relief at her real-life departure in the shape of Lottie Brace, Alun had suddenly come up with a waspish sub-plot to cast her character – Mrs Wiggins – into a less favourable light; this was so that, when the scene of her death was shown, there would be less viewer sympathy than what the actress had taken to social media to engender: indeed, Alun hoped that some might even think she had received her just desserts, which the production team's loathing for the real-life person was intended to convey. The scenario would also fit in nicely with the penultimate episode before her death, which, although involving some cuts and re-writes to the script, would be well worth it. This he had finished but not yet submitted but its inclusion would have another benefit: it would mean another sub-plot where Jenny, the whore from London Bridge, openly using her wiles to ensnare Justice Jonquil, was doing much the same to the reviewers and TV audience – especially as she had suddenly dispensed with any hesitation in baring her breasts at any scripted opportunity as it gave her extra exposure – and fame. In fact, they had become known in the gutter press as 'Jenny's jewels' and the ratings had peaked accordingly. So Alun discussed with Jonathan the idea that she should do so far more frequently. Jonathan loved the idea (although his tastes, of course lay in a different direction) and so Alun went to work.

JONQUIL'S JOURNALS:

EPISODE 151. SCENE 15. JONQUIL'S DINING-ROOM. EVENING.

	JONQUIL AND JENNY – NOW BEAUTIFULLY ATTIRED, BEWIGGED AND MADE UP AS A LADY – ARE SITTING HAVING DINNER, WITH MRS WIGGINS BUSYING ABOUT LADLING OUT VARIOUS DISHES OF FOOD ONTO THEIR PLATES AS EDMUND POURS CLARET INTO THEIR GLASSES.
EDMUND:	(MOVING TOWARD JENNY). Claret, Miss Jenny?
JENNY:	(WITH A DEFINITELY MORE AFFECTED ACCENT THAN PREVIOUSLY). No, thank you, Edmund; a glass of the buona roti, if you please…
EDMUND:	Certainly, Miss Jenny…
JONQUIL:	Edmund! Would you please now address Miss Jenny as *Lady Jonquil*, please.
EDMUND:	(POINTEDLY). I'm sorry, m'lord, but I wasn't aware that you had tied the knot with Miss Jenny yet.
JONQUIL:	Well, we haven't… but I want her to get used to the title as we will soon… (JENNY GIGGLES WITH ANTICIPATION).
EDMUND:	(ANNOYED AND WITH A MUTUAL LOOK OF DISGUST TO MRS WIGGINS). Yes, m'lord.
JONQUIL:	That's enough of the beef, thank you, Mrs

Wiggins.

WIGGINS: Certainly, sir... (SHE MOVES OVER TO JENNY AND FROSTILY DOLLOPS A PILE OF BEEF ONTO HER PLATE).

JENNY: Be careful, Mrs Wiggins – you'll splash my fallalls.

JONQUIL: Yes, careful, Mrs Wiggins; and some discretion and respect for Jenny who, as I have just intoned to Edmund, is now to be treated as the lady of the house. And those fallalls cost me a pretty penny to adorn my little treasure, too. (THEY MOUTH KISSES AT EACH OTHER). So go easily with your serving...

WIGGINS: Sorry, sir – no malice intended... (WHICH IS QUITE OBVIOUSLY THE OPPOSITE).

JONQUIL: This beef is a little tough , Mrs Wiggins – where *did* you get this from: Scrag End? (HE AND JENNY LAUGH).

WIGGINS: Oh, no, sir – the same young butcher as usual.

JONQUIL: Hmmm... Not the usual standard from Mr Orchard. Has he been giving you of his best, recently? (EDMUND SHOOTS WIGGINS A KNOWING LOOK).

WIGGINS: (POINTEDLY AT EDMUND). He certainly has, sir!

JONQUIL: Well, this is not good, Mrs Wiggins. Is your housekeeping allowance not sufficient for my tastes?

WIGGINS: Well, sir, it is sometimes difficult to get the best shanks on the money you provide...

JONQUIL: Hmm... Well, Lady Jonquil – here - seems to think that there's less in my coffer than before and I tend to agree. There are only two people with a key – you and I. Is there a reason for that?

WIGGINS: Not that I would know, sir… Have you given the key to someone else, sir? Like Jenny – er, Lady Jonquil here?

JONQUIL: No, she needs for nothing – I give her an allowance.

WIGGINS: So how does she know there's less, then, sir?

JONQUIL: I don't like your tone, Mrs Wiggins. Come and see me at 9 o'clock tomorrow morning over breakfast. But in the meantime, please give me your coffer key. (WIGGINS AND JENNY EXCHANGE LOOKS WHICH COULD KILL).

WIGGINS: Yes, sir – certainly, sir. (SHE TAKES IT FROM AROUND HER NECK AND GIVES IT TO HIM).

JONQUIL: That will be all for the minute, Mrs Wiggins… But Edmund, you stay – I'll be wanting another glass of that splendid claret presently. (WIGGINS CURTSEYS AND LEAVES THE ROOM.)

*

JONQUIL'S JOURNALS:

EPISODE 151. SCENE 16. WIGGINS' PARLOUR. EVENING.

SHE ENTERS DOWN THE STAIRS WITH THE TRAY AND POT OF BEEF IN A HURRY.

WIGGINS: (WHISPERING). Jonas? Jonas! (THE PANTRY DOOR OPENS AND ORCHARD LOOKS OUT).

ORCHARD: Hattie!

WIGGINS: Quick! I think the master's onto me and Edmund's not far behind. Look in there and find the pot of oats at the back... (HE GOES INTO THE PANTRY AS SHE BUSIES HERSELF WITH THE NEXT COURSE. HE COMES BACK WITH IT).

ORCHARD: What d'you want oats for? (SHE SLAPS THE POT ON THE TABLE, THRUSTS HER HAND IN AND RUMMAGES AROUND, EVENTUALLY PULLING OUT A LARGE BAG TIED AT THE TOP, WHICH JANGLES AS SHE EXTRACTS IT). What's that?

WIGGINS: My savings! But I think he's twigged. Take it, my love, and look after it – hide it; but don't you dare spend it or you'll be off to Tyburn again!

ORCHARD: And you, my dear, too, I think – if this gets out.

(THEY HEAR EDMUND ON THE STAIRS.)

WIGGINS: Quick – go!

(HE TAKES THE MONEY AND RUNS, JUST MANAGING TO QUIETLY CLOSE THE AREA DOOR AS EDMUND APPEARS.)

EDMUND: What are the oats for?

WIGGINS: Me. I'm not getting enough!

EDMUND: Is that little...? (HE GOES TO THE PANTRY BUT NO-ONE IS THERE). I bet he was here – I can smell him. And now that little trollope upstairs is taking over, she'll be bringing in her own servants afore long. It's all your fault... And now she's got him thinking you're stealing from him. You'll have to go – I can't be seen with a thief!

WIGGINS:	You are *now*! And it's been to your benefit, too, over the years. Without it, your beer money would have been much less. And you wouldn't have been able to afford Dulcie, neither!
EDMUND:	(DEFENSIVELY). I don't know what you're talking about…
WIGGINS:	Funny – everyone else does!

*

Alun was pleased there was now another reason for Edmund Wiggins to want to get rid of his wife, which had seemed a little sparse up until that point – except for the fact they just didn't get on. Rather like him and Dilys. It was all in the script…

*

A couple of weeks passed: but soon the filming day when the scene where Mrs Wiggins would meet her end was imminent; it was all over social media… The papers had covered the story too and there was mounting speculation as to how she would be dispensed with, as no hint had been divulged. Yet the one person not enamoured with the proceedings was, of course, Lottie Brace, who played Mrs Wiggins. Especially as she was going to be killed in a supposed duel between her husband and lover. It particularly galled Lottie further as she had recently come out as gay to her close friends and so her scripted despatch at the hands of two men made her very angry indeed. *Typical, of course*, she thought, but it had given her the excuse to cause some havoc on social media. Indeed, unknown to Alun and the production bosses, she was planning to create a little diversion of her own…

The filming schedule day and location had been sent to Lottie some week or so before: it was then that she went into action. Despite the request for secrecy, she had sent the details to all her friends and posted it onto social media, with the statement that the final insult from the TV company had been not to have her murdered by some female lover – despite this being almost anachronistic at the time, as that sort of behaviour would almost certainly have been kept quiet. But she had the sexist Jonathan in her sights, as well as that slippery Alun, and she was going to go out with a bang, so to speak. What had not occurred to her in this fit of manufactured pique was that Jonathan was gay, too …

A few days prior to filming, Leini – sensing that Lottie might try a final display of fireworks in some way – had done some research into Lottie's Twitter account to find she had set it ablaze to harness the righteous indignation of the lesbian community, who – in solidarity with her social media fanbase – were planning to obstruct filming and had been told to vocally picket the location and hamper the shoot. Leini told Alun and Jonathan immediately: so a counter-plan was immediately devised. As Lottie had let the cat out of the bag as to her demise, there was little they could do on that front other than to tell the press they should 'wait and see' what actually transpired…

All the actors involved in the scene – with the exception of Lottie Brace – were suddenly informed that their cars to take them to the filming location would arrive earlier than previously planned. But the fact that no mention was made of the new location address was deliberate…

So on her final filming morning, Lottie sat in her car, fulgent with delight at the chaos her little farewell prank would inflict upon the series she had been in for five years – and which had made her a star. However, when she was delivered by her driver to a remote location in Norfolk rather than the one she was expecting in Hertfordshire, she was furious: indeed, there was no sign of her demonstration there at all. She was even more discomfited when she tried to get onto her Twitter account to find that she had no mobile signal; Leini had deliberately ensured that they were in a dead spot. Her fury heightened, she made straight for Jonathan and the director, but she had been called last 'so she could arrive later at the location, love' as the location manager told her – which meant that the scene had already been partly shot and her scenes would be filmed last – so there was no way she could capitalise on the situation or she would have been in breach of her contract by refusing to act her final scene. Deflated and furious, she acted her final lines, the wailing needing no acting skills at all as they were all for real. Jonathan, Alun and Leini were, of course, delighted as the scene was shot and all the pent-up fury of her supporters was being directed at a location to which no film crew had arrived. Added to that, the indignantly resentful Twitterstorm would help the ratings no end – especially as this would set up an almighty furore with pro- and anti-Lottie Brace fans. As if to compound the put-down, Jonathan, Alun and Leini approached her after the filming with a huge bouquet of flowers, champagne and an expensive wrapped gift. She resentfully accepted them in her caravan, with Leini and Alun leaving as quickly and as graciously as possible, but Jonathan announcing as he departed that he understood her feelings as he was gay, too. This dumbfounded Lottie, as how could she now accuse him of being sexist? And of *course* he understood her concerns as he suffered them, too, albeit from the other side. In short, she realised she did not have a leg to stand on, which disgruntled her further – a blazing *adieu* would have bolstered her sense of self-importance mightily as she steamed off the location into the sunset. As a final affront, Alun explained that the location had been chosen only for practical reasons and he was *so* sorry that the planned demonstration had been 'dis-located' as he smugly termed it.

Lottie left the set a deflated and bitter woman; worse, her agent had not rung with any new offers of work… although this might have had much to do with Leini discreetly putting about rumours in the media that she was difficult to work with. TV is a cruel business – even when set in the 18th century.

Yet the aftermath would all be extremely good for the programme…

*

JONQUIL'S JOURNALS:

EPISODE 152. SCENE 56. A DESERTED SPACE IN A WOOD. DAY.

> WE HEAR WAILING AS MRS WIGGINS PLEADS WITH ORCHARD AND EDMUND NOT TO FIGHT OVER HER BUT COME TO AN AMICABLE

UNDERSTANDING. TWO 'SECONDS'
STAND BY, INSPECTING A BRACE OF
PISTOLS, AS AN ADJUDICATOR LOOKS
EARNESTLY ON, WORRYING THAT
THE WATCH MAY ARRIVE AT ANY
MOMENT...

ADJUDICATOR: It's time to settle this, gentlemen; so would you both come here, please? (THEY FEARFULLY COME TOWARDS HIM). Now, are you both sure that you wish to proceed with this duel, knowing that one or both of you might be killed or seriously injured?

WIGGINS: No – please don't!

BOTH: Yes. It won't be me/I will prevail, I know...

ADJUDICATOR: Very well; please each inspect one of these pistols and, if you are satisfied with its condition, follow me to the centre of the field.

(HE WALKS AWAY AS THE TWO
SECONDS OFFER THEM THE PISTOLS.
THEY INSPECT THEM AND EACH NOD
SATISFACTION, THEN FOLLOW THE
ADJUDICATOR TO THE FIELD'S
CENTRE. THE WAILINGS OF MRS
WIGGINS DROWN ALL OTHER
NOISES...).

ADJUDICATOR: Do either of you have any possibly last words?

BOTH: Quiet, Hattie!/Silence, woman!

ADJUDICATOR: Very well. Please stand back-to-back. (THEY DO). When I drop my handkerchief, you will each take six steps away from each other, then turn and fire at will. Is that understood?

THEY NOD. MRS WIGGINS STARTS
WAILING AGAIN AS THE

ADJUDICATOR DROPS THE HANDKERCHIEF; AS THEY START WALKING AWAY, HE RUNS FOR HIS LIFE IN A DIFFERENT DIRECTION TO THE TWO SECONDS, WHO ALSO SPLIT IN TWO AND WALK QUICKLY IN OPPOSITE DIRECTIONS, LEAVING MRS WIGGINS ON HER OWN.

AFTER THE SIX PACES, THEY TURN TO AIM AT EACH OTHER... THEN TURN TOWARDS MRS WIGGINS AND BOTH SHOOT HER! SHE CRUMPLES INTO A PILE OF CLOTHING, WITH TWO SHOTS IN HER – ONE IN THE HEAD AND ONE IN THE CHEST.

THE ADJUDICATOR AND SECONDS – AWARE THAT THIS WAS GOING TO HAPPEN – RUN OVER TO HER TO INSPECT THE DAMAGE, BUT SHE IS DEAD.

ADJUDICATOR: 'Pon my soul, poor woman – she is dead...

BOTH EDMUND AND ORCHARD EMBRACE EACH OTHER, WITH SMILES OF HAPPINESS.

EDMUND: Dulcie – here I come, my sweetheart!

ORCHARD: Helen – you shall be mine!

(THE CAMERA PULLS BACK TO PONDER THE SCENE... AS A POSSE OF THE WATCH SUDDENLY APPEAR ON HORSEBACK AND EVERYONE RUNS IN DIVERSE DIRECTIONS!)

SERIES MUSIC THEME AS END CREDITS ROLL.

CHAPTER 23

At around the same time the above scene was being filmed, a somewhat nervous Dilys had started preparing for Alun's visit and was putting all his effects into a series of cardboard boxes. Clothes, scripts, personal belongings, photographs, his writing awards, PC and hundreds of reference books were all making their way to the edge of his study in a neat, boxed row. She just hoped his van was big enough...

*

It was the next day and Nathan Grubb was nervous, too. He had gone to Dilys' farm that morning because she had said she would be out; once there, he found the key she kept hidden under the ceramic frog in the garden and made for the loft with the intention of going through the boxes, deposited there by Norris Griffiths, her first husband, before he had died, which Dilys had carelessly mentioned. Although sealed, he was determined to open them as he knew that there would soon be one of two outcomes: either Dilys would be dead or she would have given in to Alun's request for divorce and her demise would be unnecessary – and these documents he was now leafing through would remain 'unopened' in this fusty loft where Dilys feared to tread. Not surprising: as he leafed through the papers, it started to appear that Norris might have been 'rubbed out' rather than died naturally, as a result of a shady deal he had enforced too heavily in Bangor. But surely not: if that was the case, it must have been *someone else* who had put these files here: Dilys? The henchmen? The plot thickened. The incriminations were damning; the receipts, contacts, letters containing threats – a few addressed to himself, Nathan – were all there to be seen. It also transpired that – unknown to Dilys, he was sure – Norris had part-owned a thriving drugs and prostitution business in Colombia, where it became increasingly obvious that many illegal immigrants, sex traffickers and drug deals had been 'processed'; it also seemed that there was a bank account in the Cayman Islands where he had millions stashed away – presumably being added to as he perused the files. It was dynamite: he, Nathan, had been on the wrong end of this man but had had no idea of his other prodigiously nefarious dealings – and he was sure Dilys didn't either. Or Alun. In fact, he began to wonder whether he should tell Alun – if he didn't know already: in which case, he could evaporate to Colombia and live off Norris' illegal earnings after Dilys had been seen to. What did concern him, though, was that it also seemed increasingly likely that Norris's bent henchmen were still operating – and certainly had been when Norris was alive; from meagre beginnings in the council offices of Aberystwyth, these men could now be running a cartel and living in drug-infused, sex-filled splendour. It was disgraceful. And he was jealous.

He pondered whether this would be grounds to tell Dilys that, if she didn't agree to divorcing Alun – and pronto – then he would divulge all this to the authorities. Then, on second thoughts, he did not want to be hunted down by a cartel hitman, so scotched that idea very quickly. Keeping it quiet could also mean he might be able to appropriate the bank account to his advantage and *also* live in Colombia... in drug-infused, sex-filled splendour... A thrill went through his body... could he manage that without Dilys and Alun knowing? Or the possible henchmen? He needed more information ... and opened another box.

In it were details of the accounts, dealers, names of traffickers, drug lords and much more. Yet now he became worried: Dilys might be oblivious to all this, but while it *could* seriously change his life, it might also curtail it very quickly, too. Let sleeping dogs lie... But his thirst for revenge on the man who had defrauded him surmounted all. He concluded that some of these boxes had been sealed and put here before Norris had faced any idea of being rubbed out and would have therefore considered them a safe secret. Suddenly, Alun's divorce from Dilys was essential. And he, Nathan, was the only one who knew anything about these finer details...

He spent the next forty minutes humping the boxes down the ladder, then the stairs, and out into his waiting tractor's covered trailer. Then he locked the front door, returned the key under the frog and drove off. He would hide the boxes in his own loft and use them as collateral to ensnare Dilys – and her fortune. And the mafia would never know where to look. Yes, the *Sodbury Chronicles* would definitely be enacted – but what he had just discovered would remain forever outside Alun's knowledge. He was going to clean up... He would need to: he had that sum of £500,000 to top up...

*

The next day, Alun left London early in an archetypal white van to go down to Wales and pick up his things; as he drove, he was creating script storylines in his mind, delighted that Mrs Hattie Wiggins was no more part of them – and soon her doppelganger, Dilys, might not be either ... He smiled, but with the skies darkening as he approached the Principality, his demeanour did, too. For what he and Nathan would do to Dilys if she wouldn't divorce him was real – not a TV drama – and he started fretting that perhaps Nathan intended a clean sweep of both of them in order to get everything he wanted... and what if the donation of the Porsche was just a ruse to soften him up so he would agree, after which Nathan would testify that Alun had stolen it? Yet somehow he didn't think so; Nathan seemed a decent chap despite his inexplicable passion for Dilys but that, perversely, was what made him more amenable anyway. And it seemed his grudge against Norris Griffiths was justified, genuine and ongoing even if he, Alun, had no particular idea why. Yes, the man had certainly appeared to be a scoundrel with dodgy acquaintances but they had not really bothered him: after all, the man was dead before he had met Dilys.

By the time he reached Tref-Y-Clawdd the skies were not just dark but solid with heavy rain which insulted the van's windscreen wipers in their uselessness; when he arrived, he parked the van behind the barn and then found Dilys waiting for him with a brolly, splashing her way to him as she once dutifully used to do, then offering a warming cup of tea and a humungous slice of her very special carrot-cake, the vegetable ingredients of which he surmised must have come from Nathan's acres.

A few minutes later, they were chatting almost as they had done when first married, each having an air of detachment with the knowledge that they both had someone else and nothing that could now be said would have any bearing on the consequences. In fact, they were getting on better than they had done for years and when he heard the sound of the car coming up the drive and saw Dilys' horrified face, he wished he had had the time to talk to her rationally about a divorce in case the impending dramatic scene could be abandoned.

But it was too late.

*

The events about to be played out in Wales were taking place the day before transmission of the episode where Hattie Wiggins would be shot by Edmund and Orchard; in London, at much the same moment, Leini was fending off all manner of questions from press critics after a viewing given especially for them – but with the very final scene where Hattie Wiggins was actually *seen* to be shot edited out; this was left as an open-ended tease because the company wanted to protect the expected surge in ratings. Leini and Jonathan were alone on the stage under the viewing screen and the main topic was around why they had jettisoned the most popular character in the series. Jonathan was trying to be as evasive and tactful as possible, with Leini deflecting all manner of intrusive questioning, which was suddenly betrayed when Jonathan snapped responding to the question, "Is it because Lottie Brace is difficult to work with?" His hesitant prevarication, then curt admission, suddenly provided the excuse for a tirade of indignant questioning, which then turned more hostile and abusive, especially from the tabloids, whose readers were generally more concerned about what form Hattie Wiggins' demise might take. The punters would not like it, Jonathan was told, and the ratings would suffer as a result – and these collective journalists would be instrumental in ensuring that. They also wanted to know why Alun Loyd was not there, who was responsible for the scripts. When Jonathan said that Alun was busy planning another set of storylines, they became even more hostile and from then on it was increasingly unpleasant, with only the more intelligent papers trying to interrogate in a more nuanced way than the vicious posturing of the red-tops. Leini was trying her best to keep things calm but – with both of them feeling somewhat intimidated by the confected anger of the press – decided it was time to make a frantic call to the TV station's chief executive, Gloria Cordobes, asking her to come down and help them out. On her arrival, her portly but glamorous gravitas had a calming effect, from whence the proceedings became less heated. Despite her hidden annoyance at being dragged out of an executive lunch, she stated clearly that characters had to come and go to keep the series fresh and provide cliff-hangers – as this decision had done – and to add breadth and drama. And when she was asked about the addition of more sex scenes being sexist – as they had only so far featured scenes with *women* exposing their bodies – she replied that she was quite happy with that because she was gay herself. Having subsequently put the press on the back foot in one comment, the journalists collectively realised that, by continuing this line of questioning, it would be them who appeared sexist instead and the invective quickly fizzled out. The aplomb, control and gravitas of Gloria was admired greatly by Jonathan and Leini, who thanked her profusely for her help in coming down at such short notice to defuse the situation and, as they left, Jonathan remarked, "I didn't know you were gay, Gloria, I have to say."

"I'm not," she said emphatically, and went back to her executive lunch.

*

As the car door closed outside, Alun – suddenly realising that Nathan had arrived far too soon – had to extract the answer to his question very fast indeed and, despite the fact that they were talking about happy past memories, blurted out: "So, Dilys, you will divorce me, won't you?" She looked at him, as the swarthy splashing footsteps of Nathan approached the door: "Please say 'Yes'", Alun pleaded, "Say yes <u>now</u>, Dilys... *Please.*"

"I can't," she said feebly. "It's because of the…"

"Because of the *what?*" Alun almost screamed at her, but then

Nathan was coming through the door and Dilys was in horror. Alun got up and went to head him off but he was now in the room and glowered at them both.

"What's all this?" he shouted theatrically – he had obviously been over-rehearsing this moment – and looked at Dilys, adding, "I thought you said you'd never see this man again," in a flat monotone - as if he had learned the words but paid no attention to their intonation.

"Er, let's talk about this," Alun suggested, winking heavily at Nathan after turning his back to Dilys. "I came to get my things," and winked ever more furiously. Nathan looked at Alun without emotion, as a whiff of beer and scotch reached him: Nathan was blind drunk, and Alun realised with horror that no reasoning would cut much ice in the state he was in.

"Dilys was just explaining that she *will* divorce me... I think...," Alun said as he turned back to the tearful Dilys. Nathan just stood there, swaying slightly.

"I can't..." said Dilys, and burst into tears. Then she looked at both of them and said: "It's the contract."

It was the turn of both men to look confused.

"What contract?" they both asked together.

Dilys took a deep breath and stated. "If I divorce Alun, I'll be rubbed out."

"Rubbed out?" Alun said, the irony of this being his and Nathan's intention as well not being lost on him.

"By Colombian drug lords. As long as I stay married to Alun, I'm safe – whatever else happens," she cried out, tears coursing down her cheeks. "When Norris was murdered by a rival gang, they took control of all the proceeds of the 'things' going on over there... but they visit me occasionally to ensure that I'm keeping my side of the bargain. They were here a few days ago, just checking..."

Alun went white, suddenly trembling as he realised the situation he had unknowingly been in over the years. "Why does it matter that

I'm married to you?"

"Because you're the insurance policy. I get money every month from them because you don't know anything about it. And when you die – or if we get divorced – " she added pointedly, "then they'll have trouble with the deeds of this place, which is the bedrock of their kingdom here in Britain; and if that leads to their fixers, secret runners and distributors being betrayed, it could bring down their whole filthy empire. And then Nathan would be rubbed out, too." Then she turned to Alun: "And probably you, too, Alun, for betraying me and, therefore, them."

"But I didn't know anything about it," he protested.

"Exactly."

There was a pause, the only noise being the drip of a leaking gutter outside and the heavy breathing of an increasingly sweaty Nathan.

Dilys completed the explanation: "In the loft are all the agreements Norris made with the first mob before he was shot dead by the second mob, and which he had made me sign, too. When I met Alun, they almost forced me to marry him as it was the easiest way to continue the status quo." Alun felt instantly furious at this – nobody ever 'forced' him to do anything. She continued: "If I – we – rock the boat, there will be repercussions. At the moment, it's all a cosy little arrangement and it works. That's all there is to it."

The silence intensified. Then Alun looked at Nathan, wondering if he had understood any of the ramifications. As if to compound this, Nathan slurred simply, "Let's just do it."

Dilys looked at Alun. Do what?" she enquired uneasily.

"I think we need to sit down and talk," said Alun.

"I'm going to get my gun from the car," stated Nathan and, bumping into various items of furniture as he made for the door, left the room.

*

Leini and Jonathan returned to their office and sat down,

exhausted; then Jonathan rose again and went purposefully to the drinks cabinet.

"Scotch?"

Leini nodded. "Double."

"That was horrible. Thank God for Gloria – I was about to get very abusive with that pack of idiots." There was a pause, then he added: "If we're not innovative, they decry us, and if we are, they do the same. I hate them."

Leini nodded and then consumed almost the whole glass of proffered Scotch in one mouthful. "Sadly, they also know now that we hated Lottie Brace, too."

"Hmm. Yes, I wish I hadn't said that. I could have gone further, though – I was in the mood to say I wish it was Lottie who was being shot rather than the character she plays… Still…"

"If only Alun had been there," Leini observed wistfully.

"Yes – that would have helped… I understand he's in Wales, writing the next batch of storylines, though. I just hope that there's more obvious fiction than hoped-for fact in his stories from now on, though."

So do I, thought Leini – and wondered how Alun was getting on with his quest to divorce Dilys.

If only she could have been a fly on the wall in Wales at that moment…

*

Alun turned to Dilys. "I knew none of this," he said with a quiet fury. "Why did I never know?"

"Be honest, dear; isn't it better that you didn't?"

"But if I don't divorce you, then…"

"Then what?"

"Never mind." He could not bring himself even to hint at her possible demise but, in contemplating it, lost his composure and

140

blurted out, "But I want to marry Leini."

"Ah! So that's who it is! I thought as much!"

Alun kicked himself for letting this out, so giving Dilys even more reason to despise him. Then, to his surprise and not a little sense of pique, she continued: "And I want to marry Nathan, too. But I can't. As you can now see."

"There must be a way out of this."

"Yes – just leave things as they are."

"But... but Nathan wants your estate, land, money..."

"Yes – but what the simpleton doesn't realise is that I want *his*, too."

Alun was astonished. "So you *know* he's after your land and money?"

"Of course. It's obvious. Which is why I want his. What would anyone want with me in the state I'm in physically unless it was for an ulterior motive? I did it to spite you, mostly... Going off with a young floozy..."

Alun ignored the insult and continued: "But what if you and I *did* get divorced? Wouldn't they go after Nathan, rather than me? I mean, I never knew about it."

"I don't think they're very selective... They'd blow us all to smithereens just to be sure, I suspect."

"But legally, they don't have a leg to stand on!"

"Since when did people like that bother about anything being legal? They pay people off, threaten them, kill them... It just works best for them the way it is now. That's *their* idea of legal cover, if you like."

There was a pause. Then she looked at Alun and continued: "Mind you, if the drugs lords were ever arrested or killed, we *could* all be happy. I'd make sure you'd be well rewarded, too, of course. Trouble is, the two other Welsh councillors that Norris was in cahoots with here are still very much alive and aware of what's going on but are keeping shtum to save their own bacon as well as all ours.

But they could return at any moment. Nobby Bowles and Sid Prentice…" Their names were spoken with an air of detached sufferance. Then she darted a look at Alun and stated bluntly: "But it's the Colombians who run everything, of course. Although I'm certain that there are others still in power locally here who are involved, as well as Nobby and Sid – kept on the payroll to consolidate the status quo."

She gazed into the empty fireplace for a moment, then said with some spite: "The Colombians run everything, though. *Every*thing. Currently, Nathan thinks he's going to get all I've got but actually they – the drug barons – know about Nathan now and he's being watched." Then she looked at Alun with a look of caring that he hadn't seen for years and said, "I can give you some of the hush money, now, if it makes things easier with your floozy – but I cannot divorce you. Much as I'd like to."

Alun's head was ablaze with contradictions, theories, plans, anti-plans, reasons to continue with their plan and why-they-shouldn't-but-how-could-he-stop-it, and more. With which, Nathan entered, carrying his shotgun, lolling from side to side. "Why haven't you got your gun?" he enquired of Alun.

"Nathan, things have changed. We have to talk this through. We can't go ahead with our plan or it's curtains for every one of us."

"What plan?" said Dilys.

With that, Nathan's gun went off…

CHAPTER 24

THE TAVERN IS QUITE BUSY; SEATED AT A TABLE, LOOKING FURTIVE AND GUILTY, ARE ABEL PRICE AND ZACCHEUS, TWO UNWASHED, UNKEMPT AND SCARRED ROGUES. ZAC IS THE MORE SAVVY OF THE TWO.

ABEL: So, Zaccheus; when we going to get the money from his lordship the Justice to take out Edmund Wiggins and Jonas Orchard?

ZAC: Tonight. And we'll do it tomorrer.

ABEL: Why does he want to knock 'em off?

ZAC: 'Cos they killed his housekeeper, Mrs Wiggins.

ABEL: Wiggins? But that was Edmund's wife, weren't it?

ZAC: Yes. But Edmund knew that the new little harlot Jenny, who's stolen Justice Jonquil's heart, wanted her gone too 'cos she knew too much…

ABEL: 'Bout what?

ZAC: Jenny wanting to become Lady Bartholomew Jonquil! *And…* she was 'aving it off wiv Jonas Orchard, too, who she was blackmailing.

ABEL: What, Jenny?

ZAC: No, numbskull: Mrs Wiggins.

ABEL: (NOT COMPREHENDING). Oh, I see.

ZAC: No, I don't fink you do, Abel; look, Jenny is trying to marry Justice Jonquil so she can be mistress of the 'ouse – right? Mrs Wiggins was 'avin' horn work wiv Orchard, the butcher, 'cos she wanted a bit of 'extra victuals', if you see my point, 'cos she weren't getting any clicket wiv 'er 'usband, Edmund. See? But Edmund wanted Mrs Wiggins gone 'cos he were bein' cuckolded by Orchard; but 'e also knew that 'is wife - Mrs Wiggins – had been nickin' money from the 'ousekeepin' for years – a tidy sum by all accounts, which he wanted for 'isself. So Justice Jonquil wanted 'er gone, too, see? So now Justice Jonquil wants *us* to snabble Edmund Wiggins and Orchard the butcher 'cos Jenny found out Edmund will get the stolen money – which *she* wants in case it all goes pear-shaped wiv 'er lordship – and the Justice wants them all gone except Jenny because 'e wants 'er and no trace of any other things. And bein' a Justice, o' course, 'e can do what 'e likes. It all makes perfect sense!

ABEL: So we're just tying up a few loose ends for 'is Lordship, the Justice?

ZAC: That's right, my friend… And one day, *I* 'ope to tie up that little Jenny for mesel' too…. 'Cos she's the one planning all this…

ABEL: Oh… So why are Orchard and Edmund in it together, then? They should 'ate each other.

ZAC: Because they each have somefing to gain. Well – that's what they fink at the moment – but tomorrer they'll be no more – and we'll be £20 richer … (HE LAUGHS A DASTARDLY LAUGH).

*

Leini was waiting for Alun's call and wondering why she hadn't heard from him; she never liked it when in the dark regarding his concerns – she liked to know everything. They were now so close, after all... Yet if she could have seen what was happening in Wales at that moment, she would have been worried on a number of counts – not least that Alun was in extreme danger and all the plans that had been made were in extreme danger, too.

CHAPTER 25

Alun and Nathan were looking at the bloody mess which was now Dilys; unlike the calm before a storm, this one followed it. Alun looked at his wife and Nathan put the gun on the table as he sat down heavily on a chair.

"Sorry," he said eventually; "I didn't mean to do that."

"You idiot," Alun said after a few moments of mental struggle; "now we're murderers and we'll also have the Colombian mafia onto us for destroying their little arrangement. Why didn't you let me explain?"

"Colombian mafia?"

"Yes; while you were outside getting your gun, Dilys was explaining why she couldn't divorce me because of them – and now we're in their firing line."

"I didn't know anything about any mafia," Nathan lied somewhat simply.

"Yes, you did; apparently, you've stolen her boxes from the loft, which were all about the bloody mafia."

There was a pause. "She *knew* about that?" Nathan slobbered, unaware that she had obviously been in the loft since he removed them.

"Yes – which is more than I ever did. You've really overplayed your hand, Nathan."

"But I didn't understand all of it – a lot was all in Spanish."

"Her husband must have spoken Spanish, then; perhaps she did, too – I don't know. But death is the same result in any language – and we're on the end of it."

"Oh. Sorry. All I wanted – "

"I know bloody well what you wanted. And I wanted some of it, too – but I didn't know the reasons why she couldn't divorce me – which is what I was trying to tell you before you pulled the trigger."

"I didn't mean to…" There was something pathetic, childlike, in Nathan's comment, as if he was a little boy playing cops and robbers and that all was really make-believe. Then he added: "But I thought this was our plan…"

"It was before the facts changed," darted Alun contemptuously. "But now we're both mafia targets so as it's getting dark I think we'd better get rid of the body; take her away in your tractor and bury her somewhere remote on your farm with a digger – the deeper the better. Then we'll disperse and wait for things to take their course. I'll go back to London with my things but say I haven't been here for ages and was waiting for Dilys to agree a divorce and you… well, I don't know what you're going to do. I'd say that you're a prime target for the mob and you're in danger so let's hurry and get out of here before they arrive."

With that, they both heard the noise of a car slowly coming up the drive. They froze. The engine cut off, then a car door opened and was slammed shut. Then there was a knock at the front door.

*

Leini wondered whether to ring Alun but thought better of it. Perhaps he had decided not to divorce Dilys after all and was afraid to tell her. Well, there would have to be a very good reason for that, she thought. Actually, it wouldn't make much difference, she then concluded: they would still have a good life together and even have children if they wanted to – Dilys could not stop them doing that. There would be less money, of course, which was somewhat of an annoyance – but her plans were watertight and all would be well. After all, she had snared the important, influential man she had had in her sights and was pushing against an open door as far as his feelings for Dilys were concerned. And whilst she knew that Dilys suspected there was a 'floozy', she had no proof as Alun said he had never admitted to it. She was in the clear on that front, at least. What she did not know was that the plan had gone horribly wrong and that she would soon be very complicit indeed as proceedings developed further...

*

JONQUIL'S JOURNALS:

EPISODE 153. SCENE 17. A DARK LONDON ALLEYWAY. NIGHT.

> TWO SHADY FIGURES – ABEL AND ZACCHEUS – ARE WAITING IN THE SHADOWS. ONE HAS A DAGGER AND THE OTHER A CUDGEL. ABOUT FIFTY YARDS AWAY, A YOUNG FIGURE COMES INTO THE ALLEYWAY, SILHOUETTED AGAINST THE FRAME OF THE DISTANT OPENING.

ABEL: (SOTTO VOCE). 'Ere 'e is... (THEY FINGER THEIR WEAPONS NERVOUSLY). Let's stop 'is claret!

> ORCHARD – FOR IT IS HE – WALKS QUICKLY TOWARDS THEM, CLUELESS AS TO HIS IMMINENT DEMISE. AS HE REACHES THEM, ABEL AND ZAC ATTACK HIM AND QUICKLY FINISH HIM OFF, THEN RUN AWAY, LEAVING HIM A BLOODY MESS ON THE GROUND.

*

Alun and Nathan looked at each other in horror. Then Nathan reached for his gun and deftly – despite his drunken stupor – loaded both barrels; with a look of casual insouciance, he went quietly out of the side door to surprise anyone who was at the front. Seeing an opportunity, Alun darted silently into the hallway and into the dining-room next to the kitchen where – behind the door – there was a priest-hole; it hadn't been opened for years and the lid was difficult to prise open but he managed it quietly enough, slipped into the damp void and shut the lid tight as the sound of gunfire was heard outside.

Nathan had accidentally discharged both barrels in an aimless fashion, missing any human intruders but killing a few bats, and was now standing in the dim light from the kitchen window, awaiting a response. It soon came.

In the priest-hole, Alun heard two short, sharp cracks and the sound of something soft but heavy hitting the ground. Then silence. Absolute silence. Alun hardly dared to breathe; eventually, he heard the front door slowly creak open as two pairs of footsteps ground the soil into the granite flagstones of the hallway, making them sound even more frightening; then he heard the kitchen door squeak open and a voice said: "They've got the package. She's dead."

Then another voice said, "Norris won't like that."

"We'd better get rid of the body. You roll her up in a carpet or something and I'll check the rest of the house. Then we'll get the boxes from the loft. The boss'll want the contents of those if *she's* not here."

Alun heard the door of the dining-room squeak open and footsteps entered the room: he dared not breathe. Then a heavy body sat on the top of his hiding-place, sending bits of 17th century dirt into his eyes; there was a pause, then a match flared and he smelt tobacco: the man had lit a cigarette. Then he stood up and Alun heard him leave the room and go up the stairs, checking every room and then opening the loft. Alun suddenly remembered that there was a narrow passage leading from the priest-hole that went under the hallway, which had been an escape route for any persecuted cleric or Catholic sympathiser; it eventually bore to the right under the kitchen and ended up at a grille in the far side wall, which was overgrown with weeds and brambles. But Alun would not go that far – he surmised that the main dialogue would take place as they took Dilys' body out and 'tidied up' after Nathan's end, too; and one thing that was burning in on his terrified conscience was mention of the name Norris. Was he alive, then, still? Had his death been a scam – and had he, Alun, been wedded to a woman all these years who was still married to a corrupt, still-living council leader who was now involved with drug cartels in Colombia? He shuddered – and not just from the draught. He manoeuvred himself quietly down the passage and knew he was under the hall by the kitchen door when he heard something heavy being dragged above him and a warm drop of liquid dripped through a crack in the flagstones: Dilys' blood, he realised.

After a couple of minutes, he then heard the man who had gone upstairs bounding down them again and, on seeing his accomplice above Alun under the hallway, say, "The bloody boxes have all gone. There's a few cardboard boxes with a load of bits and pieces in them at the top of the stairs – must be the husband's. But he hasn't got anything we don't want him to have in them."

"You reckon that dead geezer outside took them?"

"Nathan Grubb? Hmm, probably. But we'll find them – we know where he lives."

"Yeah – but what *he* didn't know was that the stupid husband of hers thought the farm was his, too." Alun was horrified: neither he *nor* Dilys owned the farm? Oh, my God! The man above him continued: "Now Norris'll get the deeds to Grubb's farm, too."

"He's got them already."

"Really? I didn't know that."

"Yeah - that silly git Grubb didn't know he didn't own the farm anyway. Norris does. Grubb *thought* he did – but he just paid all the bills." Alun heard them laugh. There was a pause as various cleaning operations were heard, then:

"We'd better get away pronto," said one, "in case the husband suddenly turns up for his things. We don't need no more digging and burying tonight – two's quite enough." Alun went even colder.

"Was Grubb her lover?" one enquired. Alun assumed a nod, as the other party responded, "He must have been desperate…"

"Well, he must have found out about the connection," which was said with a dismissive laugh. Then: "D'you think the husband knew?"

"Nah – she kept him in the dark. Might be a good idea to leave him out of this. He'll never know what he's missing 'cos I don't think he ever knew."

"Best to keep it like that, probably, then."

"Hmm. You're right. And he'd effectively left Dilys anyway. He's got a gorgeous bit of stuff in London – phwoar, I saw her once – she's gorgeous. Bought a flat in Putney together." Alun was horrified – they knew everything about everyone – even him and Leini! His heart seemed to beat louder in the confines of the passage as another silence ensued whilst the 'cleaning' continued. Then one of the men said: "We'll get another Dilys lookalike in for the short-term for anyone who tries to see what's happened to her and then she can disappear while we just keep this heap going until it's a good time to sell it. With all its lovely memories."

"Sounds good to me."

After that, Alun heard them putting off the lights then leave, closing and locking the front door behind them. He was horrified: they even had a key! Then there were two thuds as the same number of bodies were deposited into what sounded like the cavernous boot of a large car – a van, even.

Then the vehicle left and silence descended on the old house again. It was a good hour before Alun dared quietly to crawl back through the passage and open the top of the priest-hole; he then tiptoed down the cold hallway and into the kitchen. In the dim twilight from the window he could see that there was no trace either of his wife or, when he eventually looked out of the side door, the now very sober Nathan. They knew what they were doing, these boys. Must have been Nobby Bowles and Sid Prentice, Norris' henchmen.

He had been spared. Time to get his boxes of stuff, put them in the white rented van he had fortuitously parked out of sight behind the barn and get the hell out of there. Never to return.

Or so he thought…

CHAPTER 26

Alun didn't remember much of the journey as he sped back to London, his senses and feeling of safety rocked by what he had witnessed, heard and learned; it was only when he got to the Leigh Delamere services on the M4 that, being so consumed by events, he remembered to switch on his mobile and ring Leini. He had switched it off at a similar point on his journey down as he wanted no mobile record of being in Wales – a prescient move of which he was even more glad, as there was now less chance of his being associated with what he had just left behind.

She sounded slightly miffed at his late call and admonished him for not contacting him earlier; yet he was loath to say anything over the phone beyond that he was well and would be home within the next couple of hours.

"You sound shocked," she ventured, after a few stuttering conversations had led nowhere. "Yup – I am. Talk later – will explain." And he rang off.

The rest of the journey continued to be a blur as the enveloping darkness eventually gave way to the illuminated section of the motorway, its womb-like warmth being a harbinger of relief at its proximity to London. It made him feel a little safer – but not much.

When he arrived back at the flat, Leini bounded out and embraced him; he put the van in the garage and they went into the sitting-room which overlooked the garden, and having poured himself a very large scotch, he started whispering the story, much to the amusement of Leini. Yet when he intimated that the reason was that their flat may be bugged, this both shocked and concerned her, as the mafia obviously knew all about them, too. "But how are *we* involved?" she said, with an exasperation he felt was slightly overdone.

"I don't know. But I think we should be very careful and keep our mouths shut; no loose talk or e-mails; just careful, quiet dialogue. In one sense, I don't think I'll ever mention 'her' – " he intimated Dilys with his lips – "and I haven't of course, seen her for many months." This last part of the sentence was said a bit louder, in case anyone was listening.

Leini looked around, as if looking for bugs; "Time to sweep the flat," she said ominously. Alun nodded and after a cursory look they soon went to bed. But neither of them slept a wink…

*

Early the next morning, as the weak sun started to permeate the eastern sky, Nobby Bowles and Sid Prentice were burying the two bodies in a small, thicket-rich wood at the edge of Grubb's land about a mile from his farmhouse. Or, rather, the farmhouse and land Grubb *thought* he had owned…

At about the same time in Colombia, Norris Griffiths raised a glass by his swimming-pool and watched as two nubile young girls cavorted sexily before him, his head honcho and bodyguard, Sander, also enjoying the spectacle. Life was good, even if he was technically dead. He smiled at the thought: he was definitely alive and now circumstances initiated in Britain were making him even happier and richer. And as the girls removed their already very skimpy bikinis, he was even happier. He had instructed Nobby and Sid to get rid of all remaining 'obstacles' to any legalities regarding the farms – and that included people, too. It had been a long-term plan and now it was bearing fruit: the farms between them were worth over £1.5 million and now his one-time wife, Dilys, would soon be confirmed as dead, too, without anyone having to risk telling him – such was the beauty of having a majority shareholding in a Colombian TV company where he could influence the programming. And he had a specific interest in *Jonquil's Journals*… Which is why he soon expected that Dilys' lover would presumably be dead too, subject to the same means of communication. Just the pansy writer, Alun, to go and he could assume either one of their identities – both, even – and discreetly run his burgeoning import-export drug, people-trafficking and arms distribution business via both countries from a position of increased financial strength as an apparently honest Welsh farmer,

153

away from the limelight and with plenty of places to hide.

*

A few days later, as Alun was walking away from his flat on the way to the station, a car driven by two uncouth-looking men ran at him as he crossed a side street; he just managing to avoid it, but the car screeched off into the main road and then turned left down another, so fast he didn't have time to get the number-plate. Was it the mafia? Were they after him? They knew everything... Perhaps it was just a warning – scare tactics to let him know they knew where he lived and to keep quiet. But his journey to the office was one of extreme caution and observation: perhaps even the lollipop lady by the school could be a mafia operative, he thought. Or even the pretty receptionist, Francine, at the TV studios... They could be anywhere...

On reaching the office, he nervously told Leini of the incident, she having preceded him into work; yet she seemed dismissive about it, as if she suddenly thought his new-found fear was becoming an obsession, so he decided not to say any more in that vein: perhaps she was right. But her insouciance surprised him... especially as she had been delighted that morning when he had received Nathan Grubb's £500,000 into his bank account. But now they would know that he and Grubb were connected: curses! Then he thought back to Leini and started wondering whether her unusually quiet demeanour was an expression of concern that this unexpected deposit from beyond the grave seemed like a demonic curse – blood money which could incriminate them both forever? Worse, as a chill went down his spine, was she going off him? Only time would tell on either count – and it was about to...

*

JONQUIL'S JOURNALS:

EPISODE 153. SCENE 28. A BUSY LONDON STREET. DAY.

> ABEL AND ZACCHEUS ARE OBSERVING THE STREET, SHIFTILY WAITING FOR SOMEONE TO APPEAR.

ABEL: Why didn't our Justice give us our money yesterday?

ZAC: 'Cos we didn't finish the job... First time in my life of nobbling people I done that... Losing my touch...

ABEL: But we done *one* of 'em.

ZAC: Yes, but we didn't get the second one, did we?

ABEL: Well, 'e weren't there, were 'e?

ZAC: No – but that's why we're waitin' for 'im now, dimwit...

ABEL: Well, 'e won't get away from *me*... I want my twenny quid – and a romp wiv Delilah!

ZAC: Well, if 'e does get away, or we're nibbed by a myrmidon, we'll be up against our own queer cuffin, Jonquil... and he'd have to send us for the drop at the scragging-post to protect 'imself...

ABEL: Mmm. He won't get away again once I've pierced 'im wiv me schliver... (AS HE FEELS THE SHARP POINT ON HIS LONG DAGGER).

ZAC: (POINTING). There 'e is! Edmund! Follow him...

EDMUND, UNWITTINGLY – BUT SEEMING SOMEWHAT FURTIVE AS IF HE'S EXPECTING AN ATTACK – GOES AROUND A CORNER TO THE FRONT OF JUSTICE JONQUIL'S HOUSE AND STARTS TO DESCEND THE AREA STEPS, WITH ABEL AND ZAC NOT FAR BEHIND. HE GETS TO THE SERVANTS' DOOR WHEN THE TWO ASSASSINS RUN DOWN THE STEPS TO ASSAULT HIM, BUT ONE TRIPS AND FALLS, CAUSING THE OTHER TO TRIP OVER HIM AND THEY END UP IN A HEAP AT THE BOTTOM OF THE STEPS.

EDMUND MANAGES TO ENTER THE DOOR AND COMES OUT IMMEDIATELY WITH A CUDGEL AND LOOKS TRIUMPHANT AS HE RAISES HIS CUDGEL...

AS WE... FADE TO BLACK AND HEAR THE CLOSING MUSIC AND SEE CREDITS ROLL.

*

Alun finished the episode, having taken the idea of Edmund getting his own back on the would-be assassins from Leini: he had originally intended the episode to finish with the outcome being the other way around. But her idea was better: and now the demise of one or all of them could be spun out, so creating a greater dramatic effect. She was really helping him with the storylines, now, and it was a huge help.

And then a thought struck him...

CHAPTER 27

Jonathan was very happy with the series of episodes Alun had written and also with the ratings: these had stayed buoyant despite the demise of the Mrs Wiggins character. Yet Lottie Brace was still desperately using social media to try to get herself written back into the script – despite having been seen to be killed a few episodes before: but this fact seemed to elude her. By now, Jonathan had concluded that Leini and Alun *must* be having an affair: they were so often out of the office together in Putney creating storylines and scripts that he presumed they were in Leini's flat. Or she was at his new flat, not far from hers. Strange, that... He had been to Alun's flat a few times, of course, but if Leini *was* living there with Alun, then it was neither that apparent nor ever mentioned. But the scripts had become spikier, grittier and more *real*, he felt, with her collusion; so as long as she did her office work for him as well, it was a good development. Anyway, although he knew she was beautiful to most men, that didn't include him, so any supposed benefit of having an attractive female presence around the office was not something he missed. The thought had crossed his mind that if Leini did leave or wish to become more involved with writing the scripts, then perhaps a male production assistant would be a pleasant distraction for him and might help him in a more personal way to offset the occasional crises and disturbances of television production.

He stopped his reverie and returned to scrutinising the *Jonquil's Journals* document in front of him. Yes, Leini's increasing involvement in the scripts really had improved the series. Yet if Jonathan had watched *'Jonquil's Journals'* every weekday with the same attention as a few individuals in Colombia, and been in tune enough to associate the characters in the series with those real-life ones they were in parallel with, he would have known exactly what was happening in reality. Yet that was lost on him and his immediate TV executives as much as it was scrutinised by those involved in the dastardly criminal processes going on between London, Wales and Colombia. But one person in each country understood every detail: in fact, they were each following the tale very closely indeed.

Because it was all in the script.

This realisation had also started to dawn on Alun just a few days before: that there seemed to be similarities with some of the major series characters' exploits to what was going on in his own life beyond his parallel ruse of using Dilys and Hattie Wiggins as one and the same – and it had started to trouble him. Yet he felt he was being paranoid, so tried to put it out of his mind. But it persisted and, along with Leini's suddenly strange quietness – and his belief that someone was trying to kill him – the feelings just would not go away. So he started to fantasise about which character was which… and who was guiding the plotlines and masterminding them. But *he* wrote the scripts, so to any observer it would all point to him. But he had been unaware of any other real-life parallels except the demise of Dilys in parallel with Mrs Wiggins at the hands of Jonas Orchard and Edmund; so who else had been killed, either in the series or real life? The more he thought about it, the more he realised that Jonas Orchard seemed to be a doppelganger for Nathan Grubb… who had been killed by the henchmen Dilys had mentioned before Nathan shot her – Sid Prentice and Nobby Bowles… was that alias Abel and Zaccheus? Yet that part made less sense: it was *Nathan* who had killed Dilys while in a drunken stupor, not Sid and Nobby. Yet, perhaps in real life – if his theory was correct – she was *supposed* to have been rubbed out by someone else but it had gone wrong. On further chilling reflection, though, this suggested he was the doppelganger for Edmund – who had wanted his wife – Mrs Wiggins – dead so he could marry the whore Jenny – or another character in the script? Was Leini one of those characters? He thought about it and suddenly his heart sank … of course – Jenny the whore was Leini! He and Leini had kept putting off Edmund's death, although Abel and Zaccheus had tried to do so in the script – but failed. And yet Edmund's demise seemed imminent: so was his, then, too? Suddenly, it became apparent to him – the person trying to kill him was Lottie Brace, who had played Mrs Wiggins and been written out of the series! Her hatred of him, Leini and all at Tellurian TV had now translated into her trying literally to rub him out for having done so, fuelled by her social media campaign! That car he had avoided was driven by two uncouth-looking men: they must have been Sid and Nobby, whom he had never seen – only heard – at Dilys' farm! And in the script, Jonas Orchard was now dead at the hands of Abel and Zaccheus – Sid and Nobby! One real farmer – Nathan/Jonas, and the other living *on* a farm, the pansy writer... which must be him – Alun/Edmund! Yes, it must be Lottie Brace! It all made perfect sense. She had used her celebrity status to bully the TV executives to create a parallel storyline where he eventually got killed. The witch! He would have to confront her. And with that, he decided to go and see her. He knew where she lived, and it wasn't far away... Yet as he drove towards her house, he couldn't help feeling that something still wasn't right and that he was missing something...

*

The day before, Leini had suddenly decided she had to get away to clear her mind; the subterfuge she had been playing had suddenly swamped her and she had to think. She would disappear and then announce from afar that her parents in Ireland had been taken ill and so she had needed to rush away for a while to see them. But that was a couple of days' time, when she had sorted herself out and knew what to say and do – she just needed to be alone. A pallor had descended upon her: was she really happy with Alun? Or did she just like the reflected praise, the money, the promise of a good life...? She knew that, in love, all people go through emotional crises, wondering if they were doing the right thing. Yet this had come upon her almost in an instant; it had not crept up on her as a tiny set of doubts, growing bigger as their relationship progressed; no, it was a flashlight realisation that she might lose him. In fact, she suddenly had to accept how much she deeply loved him.

And that was definitely *not* in the script...

*

159

Norris Griffiths gently pushed one of the two girls away with whom he had shared the afternoon, covered her naked body with a light blanket so she could sleep off the effects of her cocaine in comfort, and went to his television. It was time to catch up on the latest episodes of *Jonquil's Journals*: he recorded every single programme with the passion of a zealot. It was his way of keeping tabs on life in Britain, even if the programme *was* set in the 18th century. Yet his various business dealings were very much of now: with only erratic and – at best – dodgy internet, mobile signal and social media here in the mountains, TV was the best way of keeping in touch with investments and the health of his empire. He was glad to see that his hopes for the flow of the story were progressing as expected and smiled contentedly at the scene where Mrs Wiggins had finally been shot by the two competing men in her life. He had never liked her character but knew she was central to the plot. In fact, Mrs Wiggins reminded him of his ex-wife, Dilys. What a strange co-incidence…

*

Alun rang the front doorbell, which seemed to resonate as distantly as the outer reaches of space at the back of Lottie Brace's vast Edwardian north London house. He then stood back, expecting a torrent of spite and venom when she saw him on her doorstep; yet when the door opened, her demeanour was more one of surprise than threatening and after his garbled proclamation that he meant her no harm or displeasure, she let him in, closed the front door behind him and ushered him into her sitting-room. Alun marvelled at her opulent tastes and thought how it was thanks to him and Jonathan that this dreadful woman lived in such luxury – the funding for which they had now cut off. No wonder she hated them.

"I suppose you've come to apologise," she said quietly. "I hope you're happy – I haven't worked since." Alun was about to say that it was less than a week ago she had been bumped off in the programme and that she could only blame herself because her hate campaign had been so intense and widely known that no producer would now touch her with a bargepole. Eschewing this for a passive, "No, it's something else," he sat down.

"Tea?" she enquired. Alun shook his head and just said, "Lottie, are you trying to kill me?"

Her face was completely impassive as she looked at him, and then with a disdainful glance, said, "What – with a poisoned cup of tea?" Alun shook his head. "No. How about by trying to run me over?"

She gave him a quizzical stare. "Why would I want to do that?"

He shrugged. "I don't know… perhaps to get me back for stopping your ability to live in this splendour?" as he waved at the opulence around him. "You did mount a pretty unpleasant hate campaign."

"Well, I was instructed to do that."

"Instructed? By whom?"

"One of the top people in the TV company, I suppose – I never knew his name. But I supposed it was to get better ratings up until the time you actually wrote me out."

Alun was surprised and not a little confused. "You're saying that someone *told* you to mount the hate campaign, and that it wasn't motivated by you?"

"Well, I was happy to go along with it, of course. Especially as they paid me a lot of money to do it. That's off the record, of course – not that it matters much now."

The sumptuous salon seemed to swirl about him: she was *paid* to mount the campaign against him, Jonathan and Leini? That was ridiculous. "So who tried to run me over, then, a few days ago."

"I have no idea." There was a pause, then: "But these TV execs are a ruthless bunch. They'll do anything to get the ratings up."

In his mind, Alun could not fathom who might do that. The CEO, Gloria Cordobes? Surely not. A major shareholder? Perhaps. But it was so outrageous… And why him? He had been writing the scripts for years, won awards, been fêted and chased by other TV channels… Although without Leini he would not have managed even that. Ah, Leini… Life had become so much better since he met her and she had started helping him write the scripts with the odd suggestion, painstaking research and often very clever plotline twists.

Realising he had obviously over-imagined Lottie's motives, he apologised for the intrusion and quickly left, his mind a jumble as all these competing and contradictory confections went to war with one another in his brain. He had to talk to Leini – she would sort it out. Yet her phone went straight to voicemail: he would have to discuss it with her later. How he needed her: in fact, he realised at that moment how much he loved her and how he couldn't be without her.

*

At about the same time, Leini was close to landing at Dublin airport and feeling much the same way about Alun, with a pronounced tear welling in her eye. She had never meant this, at the beginning, to be more than a passing bit of fun – all part of the ruse she had agreed to – especially when she first met him in all his scruffy squalor. But he had improved so much and become her soul-mate so comprehensively; he had been generous, patient when she refused sex with him for so long, had bought a beautiful flat with her and given her a wonderful car into the bargain – whatever shady circumstances had produced it. Not that she could talk about shady circumstances; here was she, supposedly going to see her parents, when all she was really trying to do was get the hell away to sort out her feelings and how to extricate herself from a tricky situation. The problem, though, was that she was beholden to others; others who paid and influenced her. Yet the job in television she had been slotted into for the reasons she had embraced but was now questioning had astonished and surprised her: she had never enjoyed a job so much, never had so much fun, never been so wealthy nor laughed so much. And she had influenced events, helped her motivator... and found a potential husband. But that was now what was causing her acute mental and physical disturbance – which was nothing to do with the dodgy landing she was now experiencing as the plane approached Dublin. Yesterday, London; today, Dublin; tomorrow, the world. Well, Bogotá, anyway...

CHAPTER 28

Alun had left Lottie Brace's flat in a state of anguish – which was made worse by the fact that Leini was not at home when he got back. Being alone, though, allowed him to reflect that this was not the result of any spleen regarding Lottie but his own confusion, doubts and vacuous helplessness that had enveloped him. He knew that in the TV business there were a lot of rotten apples but he hadn't expected it to be a full barrel of them. Who could he trust now? He now even had doubts about Leini. And as for his ex-wife, Dilys, how had she become involved in what he was now beginning to suspect? Was she a useful idiot or a guiding star in the darkest of collusions? He would never know now, of course. And where was Leini now when he needed her? Or did he? Was she one of those rotten apples, too? He castigated himself for allowing himself to fall so willingly under her heavily-scented fragrance, beauty and intelligence, pondering whether she was really as clever, devious and manipulative as he was starting to think she must be. Or just misguided? Blameless, even? No, that was being too charitable – she had stitched him up. And how…

Lottie's parting shot had intrigued him, too: as he left, she had just said, "I think you should look more closely at your own scripts – what you have actually written. I think that's where you'll find some clues to all this." Yes – he had started having the same concerns only a few days ago, too; he thought his scripts were clever – but now wondered whether it was due to someone else, not him. Or was that just his inverted infatuation? Either way, it all came back to the same person: Leini.

*

Leini, for her part, was sitting in Dublin airport, awaiting the first of her connecting flights to Bogotá and sharing many of the same contradictions which had plagued her on the first flight, her sense of guilt and betrayal mounting all the while. She had tried a strong drink to loosen her mind but that hadn't worked; when she was chatted up by a pleasant Irish businessman it meant nothing – all she could see was Alun and how he must now be wondering where the hell she was and why had she suddenly disappeared. Yet if she reneged on the business deal, the careful placing in the TV company which it had been set up for, the help and the money that had been paid, the subterfuge, the risk, the treachery, the retribution if it all went wrong... well, it was terrifying. It had all started so innocently, too: she had met this good-looking South American guy, Sander, at a party in London, liked him and met with him again a few days later. At the time, she had just written her application for the job as Jonathan's PA at Tellurian TV but knew she was short on experience; Sander had asked to see it and suggested some changes and improvements, most of which – although tailored to her particular situation – were untrue but which he said he could easily substantiate and vouch for with a little bit of creativity. Flattered but keen for some help which might get her in there – and even more grateful when he said he actually knew the owners of the company – she went along with it; they had a brief affair when she got the job, then he suddenly had to return home to South America, but he didn't say where... It was all so mysterious... then she had started getting the instructions – and occasional £5,000 payments into her bank account; a few weeks later, she was told to ingratiate herself with the scriptwriter... and that's where it had all started. Then she was on cloud nine when it all went so unexpectedly well with Alun and the little nudges and tweaks from Sander regarding the plots were always so amply financially rewarded that she suddenly started to wonder what it was all about. And when Alun had realised the only reason he could marry Leini was by divorcing Dilys, it was far too far down the line to do anything about it and her happiness occluded everything. Then she had met the real script doppelgangers for Zaccheus and Abel – Nobby Bowles and Sid Prentice. That's when she had started to realise that all was not well and that their demands were almost certainly being pushed by the very man who had got her into the TV company – Sander. It had only been a few days before this that she had discovered Sander was the factotum for a much more influential person: a Colombian drug baron. This had slipped out on their last evening together after a surfeit of drinks and sex. What had surprised Leini further was the fact that this shady drug baron was a major shareholder in Tellurian TV. She had been compromised – in more ways than one…

Yet she still had no idea that this boss she imagined to be Colombian was, in fact, a bent and nominally dead Welsh ex-council leader.

*

Alun was beside himself with tears and worry when his mobile rang a few moments later but joyful it was at last Leini – who was also crying and peppering every few sentences with 'Sorry' and declarations of love, but she was in a terribly awkward position. Hearing her contrition and a vague, not over-explicit reason for her sudden departure lest her phone was being monitored, she told him she would be home soon and would explain everything and then they could get on with their lives together – and bluntly rang off.

Alun collapsed onto the sofa in their sitting-room, which seemed so empty since she had disappeared. But at least she seemed safe; and her proclamations of love and fidelity were obviously real: she had just put herself into an awkward position which she had to get out of. Yet the more he thought about the little she had divulged, the more he saw connections and subtleties that had been fed to him to put into the scripts. But what on earth did it all mean? It would not be long before he found out.

*

Leini put the phone down and looked at the flight bag by her feet, then turned around to see that the previously crowded hall was empty and that the gate was not staffed by air crew any more. With a sudden horror, she realised she had missed her flight: her lachrymose disposition, tortured soul and missing Alun had inured her to all around her – but she was furious that no air crew had come to check if she should have been on the flight: then realised that she was sitting behind a pillar and that they would not have seen her. And suddenly, the panic, the stress, the indecision all became calm. A sense of relief and happiness came over her and she vowed to get back to Alun that night if it were possible. And also that, from now, all would be different: it wouldn't be a Colombian drug dealer calling the shots but she and Alun. Furthermore, it would, definitely, still be all in the script – but engineered from a different angle and with a very different outcome.

CHAPTER 29

Thirteen hours later, the flight landed and a black limousine pulled up outside the terminal building, jostling with the yellow taxis whose drivers hooted him because he was in the wrong place – but he didn't care: he was a king around these parts and money blared louder here than taxi horns. The drivers could tell he was wealthy and influential as soon as he got out of his car, his svelte good looks, immaculate dress and chains of gold jangling on his hirsute chest a clear statement of power and seniority. Having a driver spoke volumes, too, who waited patiently as Sander entered the terminal. Looking at the flight boards, he noted that the connecting flight from Atlanta had landed and went to the arrivals area. He hadn't seen Leini for over a year and he wondered what she'd look like now; well, he wouldn't have long to wait…

*

Having missed her flight – inadvertently but thankfully – Leini had walked to the bookings desk and enquired about the next flight back to London. Being quite late at night, there wasn't one until six in the morning but she booked it. Then she went for a meal and another stiff drink: she knew her decision would cause turbulence. But she had to get out of what she had unwittingly got herself into and shuddered again when she thought how she had sold herself to that handsome Latino, Sander. Well, she could get over that – she was still young. But there would be recriminations, she was sure.

The flight passed without incident and soon a very tired and distressed Leini landed at Heathrow. She passed through customs and out to the taxi area, where she joined a short queue and was soon travelling back to west London. She decided to put her phone on and call Alun but the moment it connected to the network it rang. She saw instantly it must be Sander as he always called incognito and all her other friends and contacts were openly displayed: the question was, should she answer it? She decided it would be better to do so – no need to anger him further – and she tapped 'answer'. A smooth, sexy Latino voice said slightly huffily: "Leini – where are you?"

"In Dublin," she lied. "I missed my connecting flight. Sorry."

"You could have told me. I've arranged a party and a meeting with the boss."

"I was in the air – only just landed."

There was a pause. "So you're not here in Bogotà."

"No."

An unseasonal chill seemed to come down the line from South America, and she shivered. *Here we go*, she thought. Sander continued. "In fact, my phone tells me you're in London, not Dublin. What's going on?"

"Oh!", she cried: "Yes, London. I'm tired and I was thinking I was still in Dublin – silly me."

An extended pause. Then: "Yes – silly you." And the phone went dead.

Half an hour later she was back in Alun's arms, sobbing and kissing him contritely and explaining all that had happened and her part in the subterfuge, only interrupted by wild sex as she tried to ingratiate herself with him and prove her despair at what she had been doing.

An hour after the final orgasm had lifted their spirits and exhausted their bodies, Alun and Leini sat in their sitting-room overlooking the garden, draped in dressing-gowns and each holding a glass of wine, looking both released and concerned. The one question that Alun kept wishing to ask was: *If you spent so much time setting all this up, influencing and controlling me, but then were about to leave me to go back into the arms of a Latino lover and put us all in a very dangerous situation, then why did you decide to come back?*

"Because I love you," she said simply, when he eventually had the courage to ask it – and which disarmed him completely. Then she added: "But I wasn't going back into the arms of a Latino lover: that part of things finished a year or so ago. It was flattering and fun, that's all. And it got me the job in television I'd always wanted. But if I'd truly known what I was doing, I'd never have done it. But then I'd never have met you." Still the gremlins gnawed at Alun's stomach; she could have had a life of drug-induced luxury in hot climes and never wanted for anything but had now – apparently – chosen instead to possibly live forever with a slightly overweight widowed writer who had been hijacked by a bunch of bent Welsh honchos who had turned out to be assassins – and she and he were probably next on the hit list.

He looked at his crusty bare feet, then the beautifully-pedicured ones of the girl he had fallen for, and decided to believe her: he supposed, at that moment, that he really must love her deeply, for the danger they were now in was palpable. He sat up, looked at her, and said resolutely, "OK; from now on, though, we do things my way. We'll continue on as if nothing has happened but – as you say – the direction of the scripts is going to change. If the series really is a discreet and very clever parallel for informing the rest of their empire what's going on in the gilded hills of uptown Bogotà, then we'll have to be on our toes."

She nodded. "And ensure our scripts mis- and dis-inform them so we can bring them to justice." Alun nodded. Then she added: "And get back the farm that's rightfully yours. It may not be sunny, but it's a lot safer than Bogotà."

"As long as we actually survive," said Alun. They laughed nervously. Suddenly life was very exciting. If dangerous…

*

Sander had arrived back at the mansion and sought out Norris. "Where's the girl?" he enquired when he saw his fixer. "Betrayed us," he replied. "Got to Dublin then went back to London – to her pansy writer." Norris looked angry. "You're losing your touch, Sander; I thought you said you had her wrapped round your little finger – or was that now just your deflated little willy?" Sander disregarded the insult and stated: "Well, I *did* have her wrapped around my finger: we got the TV company under our control and the firm knows what's going on thanks to compromising the writer; both farms in Wales are now completely yours for the taking and will soon be helping your global cocaine connections to expand along even more undetectable routes. I'd say my deflated little willy has done quite well." Norris glowered at him. Sander turned away in annoyance and then spun back to add the *mot d'escalier*: "So if my little willy *was* any bigger, you might just be king of the world by now." He turned away again, only to be stopped by Norris' next question: "Is Tellurian TV still safe?"

Sander shrugged: "Why not? Their CEO, Gloria, is onside… Our cartel money will soon be funding another international soap from Spain, too, so we'll soon need to talk about starting a TV programme based there, of course; but it'll be easier to sell our stuff there when we do because of the language."

"You mean, sell more of the lucrative stuff?"

"The narcotics, yes. But for the rest of the world and North America, we'll still be able to get into those places easily as our products won't appear to come from here but Spain, Wales or London… the world's financial centre."

"You're right. But I don't trust the girl any more. And with my wife Dilys now dead, she might tell the writer – what's his name?"

"Alun Loyd."

"Yes – well, leave the writer out of it and just make sure he continues delivering the goods – propaganda-wise. But rub the girl out – she knows too much and might tell that Alun Loyd everything."

Sander hesitated. "But she's the reason this has all worked so well," he protested.

But Norris was unrepentant: "Just get Sid and Nobby on the case and do it," he responded tersely, and walked off. Sander was deeply upset. He really liked Leini and still thought he could bring her round. But his ego was hurt: she didn't really like that silly writer more than him, did she?

Well, if she did, then Norris was right. She had to go. Unless, of course, he rubbed out Alun instead. Then she'd have a sudden, terminal reason not to stay with Alun and would come back to him. Perhaps she could set up the TV station in Spain for him. As sunny as Colombia but a lot safer: she might just buy into that...

CHAPTER 30

As Leini had, indeed, told Alun everything, they were both very aware of reprisals. But changing the direction of the scripts was going to be difficult, especially without raising Jonathan's suspicions: Leini said that he knew nothing about what information the scripts had but neither of them could honestly be sure. And now that Leini was wondering whether Gloria was in on the subterfuge as well added another unknown. Yet what griped Alun most was that he thought it had been he who had cleverly instigated the idea of the parallel story with regard to getting rid of his wife Dilys as analogous to the Mrs Wiggins character: but he reluctantly and slightly angrily conceded that Leini must have infiltrated his conscience with regard to storylines far earlier than he had imagined – and with a wicked intent. But now she had come clean on all this, it was important to trust her. And keep playing Jonathan – and Gloria – as if they did not actually know anything. It was also a good double bluff if things got sticky...

Then the unanswered question returned: who was the character analogous to Edmund, who he had just implied in his script had been killed by the programme's Abel and Zaccheus? It took him a few moments to work it out; then, with a chill – and concern at how he had been compromised by Leini – realised conclusively who he had feared it was: him.

*

Sander sent the text and waited for a reply. It read: *I'm coming over. Much needs sorting out.* Then he went to one of the clubs they owned in Bogotá and availed himself of one of the choicest young ladies who had been recently trafficked from the mountains. The distraction would clear his mind. He wondered whether he would get a reply, but kept his phone beside the bed in case...

Leini looked at it and decided not to do so: she suspected Sander would be in touch with the remit of 'sorting her out' so she would know when he arrived, whatever. But she was ready for him: she would seduce him and get him drunk, then ply him with some of his drugs he always had with him and get some shady character to rub him out instead. Perhaps even Sid and Nobby, if she could swing it. Because, without telling Alun, she was fairly certain that this would be the instruction from Norris. She was now a danger to the project. What Sander did not know, though, was that she had second-guessed him and knew how to respond… She would more urgently have to start influencing Alun with the storylines of the script again, and started to think…

Having made some notes, she then thought she had it; originally, Abel and Zaccheus were going to be beaten to a pulp by Edmund – her idea, which Alun had already written. But now the storylines had to convey what she and Alun wanted them to *believe* – not confirm what Norris Griifiths *wanted*: so they had to change tack and spin *their* version of what would become the truth. So now the changes could start. She decided that this was the moment the tables would be turned and went to her computer to start re-writing the relevant part of the script; Alun would blend it in with the rest of his episode, but the message was there for all who could read it. They would not like it in Colombia, of course: but now it was time to confuse, mislead and suggest. And, to be honest, to play dirty.

She started to change it: it ended up like this:

JONQUIL'S JOURNALS:

EPISODE 154. OPENING TITLES AND MUSIC. SCENE 1. WIGGINS' PARLOUR. NIGHT.

> WE MIX TO EDMUND AS HE DRAGS IN THE SLUMPED BODIES OF ABEL AND ZACCHEUS FROM THE BOTTOM OF THE AREA STEPS AND CLOSES THE DOOR, LOCKING IT. HE HAS SOME BLOOD ON HIM, AND

THE OTHER TWO LOOK QUITE DEAD.

EDMUND: So you thought that you'd get me the second time, did you? (HE KICKS EACH OF THE FIGURES). Well, I got to you first! (HE STARTS DRAGGING ONE OF THE BODIES TO THE PANTRY, THEN THE OTHER. AS HE DOES SO:) Who told you to kill me, then, eh? Was it his lordship? Or his little lady, Jenny, on his behalf? After all, I know who provided her to him, don't I? That knave Sander! So... *was* it Sander, on his say-so? Hmm. (TO THE CORPSES). And *I* think it was you two who killed Jonas Orchard... Makes sense ...

(HE JUST GETS THE PANTRY DOOR CLOSED WHEN HE HEARS LIGHT FOOTSTEPS ON THE STONE STAIRS AND JENNY IS THERE.)

JENNY: Edmund – you're here!

EDMUND: (SUBSERVIENT). Ah. Milady... How can I serve you, pray?

JENNY: His lordship's asleep...

EDMUND: Then step into my parlour, Milady...

JENNY: You don't need to call me that, Edmund...

EDMUND: So what should I call you, Milady?

JENNY: Your true love and future mistress...

EDMUND: But – I mean... you're betrothed to the master Jonquil, as far as I can see...

JENNY: Oh, you don't understand! I loved you the moment I saw you in the tavern... and then Sander got me in here and I saw an opportunity for both of us... For even if I have to marry that relic upstairs we can be together and when he dies... you can wed me and you'll be the lordship because by then I'll be the lady of the house!

EDMUND: Oh, dear Jenny! I had no idea... but... yes! (THEY EMBRACE.)

JENNY: What if someone comes in?

EDMUND: Apart from his lordship, there's no-one else in the house. And the door's locked...

JENNY: Oh, Edmund!

EDMUND: Oh, Jenny! (THEY KISS).

JENNY: You like me more than that strumpet Dulce, don't you?

EDMUND: Of course, my poppet...

JENNY: I think Sander has been told to get rid of you.

EDMUND: By whom?

JENNY: My intended old fossil upstairs. 'Cos I think he suspects I like you more than him.

EDMUND: Hmm, I wondered...

JENNY: Why?

EDMUND: The evidence is in the pantry... Two of them... They assaulted me on the steps outside but fell down the steps and knocked themselves out. I think they're dead but I was going to skewer them in the pantry so's nobody saw me...

JENNY: You mean...? (HE NODS). Who are they?

EDMUND: Sander's fixers, I think. I've heard them in the tavern, talking about him.

JENNY:	Abel and Zaccheus?
EDMUND:	If that's their names… (SHE GOES TO THE PANTRY AND LOOKS.)
JENNY:	Yes! Oh, my lordship must not find out – not for a while, if ever…
EDMUND:	Of course not. But then you must marry him soon or you won't inherit the house and his title…
JENNY:	… and then *we* won't get anything!
EDMUND:	And if Sander is the one organising the deed…
JENNY:	Then we have to stop his claret, too?
EDMUND:	It looks like it…
JENNY:	I think I know how to do it…
EDMUND:	How?
JENNY:	Go to the tavern and tell him I'd like to see him, when Jonquil is at the assizes… upstairs in my bedchamber then –
EDMUND:	I don't *want* you to see him in the bedchamber!
JENNY:	Don't worry, dear Edmund – I'll only *suggest* I want to bed him… he likes a glass of claret… I'll put some laudanum in it, he falls asleep and then, you… you know…
EDMUND:	Ah, I see…
JENNY:	Shall we go to your room for a nightcap…?
EDMUND:	Well, yes… but… what about <u>them</u>?
	SHE GOES TO THE PANTRY DOOR AND OPENS IT, LOOKS AT THE BODIES AND THEN CLOSES THE

DOOR AGAIN.

JENNY: They're dead. Clear them away later, after....!

EDMUND: Whatever the lady of the house wishes, ma'm! THEY QUIETLY LEAVE UP THE STAIRS.

CUT TO:

JONQUIL'S JOURNALS:

EPISODE 154. SCENE 2. WIGGINS' PANTRY. INT. NIGHT.

THE TWO BODIES ARE SLUMPED ON THE FLOOR. WE ZOOM IN ON ZAC'S FACE. SUDDENLY, HIS EYES SHOOT OPEN...

*

Leini stopped writing and smiled to herself; this episode wouldn't be transmitted for another month or so, by which time what would be would be... She started to sketch out how Zac and Abel would both come to and also decide that escape was the better course than retribution – and the shame at having muffed their murder of Edmund would force them to disappear for a while; their actual demise could be scripted later – both in the script and in reality. She and Alun needed more time, so that their murder must not yet be flagged. But it eventually would be when the time was right... After all, she knew that Sander – the real one rather than the character in *Jonquil's Journals* – would soon be arriving to do some pressurising at best and an assassination at worst. Whether that was of her or Alun – or both – was an open question. But at least, if it *did* potentially all go wrong for her and Alun, the writing would be on the wall.

But also in the script.

*

Two days later, Sander walked into the TV studios in London and announced himself as arriving for an appointment with Gloria Cordobes, the company's CEO, and was shown straight up. Leini had anticipated the visit and been alerted by the CEO's assistant, Iris, having asked her to be notified of any visits from him – being, as he was, a representative of a major shareholder in the company with a particular interest in *Jonquil's Journals*. Well, that was her official excuse: what Iris probably didn't know – and, just possibly, even Gloria Cordobes herself – was the financial connection and importance to the programme of this man. Yet Leini had to see Sander on her terms, not his: he would text her soon, she knew, and suggest a meeting. What must happen, though, was that Sander had to be compromised (for want of a better word) and that he was not around by the time the recently-written episode was recorded towards the end of the next week. That would give their whole game away.

So it was essential that Sander would never return to Colombia – just as it would soon be in the script: except that the small tavern in the programme was the substitute for the much larger country of Colombia. She shrugged: poetic licence…

*

JONQUIL'S JOURNALS:

EPISODE 154 SCENE 49. JONQUIL'S BEDCHAMBER. DAY.

	JENNY IS LOOSELY ATTIRED, FURTIVELY WAITING FOR SOMEONE. THEN SHE HEARS VOICES ON THE STAIRS AND THERE IS A KNOCK ON THE DOOR.
EDMUND:	(OUTSIDE). A Mister Sander Montoya to see, you, milady…
JENNY:	Ah, send him in. (THE DOOR OPENS AND EDMUND SHOWS SANDER THE TAVERN-KEEPER IN, WHO HAS CLEANED HIMSELF UP SOMEWHAT. HE BOWS TO HER). That'll do, thank you,

Edmund…

EDMUND EXITS AS SANDER COMES FORWARD TO KISS HER HAND.

SANDER:	Milady Jenny – how splendid to see you…
JENNY:	(NERVOUS). And you, good sir.
SANDER:	Where is his lordship, Bartholomew Jonquil, esquire?
JENNY:	At the Assizes, good sir.
SANDER:	Then we have some time together…?
JENNY:	(CHEEKILY). Indeed, sir… (AND SHE LOOSENS HER BLOUSE A LITTLE). We have *much* time to discuss things together!
SANDER:	Just like old times at the tavern, then?
JENNY:	Yes! But I'm a lady now… going to marry his lordship, don't you know…?
SANDER:	I heard. But in the meantime… you and I used to have some good *bomba de rumpy* together, didn't we? Do you wish for a little more?
JENNY:	Oh, Sander, it was always so good with you… Why did you not make me an honest woman then?
SANDER:	I had all my other ladies to keep happy…! But I introduced you to his Lordship… Now look where you are…
JENNY:	Indeed, kind Sander; and it's all thanks to you. So would you like a little reminder of what we did together? (AND SHE LIFTS HER SKIRT).
ANDER:	You were always my favourite, Jenny…
JENNY:	You said that to all the girls!
SANDER:	But it is true…

JENNY:	You said that, too! (HE GOES CLOSER AND THEY EMBRACE). Would you like a little glass of claret to get us both in the mood?
SANDER:	Whyever not, Miss Jenny. Not that I need it with you…
JENNY:	Ooh, sir – you say the nicest things… (SHE GOES TO A SIDEBOARD AND POURS A LARGE GLASS OF CLARET, WHICH SHE GIVES TO HIM).
SANDER:	Not you, too, my pretty missy?
JENNY:	Oh, no, sir – I never drink at work!
	(SHE GIGGLES, AS DOES HE. HE DOWNS THE DRINK IN ONE AND GOES TOWARDS HER…
	WE CUT OUTSIDE TO SEE EDMUND LISTENING AT THE DOOR, FINGERING A CUDGEL).

CHAPTER 31

It was mid-afternoon. Alun had agreed and fleshed out Leini's plan: now they were about to put it into practice...

He was hiding in the ballroom above the garage when the taxi arrived, crunching over the gravel. Leini danced out of the front door to meet its occupant, who stood admiring the yellow Porsche but wondered why such a beautiful car was parked outside the garage rather than in it. Then all was dismissed as Leini pecked his cheek flirtatiously and took him into the flat as the taxi departed.

Inside, she seemed nervous but pleased to see her guest. "It's been a long time..." as she eyed him mischievously.

"Indeed it has. But you didn't come to see me, so it's your fault..."

"Well, things have changed... I'm about to be married to Alun."

"So I heard. But we used to have some good times together, no?"

"Yes – we did. So why did you not make me an honest woman, then?"

"I had too many other things to do, to keep in order... on track. But you were always my favourite."

"I heard you say that to all the girls."

"But with you, Leini, I meant it."

"You used to say that to all Norris's girls, too." There was a pause, then: "But if you'd like a taste of old times, then I have a nice bottle of fizz in the fridge..."

"What about Alun?"

"Oh, he'll be at the office for ages. There's been a problem with a location, so he's thrashing out a new storyline with Jonathan."

"One that still follows the lines of our agreement, I hope?"

"Of course…" She gave him a concupiscent look, went to the fridge in the kitchen and pulled out the champagne cork, which gave a loud 'plop' as it did so; the contents coursed out as she entered the room, just as she had hoped. "Oh, dear," she said, "I'll just go back and wipe this up. Back in a mo." And she went to the kitchen again. Once there, she picked up another identical bottle which had been opened not a half-hour before and came back into the room with it, and poured a glass for her guest…

*

JONQUIL'S JOURNALS:
EPISODE 154. SCENE 51. JONQUIL'S BEDCHAMBER A/B.

SANDER AND JENNY ARE GETTING INTO A COMPROMISING POSITION WHEN HE SUDDENLY STARTS TO FALL ACROSS HER, AS HE FIGHTS OFF FALLING ASLEEP.

SANDER: Oh, I feel so tired, suddenly…

JENNY: Ooh, you naughty boy… Overdoing it with Dulce and the other girls last night, I shouldn't wonder…

SANDER: No, that's not true, I… I… (AND FALLS ASLEEP ACROSS HER. JENNY'S PLAYFUL DISPOSITION HARDENS). Edmund?!

EDMUND BOUNDS INTO THE ROOM AND PULLS SANDER OFF HIS LADY, WHO QUICKLY PUTS HER DRESS BACK TO NORMAL. THEN SHE WRAPS SANDER IN A COARSE CLOTH WHICH SHE FOLDS AROUND THE COMATOSE BODY, WITH EDMUND'S HELP. THEN THEY PULL THE BODY OFF THE BED, THERE BEING A LARGE BUMP AS THE HEAD HITS THE

FLOOR.

JENNY: Where shall we do it?

EDMUND: In the kitchen: if there's any blood then I can say it's from a fresh haunch of venison I've been skinning…

THEY PULL THE BODY OUT OF THE BEDCHAMBER AS WE HEAR IT BANGING DOWN THE STAIRS, MAKING A LOUD BUMP EVERY TIME THE HEAD HITS THE NEXT STEP.

*

By now it was 2 a.m. in the morning and very dark: Leini and Alun pulled the drugged body – wrapped in a body-bag acquired through the good offices of the TV company props department – through the underground passageway to the garage in which the unmarked van stood waiting. Alun opened the rear doors and they lifted the body inside the vehicle, closing and locking them as quietly as possible so as not to wake the neighbours. Then Alun got into the driving seat as Leini opened the garage doors and moved the Porsche out of the way. Alun reversed out, whispered "See you in Wales – be careful," as he passed her and disappeared into the sodium-lit sleeping suburb and then on to the deeper night of the M4 motorway…

Leini drove the Porsche into the garage, quietly closed the doors from the inside and went back to the living room to clear up any evidence of Sander's presence. Especially the empty box of sleeping pills….

There had to be no clues at all as she knew that Nobby and Sid would eventually turn up: in fact, she purposely stayed behind for a few hours in case they did, when she would say Sander had never arrived and were welcome to search the place. Even the so-called taxi driver who had picked Sander up from his London hotel was a friend with a beautiful black limo whose silence had been bought by a large sum of money. Likewise, a television extra with a striking similarity to Sander had been given the man's hotel key and would check out early in a few hours' time, never to be seen again. Leini would leave for Wales at the crack of dawn: there was more essential cleaning-up work to be done before this could all be concluded...

At about that same time, Nobby and Sid's car passed Alun's van on the M4 – each going in opposite directions.

*

Four hours later, Alun arrived at his Dilys-less house in Wales, having hidden the van in a copse some half a mile away in order to check that the house was not occupied by Nobby and Sid – or, indeed, anyone else.

The house was dark and he quietly let himself in by the side door, locking it carefully and quietly checking every room, the squeaky stairs possibly betraying his presence had anyone actually been there. He even went into the loft, to find that the legal papers had been retrieved from Grubb's farm and had been packed into a large box ready for transit to Colombia, where they could be doctored – and names and dates changed to fit into the accoutrements of Norris' expanding drugs empire.

Finding the coast clear, he went back to fetch the van and hid it behind the barn, where it was unlikely anyone would go. Hearing movement from Sander as he got out, he injected a large dose of heroin into the man and re-checked that he was still well-bound but that his nose and mouth were unobstructed. It was all part of the plan... Then he went back into the house and closed the bedroom curtains so no light would be seen as he undressed and got into his old bed for a few hours' kip before Leini arrived.

*

The TV 'extra' playing Sander paid the hotel bill in cash and walked out into oblivion, about an hour before Nobby and Sid arrived for their supposed instructions. Finding neither these nor the man in question, they became panicky and interrogated the young receptionist who had taken the money when checking Sander out. At which point, they were asked to pay for a very large mini-bar bill which the man had omitted to mention. (In fact, that very same man was now sitting in his flat in a very drunken stupor).

Having reluctantly paid the drinks bill, the two men stood on the pavement outside the hotel and debated what to do next. "Let's go and see Leini and Alun for breakfast," Nobby opined to which Sid agreed, then added, "Something's fishy going on." "Good – I like kippers," said Sid. Nobby knew not to explain what he really meant and they went back to the car park and drove out, having received no answer from Sander's mobile, which had gone immediately to voicemail.

By the time they arrived at Alun and Leini's flat, the latter had already left. So, finding a key she had purposely left slightly uncovered under a stone by the front door (to hopefully avoid any breaking in), they entered the flat and looked around. Leini had also carefully left a note or two on the fridge to give the impression that they were away for a few days together, like 'Take the cat to the cattery' and 'Pack anorak for Wales'.

"D'you think they've gone to Wales?" asked Sid as he read it.

"Bloody hell – looks like it. The cheek of it – it's our bleedin' 'ouse now and she knows that." He pondered for a moment, then, "I didn't know they 'ad a cat, neither."

"No – nor me. D'you think they're up to something?"

"Looks like it… Let's get back to Wales pronto. Sander's not answering 'is phone, neither, is 'e?"

"Nah – tried again a few minutes ago."

"Let's ring Leini. She'll know what's going on."

She did. In fact, Leini was hiding in the ballroom above the garage, monitoring Sander's phone, which she had put on silent. On her own phone next to Sander's, she was also monitoring the conversation over their intruder system camera; they were right – she and Alun *didn't* have a cat.

When her phone vibrated, she knew it was Sid: not only did his name come up on the screen as a known alias but she was watching them. She did not answer it. But neither did they leave a message.

185

Realising they were in the wrong place and behind the curve, Nobby and Sid left in somewhat of a hurry; as soon as Leini observed this, she rang Alun to tell him that the plan was working and the two fixers were on their way to Wales… Then she went back into the flat, removed the stickers from the fridge, hoovered the men's dirty footprints and locked up. Then she got into her Porsche and left for Wales, with almost as much haste as the two who had recently preceded her.

Alun had been woken by Leini's call but knew he had a few hours to spare before Nobby and Sid arrived, so he showered, dressed and found some old cereal bars which he consumed for his breakfast and then went out to the van. Finding Sander moving more than he would like, he injected him with another dose of drugs – this time including an additional shot of a sedative which would make it appear that Sander was so still as to appear dead. Then he drove the van to the front door, pulled the bagged body into the house and heaved it onto the kitchen table - together with the same large cudgel used by the actor playing Edmund in *Jonquil's Journals*. Then he locked the side door again as he left and drove to a layby a mile away where he knew there was a rare good mobile signal, and waited…

Leini was aware that the men's plans had been disrupted and suspected that – both being big men who had had an early start – would need to have breakfast. To ensure this, she pulled into a quiet cul-de-sac and rang Sid on his mobile.

"'Ello, doll," the dulcet tones of Sid answered: "Where are you? I tried ringin'…"

"Yes, I saw your number. I must have been on the Tube when you rang. What is it?"

"Sander's disappeared. And where's your bloke?"

"He went into work early – it's a filming day."

"Where 'is 'e, then?"

"No idea. The location was changed at the last moment – but I'd imagine he's somewhere in Hertfordshire. Why d'you want to know?"

"No reason."

"Oh. So what do you want? Where are you?"

"On the way back to Wales. Did you see Sander?"

"No."

"I thought he was going to pay you a visit."

"Well, he didn't. I heard he was staying at a hotel in London but we try not to see each other now in case things get difficult. After all, Alun mustn't know our 'connection'..."

"Oh.... yeah."

There was a silence. Then Leini said: "So you're going back to Wales... Whereabouts are you?"

"On the M4 near Newport Pagnell."

"Having breakfast?"

"That's a good idea. Yeah, we need somefing to eat. The service area's coming up."

"So why not stop for a bite if you're hungry? No-one's going to know when you left for Wales or what time you'd arrive. And I won't say anything. Go on – you need to eat."

"Yeah. 'Ere, Nobby – pull into the services and we'll 'ave some breakfast. Leini says we can. Just there – go on..." Nobby did so.

"We'll talk in due course," Leini confirmed, without the boys realising where that would be, and they each rang off.

Twenty-five minutes later she raced past the services and on into Wales, just as a huge megabreakfast was being put in front of each of Norris's henchmen...

CHAPTER 32

After half an hour, Leini used her hands-free mobile to call Sid again, who had only just finished his breakfast.

"Sid, there's been a development," she said breathlessly, "and now I'm on my way to Wales, too — just got onto the motorway. God, I had to lie through my teeth to get away from work, but no matter."

"Why — what's up?"

"I've heard from Sander."

"He hasn't rung us."

"No. That's because he was having trouble with his phone. He got me on my office one. And I've found that Alun's not on location as I thought but in Wales — and Sander thinks he's discovered what's going on, which could be terminal for all of us, so he's instructed us to dispose of him as fast as possible. Sander's in a car behind me because he wants me to distract Alun while he disables him and trusses him up to make it easy for you to finish him off — your job. Where are you now?"

"Still at Newport Pagnell services. But we're leaving."

"OK. I'm ahead of you now, so I'll surprise Alun and say I found out he wasn't at work and thought he might be cheating on me — and the only likely place he could do that is in Wales, under the pretence of clearing up a few more of Dilys's things."

There was a silence, and she could tell that he was not convinced. "But he finished doing all that already," he said after a slight pause.

"So I thought, too — but that makes it all the more likely he's having an affair, if you think about it. *We've* got nothing to hide but he didn't tell me he was going to Wales so I'm going to confront him."

"OK. We'll be right behind you."

They rang off. Leini smiled. Then she rang Alun and told him that all was still well on track. "Is the body on the table?" she enquired.

"Was when I left. And I don't think he's in any position to go anywhere."

"Good. Well, I'll be there soon and well ahead of the boys so it should look as though I've had enough time to drug him – you – and truss him up. And Sander can help with that."

"Eh?"

"I've told them that Sander's in the car behind me, so I'll theoretically have distracted you while he also theoretically trusses you up. Then the boys will finish you off."

"Charming. I hope you don't really mean that…"

"Course not, silly; I love you too much for that."

"I hope so. But won't they expect to see Sander there?"

"I'll tell them that he had to leave quickly after helping me as he had to urgently catch a flight back to Colombia."

"OK. I'd better get back to the farmhouse again, then; I don't think anyone's been or gone. I'll hide in the priest-hole again."

The next few hours would be very interesting. And eventful, she felt.

Yet they would not turn out quite as she and Alun had expected…

*

There was no sign of Alun's van when she arrived at the farmhouse and she ostentatiously parked the Porsche at the front to ensure the boys knew she was there, its bright yellow paint contrasting against the grey stones of the building like a bright sun in the dark void of space.

She unlocked the door and saw the body-bag containing Sander on the table as Alun had attested, with the cudgel next to it. It seemed motionless, bar a slight breathing motion. Then she quietly went to the priest-hole and lifted the lid to reveal a terrified Alun until she smiled, put a finger to her lips and quietly closed it again.

She returned to the kitchen and, noticing slightly more movement of the body, opened her bag and took out a syringe, into which she loaded some more strong sedative; she then unzipped the bag enough to reveal an arm and plunged the needle in, emptying its contents. She reflected how her youthful training as a nurse would always come in handy as she did so – then wondered if Alun had already done the same. Damn, well, too late: he might already be dead before the boys got here – but no matter: he would be dead soon enough anyway by the time those two finished with him. She was about to go and ask Alun when she heard the sound of a car coming up the drive: surprised at how well the boys had done to get there she quickly but went out to greet them – only to find that it was not them at all…

In the priest-hole, Alun heard the car too and stiffened: this was it. He was going to aid and abet the murder of a murderer, then, perhaps, actually murder two more himself. A chill went through him but he knew it was the only way to get Leini, his farmhouse, Nathan's farm, a lot of money… and hopefully bring Norris Griffiths to justice, so destroying his criminal empire for good. Then he heard a female voice – but it wasn't Leini's. What was happening?

CHAPTER 33

In London, Jonathan was reading the plotlines for some future programmes which Alun and Leini had submitted and was surprised to see that they were going off in a somewhat different direction to the ones they had discussed. Slightly baffled, he went to find his own notes: no, they had *not* talked about Sander the tavern-keeper being knocked off – or the hinted demise of Edmund at the behest of Jonquil, who was now colluding with Jenny... or the blossoming relationship between Jenny and Edmund. Or, he was astonished to see, Abel and Zaccheus being murdered by Edmund. At this rate, they'd need a completely new cast – and very soon, too!

He reached for his phone: he must call Alun immediately. And why had he not seen Leini for two days? He knew they would both deliver... but they had never been so out of touch before. He dialled a number...

*

Leini was somewhat surprised to see a rather portly, overweight and grey lady with wispy hair get out of Dilys's car – who looked just as surprised as Leini at their mutually unexpected meeting.

"Hello - who are you?" asked Leini, suspiciously.

"I'm Dilys," the lady replied, in much the same tone. "And I live here," she added. Can I help you?"

Inside, Leini was panicking: Dilys was dead! She had never met her but she certainly resembled the photograph Alun had shown her once. "And who are *you*?" the woman blurted at Leini. "Alun's floozy, I'll be bound." Then, seeing the Porsche, she exclaimed, "And that's my Nathan's car! I thought he'd crashed it or something. Why have *you* got it?"

Leini was flummoxed: how did this stranger know everything about them and who she was when she thought the real Dilys was now dead? Added to that, she could not allow this woman into what she would profess was 'her' kitchen as Sander's body was on the table there!

Alun – having been terrified when Leini had unexpectedly exposed him in the priest-hole – had crawled along the passageway and was now under the front door – before it turned right beneath the kitchen – and had heard the lady say, "I'm Dilys." He also heard her talk about Nathan's car – his Leini's Porsche! – and panicked: Dilys still alive? Just like Norris Griffiths? What had they got themselves into here? And yet... and yet... The voice was not that of Dilys – it was lighter, less bronchial, less lilting...

"Well, if you're Alun's floozy, you *definitely* have no right to be here," the woman was saying. "This is my house, my land, so get off it, you harridan!" Hearing this, Alun realised he had to get out of the priest-hole and accost this lady for the impostor she must be: yet he was concerned that the boys would soon be here and then things would become very tricky indeed. Dangerous, even. Speed was of the essence – she must be exposed and banished forthwith, before their plans were wrecked forever. He crawled backwards as fast as he could, hitting his head several times and causing a trickle of blood to drip down his face – and tearing his trousers to boot. He quietly opened the priest-hole, climbed out, strode down the hall to the front door and dramatically opened it.

Leini's back was to him and the woman was advancing threateningly towards her, a rolled umbrella being waved as she did so. But she stopped as the front door opened and Leini turned back towards this man with the torn trousers and blood dripping down his forehead. Then she asked the question that Alun was hoping she would: "Who are you?"

*

Jonathan had not got through to Alun; it kept going to voice-mail. So he tried Leini. It rang! In the kitchen, where Leini had left her handbag, it vibrated away and sang its ring-tone; Leini heard it but was too frightened and confused to answer it, even without this alien woman who had been bearing down on her. But seeing Alun at the front door, the woman's advance had stopped, frozen in astonishment.

"What are you doing in my house?" the Dilys thundered at Alun.

"I'm Alun, your husband, you daft woman – and if you don't recognise me, you're an impostor. So what are you doing here in *my* house?"

There was a pause, then she shot back: "But you can't be – you're dead."

The confirmation of that intended outcome caused a wobble in Alun's voice as he retorted, "No – *you* are."

"I was told you had returned to London with your things, then been eliminated, never to return."

"By whom?"

"People."

"Not unusual," Alun said sarcastically. "But *what* people?"

"The people who told me you were dead."

"Well, here I am – the real thing; alive and well."

"Well, you *were* dead," she added for terminal effect.

Leini felt as if she was watching a tennis-match as she turned from one to the other, then discreetly backed off to allow them free abuse of one another. As she did so, she saw the sun glint off a distant windscreen at the end of the drive and realised with horror that the boys had arrived…

Alun saw it too, and dived back into the house, slamming the front door shut. "I can hear my phone ringing," Leini said, and ran into the house through the side door. She got to the phone but found that it had somehow become wedged under Sander's corpse; she managed to free it and found herself talking to Jonathan, who started asking searching questions about the script plotlines.

"I can't talk now," she shouted at him: "In a tricky spot. Will call you later. Sorry. Thanks. Bye."

She ran outside again just as Sid and Nobby drew up and got out of their car.

"Hello, Mildred," Sid said airily. "I see you've met Leini…"

The two women darted hostile looks at one another.

"Yes," said Leini, and proffered a hand to shake. But Mildred was having none of it. "You're Alun's floozy," she said.

At this, Sid and Nobby started laughing. "Don't worry," said Nobby, "she's wiv us. She's on our side. Good to see you did yer 'omework properly, though!"

"What about the other one, then?" the woman demanded, as Leini's heart sank. Now they were in trouble. Sid and Nobby stiffened. "What other one?" asked Nobby.

"The one inside. Alun – who you told me was dead."

"Inside?" said Sid.

"Yes, he was standing in the front doorway just before you arrived."

The men's gazes turned to Leini, and not without a smidgeon of hostility.

"Well, *we* told Mildred 'ere 'e was dead to avoid complications: but *you* said 'e was filming in 'ertfordshire. By you, Leini. So is 'e 'ere, then?"

"I found him here – having an affair as I told you I suspected when I rang you."

"So you mean there's a *real* floozy 'ere as well, then, Mildred?" Mildred neither nodded nor shook her head but gave the impression that there might be as she had hated Leini on sight.

Sid and Nobby looked at each other, then whispered and finally nodded.

"Mildred… I think fings might get a bit difficult 'ere now, so, er, probably best if you go 'ome and don't say nuffing. We'll tell the boss you played your part admirably pretending to be Dilys and I'm sure 'e'll slip you few more spondoolies in recognition of that. But for now, I fink you'd better scarper – and you've seen nuffing, right?"

She nodded, cast Leini a look which could kill, climbed into her car and left. Then the men turned their gaze to Leini…

*

Upon the arrival of the two men, Alun had not gone back to the priest-hole after his rapid disappearance but entered the kitchen and got Dilys's gun from where it still was by the back door, loaded it and then went to the priest-hole and disappeared down it. He could hear muffled conversations between Leini and the boys but it was too indistinct, so he crawled down the passageway again to get closer.

"You can't 'ave done," he eventually heard Nobby say in disbelief. "You've killed Alun?" Hearing no reply, he presumed Leini was nodding animatedly – and he was right – but she had tinged it with a look of acted deep regret.

"So who's the geyser Mildred said she saw at the front door, then?"

"Sander."

"Not Alun?"

"No. I killed him – with Sander's help. Alun's dead on the kitchen table but… I'd be grateful if you could smash him up a bit so he'll never be recognised. It really hurts, you see, and I never want to see his bastard face again," and she started sobbing.

"I fought you was 'avin' an affair wiv Sander?" Sid intoned. "No wonder 'e 'elped you kill Alun." They laughed. But not Leini, who was now in serious acting mode – and enjoying it. She hadn't watched hundreds of episodes of *Jonquil's Journals* without learning a few acting tips…

"Sander and me were a long time ago. But he's heading back to Colombia now. He left immediately after helping me kill Alun – had a flight to take back to Colombia."

"So where's the lover, then?"

"She scarpered when I arrived – ran off. I was so angry, I didn't

195

care. All I wanted to do was kill Alun for promising me so much and then letting me down..." and she started sobbing again.

So where's Alun's body, then?"

"On the kitchen table, as I said. In a body-bag."

"A body-bag?"

She nodded. "I found it here – I think it was meant for me if I found out. Or his lover... no, must have been for me because he *knew* I'd soon find out..."

Sid and Nobby looked at each other, moved to the side door and entered the kitchen where there was, indeed, a body-bag with a corpse in it. Alun heard the heavy footsteps above him and then the sobbing tones of Leini saying, "No, please don't open it – trust me – it's Alun – and I never want to see his face again... Please."

"All right, then..."

There was a pause, and then the sound of a body being beaten to a pulp. Below, Alun felt every blow – as if they *really* were aimed at him. Then a few drops of blood dripped through the flagstones as they had when these same two men had murdered the real Dilys. And all the while, Leini sobbed.

After a few minutes, he heard the body being pulled off the table and it clumped to the floor. Then he heard them lifting him – no, not him, Sander – outside and the body was put in the back of their van. As he heard it drive off, Leini's sobbing curtly stopped and she stamped on the floor above him three times. She knew he was there. He crawled back up the passage and out of the priest-hole to find her there waiting for him and threw her arms around him, kissing him as if it really was him who had been butchered and was glad he'd come back to life without a blemish. Except the one on his forehead.

"Now we must prepare for their return and part two of the plan," she said. He agreed and they went into the kitchen and waited. There was no need to clear up the mess: there would soon be more of it ...

CHAPTER 34

As the sun was setting behind the hills, Sid and Nobby drove the van up to the edge of the copse - where Dilys' and Nathan's bodies were already buried – and dumped the new one. They then drove the van back to the lane and went to get the digger. Nathan's farm now looked deserted and nature had started to take over its previously more-tended appearance – and most of the crops looked in need of attention and water.

"We'd better get someone in to tend this place," Nobby noted, or people will talk." Sid agreed: "The local farmers'll be the first to notice," he concurred. "Better get in a tenant farmer from far outside the area," Nobby suggested; "Somewhere like Colombia."

They laughed, then Sid said, "Good idea. But will the drugs we sell grow in this wet place?"

"They will under polytunnels," he replied. "And blast them with warm air..."

Then they got on with fetching the digger, and the extra body was soon buried alongside the others.

It was quite late when Leini and Alun heard the van returning towards them and realised that they, too, would soon be imitating what these two did for a living – and it was a thought which chilled them to the bone. Again.

*

Jonathan was becoming agitated, annoyed, and not a little angry: where was his PA and his star writer? He knew that Alun went into deep mental hiding when he was obsessed with a script but Leini had never let him down. What was going on? Despite his homosexual perspective, he had pretty much concluded that they were having an affair but had always resisted the idea of believing it because he could see that Leini was truly beautiful but Alun… well, was not really much of a looker at all. Even with a lot of imagination, even he could never find him attractive – which was probably a good thing, actually, or it would have got in the way of the plotlines and the scripts. And yet, he was jealous: not just of one, but both of them, for neither finding *him* attractive. And now this: the plots were going awry, he couldn't understand why they had been changed without his agreement and now he was unable to get in touch with either to censure them.

Yet, if he had realised the parallels and subsequently paid more attention to the scripts, he would have been much more in the know regarding reality...

*

Leini was waiting in the kitchen when Sid and Nobby returned, a bottle of whisky and a used but now empty glass on the table, surrounded by a number of damp, used tissues. The only item missing from before was the cudgel…

"Why haven't you cleaned up?" asked Sid as they entered. "What if someone came in – like the police?" Leini shrugged, dabbing her tearful eyes. "I really loved him," she said, as if that answered everything. Then she looked at them and said brightly: "Where did you put Alun's body?"

"Same place as the uvvers – Nathan's farm."

"Where's that?"

"'Bout ten or fifteen miles away." There was a momentary silence, then he added: "In a copse at the top of a small 'ill… on the left as you go down the drive… if you want to pay your respects…"

"I might want to go there," she said simply. Then: "Where is it?"

"I'll write it down for yer."

"Can you do that for me now – before we forget?"

"Er, yeah. But what's the 'urry? We'd like somefing to eat, if you got anything 'ere."

"Certainly. But please write down the address." Actually, she knew

198

it – it was in the papers they had retrieved – but she had to play dumb on that point…

Nobby looked around. "Got a pen?"

"Over there."

Nobby went to the dresser and picked up a pen and a pad, noticing a box of blue surgical rubber gloves in a half-open drawer.

"What are they for?"

"Cleaning up, I suppose," she said nonchalantly, angry that she had left it open.

"Don't remember seeing vem before…"

"You were a long time getting back," she parried, changing the subject as he wrote down the address.

"It would 'ave been longer wivvout the little digger," Nobby replied. "There," he continued as he finished writing the address. Now could we trouble you for somefing to eat?"

"Oh. Right. Yes. I'll knock something off for you."

"Don't you mean 'up'?"

She paused. "Actually, I don't know what I mean at the moment… so confused, betrayed…"

"You'll get over it," Sid said, with a catch in his voice. "*We* always do." Nobby gave him a patronising look. "Bit late to start getting sentimental," he said curtly.

Leini turned to Sid and said, "Sid, as you probably know, there's a freezer in the barn with lots of meat and veg in it. Go and get what you want, bring it back and I'll cook it for you both. Then I must get back to my empty flat…" and she burst into tears again.

"I'll come wiv you," Nobby said to Sid, but Leini put up a hand and said, "No, don't go, Nobby – I need someone to talk to… Sit down opposite me for a moment…"

"OK." As he sat down, he intimated to Sid to go and get the food.

Nobby's back was now to the door – outside which waited a

trembling Alun, clutching the very same cudgel that the boys had beaten Sander to death with...

"Do you enjoy your work?" Leini enquired in an unnaturally loud voice. Nobby looked at her strangely: why did she say that so positively? But it was Alun's cue and he burst into the room with the cudgel held high above his head, bringing it crashing down onto Nobby's skull. Dazed but having a cranium composed of very dense bone, Nobby fell off the chair onto the floor, turning to his assailant as blood spurted from his head. "You? Then who was...?" were his last words as Alun brought the cudgel crashing down again and the big man's life ascended to the heavens – or, more likely, to hell.

Instantly, Leini had taken a damp cloth from the sink and was wiping the blood off the table as Alun dragged the body along the hall and into the room with the priest-hole, whereupon he heaved him in as Leini followed with another cloth and a bucket to wipe up the trail of blood on the flagstones. But Nobby's body was much bigger than his, and it got stuck head-first halfway down the hole, the boots – covered with earth from their last job – sticking up so high that Alun could not close the top. "Never mind – get back," Alun whispered furtively. He kept shoving for a moment but gave up as they heard Sid calling from the kitchen and Leini went back into character, sullenly entering the room as she dabbed her eyes and blew her nose.

"Where's Nobby?"

"Gone to the toilet. I was showing him where it was."

"'E knows where it is."

Almost caught out, Leini just said, "Well, I was telling him anyway. Would you like a drink, too?" Sid's countenance brightened. "Don't mind if I do," he said as he dumped a large amount of frozen food on the table.

"Sit there," Leini said, pointing to the righted chair which moments ago had contained his accomplice.

"That's Nobby's chair."

"Nobby can sit over there, when he gets back," as she pointed to another chair and poured him a drink. As he did so, he looked at Leini and said, there's blood on your blouse."

"Nosebleed. I get them when I'm upset."

Nobby looked at the floor under his chair as he sat down.

"Must have been a hell of a nosebleed," he said suspiciously, eyeing up what looked like a lot of fresh blood on the floor.

"Yes, it was," she said, as Alun's cudgel repeated its dastardly deed and Sid slumped instantly down the chair and onto the floor.

Alun looked at his handiwork as Leini brightened up and came over to give Alun a hug. "This farm will now soon be yours again," she whispered, and started cleaning up the mess contributed by three bodies in such a rather short space of time. "*Ours*," Alun said as he stood there, breathing heavily, holding the cudgel as its end rested on the floor. "I need a drink," he said.

"I just poured one for Sid," she said discompassionately; "but he won't be needing it now."

Alun downed it in one and, refreshed, started helping Leini. The two other body-bags were brought in and soon the kitchen looked as though nothing had happened – except there was only one full bag by the side entrance: it was still going to take them somewhat longer to prise Nobby out of the priest-hole...

*

Norris Griffiths put down his gin and tonic and plunged into the pool, which he often did when things did not seem to be progressing right; the water cooled him but when he surfaced he was still worried. He had not heard from Sander for over a day and – whilst he knew that the mobile reception was patchy in Wales – Sander always managed to get in touch somehow. Norris knew Sander had checked out of his hotel, of course: Nobby had confirmed that. But now there was no word from him or Sid either...

He decided to wait a bit; any contact to England was risky. So he went inside to watch the latest episodes of *Jonquil's Journals*, and grumpily turned his back on his garden of Eden for an hour to see if there was anything to glean…

*

After the dispatch of the two miscreants, Alun and Leini had donned rubber gloves and aprons and washed everything they had touched – especially in Leini's case, who could not ever be known to have been there; Alun's fingerprints and DNA were, of course, to be expected – but not hers. Alun was now heaving Nobby's body upwards whilst Leini pulled at the legs of this stocky individual jammed in the priest-hole; but finally the body moved, then eventually bumped lifeless onto the floor with a dull thump. They were both sweating with the effort but relieved they had finally managed it. Then they put the body into its waiting bag and zipped it up. It was starting to get dark when they looked around outside to make sure that the fake Dilys had not returned and, as quietly as they could, put the two bodies in the back of Nobby and Sid's van. Just in case the digger the two men had used had been hidden – or they could not start or work it – they had also put some spades and forks into the van. As a final act, they took the boxes of legal papers from the loft and put them next to the bodies: then Alun drove the van down the lane while Leini followed in the hired white van that Alun had travelled down in.

Half an hour later, they arrived at what was still termed as Nathan's farm and looked out for the copse on the hill the boys had mentioned. It was easy: where the fence was broken and digger tracks led into a field and up a hill was quite the giveaway – and also somewhat chilling as it was obvious the two reprobates had expected more bodies before they bothered to mend the fence and cover the tracks. The gradient was not steep, and the gentle slope meant the copse was still some distance away, but soon Alun's van was in the copse, where a large expanse of disturbed ground was the obvious resting-place of Alun's wife – and probably Nathan to boot. The digger stood proudly beside the graves, too, hidden from the road by the trees but a ghostly sentry standing witness to previous dark deeds – and the one about to be perpetrated…

*

Norris came out of his palatial living-room an hour later, to find his girls asleep and an afternoon torpor hanging over the place. The programmes had divulged nothing of any import, although what he did not know was that the salient parts of the story which would soon affect him would not be broadcast for another week. As a result, nothing seemed awry, so he stood and looked at his empire. He lasciviously studied the somnolent, pretty girls by the side of the pool, took a quick snort and a second G&T, and soon felt more relaxed... but the lack of information from Sander was still gnawing at him. He hated not knowing things. He was the boss and had minions to keep him constantly updated – which they were now not doing. He didn't like using his mobile phone – even when it sporadically worked up here – because it gave a fix on him that he would rather not divulge. This silence was becoming disconcerting, though. And suddenly his feeling of unease turned to anger.

So he decided to throw caution to the wind and, picking up his phone, he walked to the end of the terrace where there was an occasional signal and rang Nobby.

*

As the ground had been so recently disturbed by the addition of Sander, it was quite soft, so Alun and Leini decided to dig the final two graves themselves, rather than risk touching the digger; that was testament and proof to the others' deeds and would hopefully exonerate their own involvement. They soon got down to the bagged bodies of Dilys, Nathan and Sander and created space for the additional two beside them. But soon after the bodies had been deposited and covered, they heard a mobile phone ringing from beneath the sod: it was Nobby's final call.

*

When the phone wasn't answered, Norris was in an even worse state of mind. Things now seemed even less right. Yet there was no-one else he could turn to in England – and nor did he want there to be. And if he sent a couple of his local drug pushers there they would probably be so addicted as to cause the collapse of his carefully-constructed empire overnight. It wasn't worth the risk. So he bit his lip and decided to wait. Sander would be in touch soon. Of course he would… And if he didn't, he would go to England himself. As someone else, of course…

*

Realising that the phone could give away the position of the body, Alun and Leini furtively burrowed for it; finding it, they then checked for Sid's, too – but he didn't seem to have one. With the phone retrieved and the battery removed, they decided to insert it again when they reached the outskirts of London, where its dwindling signal might attract the law away from this part of the country. On the way back onto the drive, Alun beat down the digger tracks with his spade while Leini mended the fence; being Wales, the lush grass would quickly grow over the tracks if they were lucky.

They left Nobby and Sid's van outside Nathan's farmhouse and dropped its key through an unclosed kitchen window; it bounced neatly onto the inside sill amongst some dead flies and looked as though it had been there for ages. Then they drove back in the white van to what would now become Alun's home again. And Leini's. If they wanted it, of course…

By the time they had got back to the farm, locked it up, taken the box from the loft with the documents in it and reached the M4 motorway, then disposed of Sander and Nobby's live phones into a skip in Hounslow, the sun was rising on Putney as Alun's white van and Leini's yellow Porsche arrived home. The van went straight into the garage for intense cleaning; then they showered, put all their clothes into a sturdy bin bag for later disposal and went to sleep. It was nearly ten in the morning when they were awoken from deep slumber by an agitated Jonathan.

CHAPTER 35

Two days later, a distinguished-looking, smartly-attired man in a white suit and hat, carrying a silver-topped walking-cane and a Colombian passport, passed through immigration at Heathrow. His name was Nicolas-Arturo Garros but through his broken English the border officer could not help but notice a distinctly Welsh accent...

Norris hadn't been to Britain for several years, ever since he had 'died' and moved to the hills – which were far enough away from Bogotà to avoid the tentacles of the law but close enough to get out in a relative hurry if necessary. Whilst this visit was one he was reluctant to make, the fact that he could not get in touch with any of his three contacts compelled him to ascertain for himself what had happened to his minimal staff by actually returning. His first action – after checking in to a very expensive, sumptuous London hotel – was to request a meeting with Gloria Cordobes at the Tellurian TV studios. He would use Gloria to get a meeting with Leini whom, he felt, must know everything. And almost certainly what had happened to Sander, Sid and Nobby. Sander had told him that Leini was very beautiful and the prospect excited him; so he only hoped that he would *not* have to rub her out after all for knowing too much. Or failing to stick to the script – in more ways than one...

*

Leini, for her part, was fully aware that this visit was likely – although unsure whether it would be in person or from one of Norris' rapidly-depleting set of accomplices. She would soon find out.

The next day, she was in the office with Alun and Jonathan, trying to placate the latter regarding the diversions from the pre-agreed script storylines. Alun had been forced to use all his ingenuity, tact and persuasion to explain that the new direction of the stories would cost less (untrue), be sexier (difficult with a dwindling cast of young men and women), more crime-oriented (challenging, when most of the offenders had been — or were about to be — killed off) and allowing more chance for cast renewal to uphold all the previous points (probably true but more expensive, as many new actors would have to be auditioned and their contracts negotiated in a series which was very popular and had a high profile). Jonathan was wrestling with these unnecessary changes (as he saw them) — as were Alun and Leini from a different perspective — when Gloria's PA arrived to ask for Leini's presence in the boardroom immediately.

Leini and Alun cast furtive glances to one another, then Leini asked, "Well, yes, of course: but whatever for?"

"There's a programme investor who wants to meet you, I understand. A Señor Nicolas-Arturo Garros from Spain, I'd think."

"What on earth does a programme investor from Spain want to talk to me for?" she asked, knowing the answer full well. "Surely that's Jonathan's department."

"Yes — that's *my* department," Jonathan said feebly.

"Well, he only wants to see Leini for now," she said firmly. "And he's waiting for you."

Alun and Leini had discussed this possibility and agreed that Alun would not push himself forward when the moment arrived: he could work better anonymously from behind the scenes. And apart from being Dilys' ex-husband — well, that's what he had thought! — he never felt he had featured in the set-up at all until Leini had come clean a week or two before. So Leini rose and went out, leaving a worried Alun and a disgruntled Jonathan to continue their conversation alone.

On arrival in Gloria's office, her heart was thumping hard. The man rose in a gentlemanly way with a slight bow of the head and kissed her outstretched hand; as he did so, Leini was sharply aware that he was assessing her hands, bust and legs with more acuity than politeness. *'He's a monster'*, was all she could think — and was especially careful not to expose her underwear as she sat down in the leather chair, swiftly crossing her stockinged legs.

"Nicolas-Arturo's from Colombia," Gloria was saying as she settled in and her PA left. "I didn't know it but he's been one of *Jonquil's Journals'* biggest investors. I think you met his business partner, Sander – as did I – but apparently Nicolas-Arturo is the man with the money."

"*You bet*," thought Leini.

"Anyway, as you knew Sander, this gentleman wanted to meet you because Sander's disappeared... so Nicolas-Arturo wanted to meet you to continue that connection."

"Disappeared?" Leini asked incredulously, the image of Nobby and Sid beating him into a pulp foremost in her mind. "How?"

"That's what I wanted to ask *you*, young lady," the man replied, with an intense look of suspicion. "Did he contact you recently?"

"Yes," she affirmed openly. That was the easy bit – it was true. "About two weeks ago, I think."

"Yes – you were about to see him in Bogotá, I believe – but you got as far as Dublin and came back." Gloria's mouth fell open: Leini had been going to Colombia? Without she or Jonathan knowing?

"No. I went to Dublin to see my parents for a weekend – I was not going to Colombia."

"Not what Sander said."

"What's all this about?" Gloria interjected. But the man ignored her and continued: "You were lovers and he got you this job here at Tellurian TV." Gloria's mouth fell open even wider. "You were his contact to me. And you're very important because you tell us what's going on and why we should continue bankrolling *Jonquil's Journals*." Gloria leaned forward to say something but his raised hand stopped her. "But now he's disappeared – as well as some other minor characters –" and he waved his hand again as if to imply their insignificance – "and I want to know how."

A silence descended onto the room and Gloria's still-open mouth betrayed a tongue-piercing Leini had not seen before.

"Well, I don't," she said emphatically. "I did know Sander intimately for a while around the time I joined Gloria here at Tellurian TV but we went our separate ways. I mean, I'm horrified he's dead but I hadn't seen or spoken to him for ages."

"I didn't say he was dead." The words were spoken with the chill iciness of a deep crevasse, as Leini squirmed, re-crossed her legs and inadvertently exposed the very part of her anatomy she had much wished to keep private. Which was much appreciated by Nicolas-Arturo.

"Well," she blustered, "the way you were speaking made me *think* that he was dead... I mean, if you can't find him or speak to him, surely that would be the implication..."

Nicolas-Arturo just looked at her. "You tell me."

"Would anyone like a cup of tea?" Gloria posited.

No-one answered.

*

Downstairs, Alun had come up with plausible, artistic and economically-superior reasons for the script changes, his mind working like a supercharged turbine to come up with solutions so he could escape Jonathan's stubborn interrogation and get to see what had happened to Leini. To say he was worried about her was an understatement and the fact that this was all due to her previously secret subterfuge was galling him anew – the only mitigating factor being that her reasons for changing sides was because she obviously truly loved him.

The general new direction of the plots confirmed, Alun left a sullen Jonathan and went back to his office to start typing them up as he waited impatiently for Leini's return, every person calling or dropping in being met with a swift, dismissive response.

After an hour, he needed to get out of the office and popped over the road for a stiff drink in Studio Six. Three brandies later, he returned to his office to find Leini there, sobbing at her desk, a torrent of tissues already adorning her position.

"Oh, Alun, darling… it was awful," she said as she threw her arms around him, wetting his shirt with large volumes of salty tears. "The man is a monster!"

"Well, who *is* he?"

She lowered her voice and said in his ear, "Norris bloody Griffiths."

"I thought he was Spanish."

"Oh, you dear, sweet, innocent man! He's here *pretending* to be Nicolas-Arturo Garros. That's his *alias*."

"Oh, my God. I thought it was another person like Sander."

"No – this is worse. He's the dead hand – literally – behind all this. But now his accomplices, murderers, whatever, are dead, he's had to come over himself to find out what's going on."

"Do you think he suspects you – us?"

She nodded. "Yes – and he accused me of knowing what had happened to Sander. In front of Gloria! He also told her we'd have to change the scripts if he was to continue funding the programme."

"I've just done that with Jonathan."

"Yes – but now we'll have to have Edmund killed in the storyline after all – not how we've just changed it with Jonathan. He *knows* what we know – that you're the parallel to that character. Obviously, he couldn't make that clear to Gloria because Gloria kept talking about you and so he knows you're still alive. And also the programme's scriptwriter, which would be tricky."

"Well, that episode hasn't been broadcast yet."

"I know – but now Gloria might soon twig and, if she does, then you'll have to disappear before Garros sees it." Then she looked even more horrified as she added, "Who knows, she might be showing that episode to him now."

"Impossible. It hasn't been edited yet." Then: "So we'll have to kill off Jenny, too, then?"

"Yes – and that's *me*."

There was a pause. Then Alun brightened. "That's great!"

Leini looked shocked and hurt.

"No – not literally, you silly thing. But once he's back in Colombia then we can pretend there's no character correlation, kill them off and carry on."

"Not that easy."

"Why?"

"I think he's just bought Gloria – brought her into his fold, told her everything regarding his financial input. Without mentioning where his money comes from, of course. But she'll then have to make sure that the scripts will reflect reality to keep the funding going – not me – now Sander's gone, I'm sure of it. I don't think she realised before, but I think she might now. And, after all, if he's subsidising the programme – and the station... Well, of course she'll fall in with his plans."

There was a pause as Alun reflected on this. Then Leini continued: "And I think she rather liked him, actually. And he her..."

Alun suddenly straightened and with an excited gasp said, "Then when the script gets to the point it's transmitted, we'll just disappear. Together. Forever."

Her face broke into a damp smile. "Sorry to have brought all this upon you," she said sweetly. I was so naïve. Will you ever forgive me?" as she pinched his cheek with her manicured thumb and forefinger.

"I have already," he said airily. "Because you've just given me the most wonderful idea."

CHAPTER 36

Events accelerated after that meeting: the threat of exposure, collusion, murder, fantasy, drugs, money-laundering, employment, love and death being a potent combination that quickened the senses – and perhaps, even, the dead…

Leini had been summoned up to see Gloria Cordobes again after Nicolas-Arturo Garros had left the TV studios and told to explain herself, which was tricky; she did not know what deal – if any – had been agreed between the two, nor whether Gloria now knew the source of his wealth which, if it came out, would have finished the TV station completely. And Gloria, of course – as well as she and Alun. So Leini gambled that this would not have been divulged by Norris – it was too dangerous for him – and all of *them*. And Leini had one up on Gloria: she knew exactly who Nicolas-Arturo Garros *really* was…

The meeting finished with Gloria saying she would henceforth be taking a keener interest in the script storylines – but whether this was to do with watching her own back and ensuring continuing funding or because Norris had threatened her, Leini had no idea. And if Gloria might have been worried about her security – personal and company-wise – then that meant Leini and Alun were very much in the firing-line too. As for Jonathan, it became very obvious that he knew absolutely nothing about anything.

Alun, for his part, was furiously re-writing the scripts to attune to what Jonathan and he had agreed, whilst keeping one eye on actual events to ensure that if Norris – aka Nicolas-Arturo Garros – ever made it back to Colombia, then he would have to change the scripts' direction *again* to reflect reality rather than what Norris was actually expecting. Which would involve more skulduggery and certainly a number of panic-stricken re-writes to keep the man at bay – and CEO Gloria Cordobes. As well as trying to explain to an increasingly pernickety Jonathan why.

With tensions rising, Alun and Leini were being forced to devise a plan: what to do about Norris. Most pressing was that the man must very soon believe that Alun was not alive – especially after the episode when the tavern-owner Sander had been killed, which could not be changed as it had recently been recorded, if not aired yet... so suspecting that this pseudo-Colombian might soon be poking around their flat, the first part was for them to drive the Porsche to Wales very early, enter the farmhouse and wait for him – for Leini was convinced he would be unable to resist visiting. There, he would not so much meet *them* but the same fate as his henchmen – especially as he and Leini would soon literally be supposed dead, as in the updated script. And if that was the case, the graves in the copse would possibly have either one, two or three additions, depending on the unfolding circumstances...

*

Meanwhile, Norris – still disguised as Nicolas-Arturo Garros – had decided to travel to Wales, as Leini had expected. Having tried to reach her several times by phone to press her even harder regarding what had happened to Sander, Leini's lack of response – she had sussed and blocked his number as it had a Colombian prefix – had now made him sure beyond doubt that she knew everything – and not just about his nefarious dealings. So she had to be accosted fast. He had therefore hired a sumptuous black limousine and commenced his journey early that morning via her home in Putney: but it was obvious she was not there. Nor her 'pansy writer', Alun, of course – he had probably fled as Norris had made it clear to Gloria that he wanted him fired – a shorthand for being rubbed out by either him or Sid and Nobby... if they still existed. He had managed, though, to get in touch with Mildred – the fake Dilys – and agreed to meet her at what had been Dilys', his – and nominally Alun's – farmhouse, to retrieve the vitally important paperwork from the loft, which he thought Sid and Nobby must have prepared but which he had never received. And that was another reason to try to glean what might also have happened to Sid and Nobby. As with Sander, he was certain something tragic had happened to them and was convinced that Leini knew what; yet he could not accuse her without the facts – just deleting her was not an option. Well, not yet, anyway. That was a future occurrence which would eventually have to be reflected in the script...

He arrived at the farm a few hours later and, as Mildred had not arrived yet, walked around the house to see if any doors or windows were open so he could escape the miasma of mist which had suddenly descended, dampening everything. But the house was all secure. So he went into the barn and waited...

Looking around, he saw three sets of tyre-marks going in and out and noted that the treads and widths were somewhat different; and also that one set was less impressed than the other two, which suggested a light car rather than heavy vans. Apart from that, all seemed normal – except for a cudgel by the doorway; at that moment, the blurred headlights of a small car appearing through the fog became visible. It was Mildred; apologising for her lateness – she had been to a cake-baking class – she unlocked the front door and they entered.

Inside, the slightly damp smell of an old house which had not been heated or much lived in for a while instantly struck their nostrils – as well as the distinct smell of bleach and soap...

*

Having escaped so early, Leini and Alun had decided to finalise their plans over a hearty breakfast at a greasy spoon en route to Wales, where there was almost no chance of anyone knowing them or having their conversation overheard. The definitive plan now in place, they were now heading resolutely towards the farmhouse, unaware that Norris had passed their location an hour beforehand and was now exactly in the same place they were heading for.

But what Alun had not told Leini was the final part of his plan. That could wait.

*

Norris had abandoned his pretence at a Colombian accent for his meeting with Mildred, and his strong Welsh lilt sat strangely at odds behind his disguise as Nicolas-Arturo Garros. He was all ears, though, as she recounted the unexpected meeting with a pretty woman – Leini, she said – who had been there when she last saw Sid and Nobby. He was even more astonished to hear that Alun had made an appearance to her because Sid and Nobby had told him he was dead – and had beaten him to a pulp themselves. Then he realised that the murder must have been immediately after that meeting, as Leini had said it was Alun and wanted him dead for betraying her for a lover.

"Did you see that lover?" Norris asked suspiciously. Mildred shook her head. "No, she'd gone before I arrived. Well, that's what I was led to believe…"

Norris reflected for a moment. "Hmmm. I wonder if the body was her?…"

"You mean, *not* Alun?" Mildred enquired. Norris nodded. Then another thought struck him. "Or perhaps it was Sander," he said quietly.

"No, it wasn't Sander. I met Sander once briefly. He was dark, muscular, swarthy, handsome… good-looking – I'd like to have – "

"Yes, yes," Norris interrupted. "That's what all the girls say. Or said."

"What do you mean – *said*?"

"I think he's no more. And that's why I want to see Leini."

"Is Leini Alun's floozy that I saw?" Mildred enquired. Norris nodded.

"And I want to see her as soon as possible."

That wish would be visited upon him far sooner than he suspected…

*

Leini and Alun approached the turn-off to the drive with some trepidation: what if Norris had sent a whole phalanx of Colombian henchmen to the house, perhaps posing as immigrant labour to pick his and Nathan's fruit and veg? To the casual observer, they would not seem out of place at this time of year…

They therefore decided to pass the entrance and hide the Porsche down a farm track in a thick wood some hundred yards further on; then they donned Wellington boots and started to walk carefully up the drive, their progress somewhat hidden by the mist. But as they got near to the farmhouse, the mist started to lift and a hazy sun burst through, exposing not only them but – outside the farmhouse some three hundred yards away – a large black limo and a small, squat, dirty little red runabout.

"Norris and the fake Dilys," Leini murmured to Alun, who nodded.

Inside the house, Norris was becoming ever more apoplectic as he had gone to the loft and found that all the incriminating papers had vanished. He almost tumbled down the stairs to a startled Mildred and asked her if she knew where the boxes with all the legal papers were. She shook her head – no, she knew nothing about any legal papers or, even, that there was a loft where they might have been.

With no other explanation, Norris wondered if he had been double-crossed or stitched up; but who would do that to him? Surely not Sander? Or was that why he had disappeared without trace? Sid? Possible… Nobby? No – too stupid and fearful. All three together? Another possibility… What about Mildred? Did she really not know anything? He turned on her belligerently: "Are you *sure* you don't know where those papers are?" he said with the voice and demeanour of the Norse god Thor.

Mildred wilted in terror and emitted a feeble, "No; no, I don't – honest."

Norris took a step back and imagined his entire empire in tatters, the Colombian police crawling all over his mansion, his bank account at nil and the looming approach of a very long court case and prison sentence. As well as extradition back to this country of his birth to face charges of fraud, corruption, extortion, drug-running and the forced repayment of many people he had threatened, compromised and stolen from when a council leader in Wales. People like Nathan, Alun – obliquely – and many more. Then he took a deep breath, calmed down and turned to the still-shaking Mildred. "Go," he said gently, "but you have never met *me*, nor Sander, Sid or Nobby; you have never been to this house and you know nothing – and especially anything about Leini the floozy or Alun. Absolutely nothing – d'you understand?"

Mildred nodded and started to go. "Wait a moment," he said, and went to a briefcase he had parked in a corner and took out a wadge of notes. "Here's five thousand pounds for your silence," he said, as he gave it to her. The eyes of the woman were on stalks as she nervously took the money, turned and ran to her car, soon careering down the lane and avoiding the potholes with the speed and precision of a rally driver.

Leini and Alun had observed movement at the front of the house and dived into a ditch behind a sparse but welcome remnant of hedgerow before the panicked-looking Mildred drove past, her ghostly white face in stark contrast against the red of the car. Leini was certain Mildred caught a glimpse of them as she bounced and swerved down the pitted lane, registering a furtive look of even deeper terror because the car suddenly seemed to go even faster until it reached the road and then disappeared.

"So it's definitely Norris there," Alun said darkly. Leini nodded. And he would be expecting them much as they had thought to expect him. But Norris had got there first. And that was *not* part of the plan…

*

Jonathan was poring over the plotlines, increasingly furious that Alun and Leini appeared to have deserted him, so leaving him to try and guess where the plotlines should go next, This perplexed him: he wasn't very good at plotlines – only changing those of Alun from time to time. Not that changes were often necessary, but done just to prove that he was the producer and in charge.

What he could not comprehend was that they had initially plotted the demise of Edmund in the script, who would be assassinated by Abel and Zaccheus under orders from Bartholomew Jonquil, who was wary of a developing relationship between Edmund and Jenny, his intended. But now, Abel and Zaccheus had supposedly been murdered by Edmund but escaped; yet Edmund had succeeded in murdering the tavern-owner, Sander, with the collusion of Jenny. Yet it also appeared that Jonquil would soon be using his influence to condemn Edmund so that Jenny could not marry him, under the guise of a cooked-up charge – perhaps, even, the murder of Sander, Abel and Zaccheus. It was all too much. So much so that when the designer rang up to suggest lunch, the temptation was too much and he only hoped that Alun and Leini would send the updated plotlines soon.

In fact, in one sense, that was what Leini and Alun – at that precise moment – were trying to conclude. For, as the plots reflected the clandestine goings-on of what was happening to Sander's empire, they were now about to find out which way they would go. Or be so dead by Norris' hand that no-one would ever know anyway. In which case, Jonathan would have to become very good at plotlines incredibly quickly...

*

Norris was looking out of the kitchen window, wondering what to do next, when he thought he noticed some movement on the drive. Peering more intently through the dirty, rain-flecked glass, he saw a woman walking nonchalantly up the drive as if she owned the place. Mildred had been sent packing, so it wasn't her; yet this lady's confident air troubled him. The figure was wearing a rucksack over an anorak with a hood, the sides of which kept hiding opposite sides of her face as she walked. Yet it did still seem familiar... Yes! It *was* Leini, he was sure... Perhaps he would not kill her, he thought; he would make her an offer she couldn't refuse – the chance of living a wonderfully easy life in Colombia with him, every whim satisfied and he having the ability to pleasure her every night... best of all, for her, she would escape the damp and cold of Britain, as he had done. He imagined himself *in flagrante delicto* with her but was brought up short by the fact that Sander had got there before him. Still, perhaps that was one good reason that Sander appeared to be missing after all…

As he dreamed, the vision of loveliness passed his view and disappeared to the side of the house: damn! – she was just a lonely walker and was not coming in! Yet something still told him it *was* Leini – he at least had to check and if it wasn't, she was pretty enough to confront as a supposed trespasser, without any consequences if it was someone else. He opened the kitchen door and stepped into the hallway on his way to open the front entrance and accost this lovely lady when suddenly his cranium met his teeth going in the opposite direction as Alun's trusty prop cudgel added another to its list of real victims…

CHAPTER 37

JONQUIL'S JOURNALS:

EPISODE 159. SCENE 57. WIGGINS' PARLOUR. DAY.

	EDMUND AND JENNY ARE CANOODLING BY THE CENTRAL TABLE WHEN THEY HEAR A NOISE AND START LOOKING NORMAL AS IF DISCUSSING SOME DETAILS.
JONQUIL:	(OFF). Jenny, dearest, my pretty maid, where art thou? Hello, I'm here... (HE APPEARS TO THEM). Ah, dearest little bunny... Er, what are you doing here with *him*?
JENNY:	Just discussing a change of victuals, dear Sir... I'll be up in a minute...
JONQUIL:	Edmund. Are you trying to seduce my sweetheart?
EDMUND:	No, Sir! It would be more than my life's worth to cuckold you, kind Sir!
JONQUIL:	Well, let's hope that's the truth... Come, my dear – I need your company in bed before I have a long session in court regarding the murder of two tyrants, Abel and Zaccheus. Pity – I wanted to use them meself... (AS HE LOOKS HARD AT EDMUND. THEN HE GOES UPSTAIRS).
	HAVING TURNED THE CORNER AND SO OUT OF VIEW, JENNY LOOKS AT EDMUND AND NODS. AFTER A MOMENT, HE PICKS UP A CUDGEL AND RACES UP THE STAIRS. THERE IS

A LOUD NOISE AS A KERFUFFLE
ENSUES AND LOUD GROANS OF PAIN
EMANATE FROM ABOVE. THEN
SILENCE. JENNY RUSHES UP THE
STAIRS AND LOOKS OFF IN HORROR.

JENNY: Oh, my darling... NO!

END OF EPISODE 159. ROLL CREDITS.

Alun and Leini – by now getting used to clearing up the mess of shattered skulls – finished the job in record time and soon the body was bagged, the forks and spades were fetched, and the stench of soap and bleach once more pervaded the fusty odour of the farmhouse kitchen.

The Porsche was almost a mile away, so it seemed expedient to use Norris' much larger limo parked outside to carry his body to the burial site at Nathan's farm – especially as Norris was the named driver. Even if he *was* dead...

Having retrieved all of Norris's personal effects – particularly his briefcase in the kitchen which contained his phone and a large wallet bristling with credit cards and British and Colombian cash – they put the body in the boot where they also found a man-bag containing the details of the car-hire as well as much else, such as his passport and flight tickets. There was a significant deposit to be repaid if the car was returned on time without a scratch, so Alun opted to drive it back to London to retrieve it. After all, it would be thoroughly cleansed by the hire company and all traces of Norris's DNA would be destroyed forever. And theirs.

But the phone presented a problem: they wanted all its details without any chance of being compromised by them. Leini had foreseen this possibility and acted accordingly, as all good PA's would; she donned rubber gloves again and connected the phone by cable to her laptop; fortunately, he had not protected it with a password so it was easy copying all Norris' contact numbers; it also had a massive memory-card, which she hoped would furnish more details, pictures and evidence of contacts and contracts, and carefully wrapped it in a plastic bag and put it in her handbag.

Then, with the body safely in the limo's boot, they extinguished the lights, locked the house up and drove to Nathan's farm once more.

By now the dusk was gathering, but the limo was too heavy to drive up to the grave-site and they did not want to risk it becoming stuck; so they re-broke the wire fence and half-carried, half-dragged the body up to the copse, where the digger still stood on guard...

An hour later, covered in dirt, they walked down to the limo again and drove to the wood to retrieve Leini's Porsche, where they both changed into different clothes. It was pre-planned that they should each look as different as possible for the return journey to London: Alun had applied a beard, a long-haired wig and thick-rimmed glasses, sporting a bland top and mis-matching trousers, while Leini did much the same in a more demure and feminine way. Alun left first, Leini departing fifteen minutes later. On the way, Alun filled up the limo on one of Norris's credit cards and Leini filled her Porsche on another a few minutes later; Alun then finally threw Norris's phone into a different skip in an even less salubrious part of Hounslow before continuing on to home.

It would soon be time to put the second part of their plan into action – the part that Leini knew nothing about.

CHAPTER 38

Jonathan was listening intently to the reasonings of the scripts' plotline changes from his cream team but, as he did not know of the deceit, was understandably struggling to understand them. It was only the sudden and unexpected appearance of CEO Gloria Cordobes (initiated by Leini) that he agreed to the new direction with a shrug and a dismissive, "OK, but keep me informed from now on and let me know the budgets for new characters and why they're necessary," as he grumpily left the room. In fact, Leini and Alun had already fleshed out the next few months' general storylines which, in parallel with *Jonquil's Journals*, followed their own lives ever more closely…

After Jonathan left the room, Gloria remarked drily, "I just hope you know what you're doing – Tellurian TV depends mostly on the success of this series, you know…" then went back to her office.

But Alun and Leini knew exactly what they were doing: yet whether it was more to the benefit of Tellurian TV or themselves was another matter…

What they also knew was that eventually, probably after a very short length of time, people would notice that Nathan, Dilys – even Sid and Nobby – had not been seen for a while… and, in the longer term, if their farms were left to grow over, people would start asking questions, especially the many providers and customers of Nathan's organic produce shop. As for Norris, they knew that many dealers and traffickers would soon be trying to take over his business – both in Wales and Colombia – the very moment they realised that neither he nor Sander were there. Time was of the essence.

These conundrums had been foreseen early on by Leini and Alun: but now Sander was no more, there was an organisational and logistical vacuum and they had to find a way of discovering who worked for him in both countries. As for Nathan, they had to find those who helped manage his vast acres of organic produce but who were unknown to them – he had done most of the work himself and only had some occasional hired hands on the farm. There was the shop to sort out, too: so they swiftly had to come up with an action plan before any interruption happened.

Which it already had – in several directions... So it was now that Alun divulged the second part of his plan to Leini.

*

At Nathan's organic produce enterprise his assistants, used to not seeing him for days at a time, had not worried – until his produce stopped coming in. Knowing the area – and the late Nathan – better than Leini, Alun decided he would phone the shop and inform the staff that Nathan had suddenly been forced to travel to Australia to see a long-lost uncle who was ill; this fiction would be embellished by other fabrications to give the story more pertinence, such as that this uncle wanted to leave him a huge farm and house there, as well as much money besides: the lie would conclude with the explanation that he, Alun, had been appointed to manage the taking-on of a new general manager until Nathan's return. That this would be 'never' he would divulge in due course.

He managed to get through to a bored girl named Bledwyn who said she was the store manager yet seemed to have no interest in the business at all. But he imparted all the pre-determined lies he had concocted – which surprised the girl but who registered zero emotion – and said he would be down to discuss things within a day or so. But he could not run the risk of being recognised, so took on the guise of a supposed friend of Nathan's; and with the help of a colleague in the TV make-up department, he construed a disguise which would fool anyone – and when even Leini didn't recognise him, he knew it was a winner.

For her part, Leini knew she would be best placed to go to Colombia as herself; her short romance with Sander had involved a few days at Norris's mansion so she was at least known there to all the domestic staff; yet she had never met Norris at that time, who had been away on a mission to acquire more suppliers. She surmised that if there was any trouble with the local traffickers or dealers, a pretty face would be more able to mollify desperate, hardened drug dealers than any man. It was dangerous, certainly; but the rewards would be enormous. As long as she succeeded, of course...

As for the Welsh connection, Alun would confront the staff of Nathan's shop when he arrived there; that was why he would pose as a friend. He and Leini were reasonably assured of success in their ventures as details of all the colleagues and peripheral contacts relating to both Norris and Sander had been found in their respective briefcases. On the drugs score at least, they knew everything: it was only their future about which they knew nothing – and were increasingly worried about...

*

In order to swiftly enact their overall plan before people started asking questions, Alun and Leini had quickly finished the storylines to suit their narrative, submitted them to Jonathan and then asked for two weeks' holiday – supposedly to 'recharge their batteries' in Mauritius; in actual fact, the next two weeks would hardly be a vacation but the most challenging and perilous time of their lives. For their plan to succeed, careful preparation and speed were essential: dealers could not delay supplying their clients when they were all hooked on substances that needed constant replenishment – and could cause them to go to other barons and dealers: all of whom would then smell a very big rat... A drugs war had to be avoided at all costs. Fortunately, Leini had not just agreed to Alun's plan but embraced it...

Two days later, Leini landed at Bogotá airport. She had tried ringing the mansion but a worried-sounding young girl answered the phone in Spanish, which she did not understand; but now knowing Nicolas-Arturo Garros' address from Sander's files – which she had not been told when she first knew him – she queued for a taxi and told the driver where she wanted to go. But three times their faces dropped and they shook their heads – "No go there," one said, which seemed to typify the response of the others. Deflated, she looked around, only to realise that she was being intensively observed by a balding, unshaven and gold-bedecked man in a black T-shirt, olive shorts and brogue shoes. He smiled at her, exposing teeth also tipped with gold, which shone in the early afternoon light. *Drug-dealer*, she thought, *Might be useful,* so she smiled back.

"You want car?" he asked hoarsely. She nodded. "I take you," he said, and intimated to follow him, as he walked off across the road towards banks of cars. She dragged her hastily-packed but heavy suitcase in his direction as he arrived at a large people-carrier. He hoisted her case into the back as if it was as light as an egg and opened the passenger door.

She slipped in as he closed the door behind her and went around to his own side, sliding into the driving-seat as if moulded for his form and no other. Then he turned to her and said, "You Leini, no?"

Leini did not know what to say or how to react, so she just nodded. "How did you know that?" she eventually managed. "I see you before," he replied. "I drive you when Sander here for you last time." She gulped – she didn't remember him: but that might have been because of her infatuation at the time with her lover... Suddenly, the fear she had been trying to quell all flight spilt out. "So you mean, you've been waiting for me?"

He nodded as he started the engine. "I come to every flight from London or Dublin via Miami, Amsterdam, Philadelphia, wherever..."

"You must have spent a lot of time at the airport recently, then," she joked nervously. He nodded, with a tired smile, and said, "Si: ever since Sander disappear."

"Sander's disappeared?" she asked, knowing she was acting very badly but could say nothing else. He nodded again, gave her a knowing look, and they departed the airport.

"So where are you taking me?" she eventually hazarded nervously.

"To Norris mansion, of course. He want see you."

A wave of fearful and conflicting misapprehension swept over her and she felt nauseous; if the man they killed wasn't Norris, then who was he?"

In her state of confused paranoia, her head was a jumble. She was going to the right place, but nothing else made sense. And how did this man know she might be on this flight? And had Norris faked death twice?

She was unsure whether she wanted to know the answer to that question. And for now, she would be living on her wits...

CHAPTER 39

Alun arrived outside Nathan's organic produce centre, confirmed his moustache was still attached and, on entering the building, noted the depleted shelves, the smell of rotting veg and a palpable air of boredom from the two staff he encountered. He asked to see the manager. The girl he addressed had viciously long designer nails with which she was typing on her phone. She looked up with a dismissive air and just said, "He's disappeared."

"Well, I've come to fix that," he said. "Are you Bledwyn?" The girl stiffened and nodded, her nails poised over the screen, which seemed momentarily grateful for not being attacked by the glittering, multi-coloured talons. Alun continued: "Well, I'm your new general manager for the moment but it'll be someone else soon. So it's you who's in charge?"

Suddenly realising the importance of Alun's presence as her new boss, the quickly put her phone down and said, "Oh, sorry, sir… I thought you was a customer."

"Well, if that's how you treat customers," he said gruffly from behind his stick-on moustache, "no wonder there's no-one else here."

"That's because since Nathan disappeared to Australia, no-one's been in charge and so we haven't got any produce to sell." *The lie about Australia's been disseminated then*, Alun thought. *Good*. "So where's Sid, then?" he enquired. "He's gone, too," she replied, slightly concerned at how much this stranger knew.

"I'm a friend of Sid's," Alun said uncertainly. The girl looked interested. "D'you *know* Sid?" she enquired.

"Yes, I'm a friend of his, too. Which is why I'm helping him out. He suddenly had to go away. Family business."

"What – him as well as Nathan?"

"Yes – family business."

"What sort of family business?"

"Erm, he's gone gay and went off with Nobby to Spain so they could get married."

Her eyes were out on stalks – of which there were a severe shortage in the shop.

"Nobby and Sid? Gay? *Married?*"

Alun nodded, enjoying his performance. "So who's taken responsibility for this place since they left, then?"

"I have," said a deep cockney male voice from behind him. Alun turned.

The voice came from a man who looked suspiciously like Nobby.

*

Leini arrived at the mansion she had last been to around eighteen months before and was deposited outside the main entrance. Her driver's name was Luis and he ushered her through the door and then went to park the vehicle. The mansion was palatial, cool and imposing, if a little vulgar, as she had noticed the last time. One of the girls appeared from the swimming-pool area at the back and recognised her.

"Hola, Miss Leini," she said, and ran to shake her hand. "Nice see you again." Leini returned the compliment, remembering Rosa as a new addition to Norris's harem when she was last there – much to the discomfiture of Maria, who then also appeared from the pool and made similar protestations of affection. Then they all stood there, not knowing what to say next. Luis arrived and offered her a drink, which she accepted, as they all moved to the pool area. She was terrified that Norris might suddenly re-appear again as Polonius' ghost in Hamlet and – despite knowing he was mouldering in a deep grave in Wales – was still expecting him to make an appearance. Yet of him – or Nicolas-Arturo-Garros – there was, fortunately, no sign.

*

No it __can't__ be Nobby, his mind was telling him despite his facial recognition informing him otherwise. "I thought you were dead," he said stupidly.

"Then 'ow can I go off to Spain to marry Sid, then?"

"Ah – well, that's what I wasn't, er, sure about. But it's what I *heard…*"

"Bollocks."

Alun stood transfixed, not knowing what to do or say.

"But Sid's dead – you're right about that." There was a pause, as Alun's lip sweated and the long-haired wig made him even hotter – making him aware that his moustache was slipping off. His mind was working so hard, though, that this seemed less important than the man menacingly facing him: he had clubbed Nobby himself and then pulled him out of the priest-hole with great difficulty… And suddenly, he saw that the man was quite a lot less portly than that man: so the man was an impostor.

As was he.

*

Gloria read the storylines and made some tweaks. Then, always fancying herself as a scriptwriter, she decided to re-write one of the scenes. After all, Alun and Leini were on holiday, and she could easily tell Jonathan to do as she requested or she would fire him. The scene would now run thus:

JONQUIL'S JOURNALS:

OPENING TITLES. EPISODE 160. SCENE 1. WIGGINS' PARLOUR. DAY.

> WE SEE INTO THE PARLOUR FROM THE REVERSE ANGLE TO BEFORE, IN THAT WE SEE JENNY'S FACE IN TORMENT AS SHE LOOKS AT TWO BODIES APPARENTLY LIFELESS ON THE STEPS BEFORE HER; FOR THE

	MOMENT, WE CANNOT TELL WHICH IS JONQUIL AND WHICH IS EDMUND. SHE FALLS ONTO ONE OF THEM AND WAILS.
JENNY:	Oh, Edmund, my darling, NO! Don't go! I love you!
	THE OTHER BODY TWITCHES AND SITS UP – IT IS JONQUIL.
JENNY:	You little hussy, Jenny! You've tried to have me murdered so you could have my money and title… but now it is Edmund who will die! (HE PULLS OUT A PISTOL AND FIRES IT AT EDMUND'S BODY, WHICH DOES NOT FLINCH. JENNY SCREAMS IN FEAR AND DESPAIR). And I *will* have you for my own, you little cockish wench!
	JENNY SCREAMS AND RUNS UP THE STAIRS OUT OF SHOT. WHEN SHE HAS GONE, JONQUIL SHAKES EDMUND – WHO SITS UP.
EDMUND:	(WHISPERING). Has she gone?
JONQUIL:	(NODS). Yes – now get out and keep low for a while to let events take their course, good sir. I'll get someone in to 'take your corpse away', don't you know… while I'll go and have that little Ma'm Pussy to ensure she's mine forever, ha-ha! (GETS UP AND GOES, AS DOES EDMUND IN THE OTHER DIRECTION).

That'll confuse them, thought Gloria – and saved it as if nothing had been changed at all…

*

The fake Nobby – of this, Alun was increasingly sure – looked away at the remains of the staff for a moment, as Alun tried to stick his moustache back on, without much success.

"You can all go now," the Nobby said to the staff, and they quickly packed up and evaporated into the wet afternoon. Then he turned his gaze to Alun.

"Pleased to meet, you, Alun. I'm Detective-Inspector Giles Marston. I've been wanting to meet you for some time."

Alun was flabbergasted, then remembered that he had to look innocent and managed a squeaky "Why?" as his moustache finally fell off. This man must know that he had killed the real Nobby and the real Sid and he'd be in prison for life for the murder of three people, deception, obstructing the course of justice and more, he was sure.

Yet the officer just asked him to sit down so they could have a talk. Alun assented, almost falling into a large garden chair which had a large price-tag on it, announcing a price reduction from £79.99 to £50.00.

"Do you know what happened to Sid and Nobby?" he enquired.

Alun was finding the wig too hot now so – knowing he was doomed whatever – took it off. Then he shook his head, as the officer looked surprised at his new appearance.

As if to return the compliment, Marston took off the wig he was wearing, too, and they both found themselves laughing.

"We shouldn't laugh," Marston suddenly said, and re-assumed his serious face; so Alun did likewise.

"No, I don't know either of them, actually. It was Nathan I knew – the owner of this place… and a farm up the road." He did not say where it was as he did not want to draw attention to the digger and all the buried corpses.

"What happened to your wife, Dilys?"

"Well, we were estranged. I collected my stuff some weeks back and moved in with my lover. In London."

"Would that be the floozy?" Marston enquired, deadpan.

Alun was shocked: how did he know that? And who told him? But he had to reply, so said, "Er, well, yes... Well, that's what Dilys called her. But they never met, and it was all speculation as far as she was concerned." Marston nodded sagely, as if willing Alun to continue. He did: "So all I know is that Dilys was having an affair with this Nathan Grubb... but I wasn't bothered because I had Leini."

"Hmm... Were you going to divorce?"

"Erm, in due course, yes. But Dilys was resistant."

"For what reason?"

"I don't know," he lied.

"We think she's disappeared. Do you think she might have gone off with Nathan Grubb?"

"Disappeared? Oh... Well, it's possible... Probable, even. But I don't know. Although I did hear that Nathan had gone to Australia – perhaps Dilys went with him."

"Hmmm."

Alun could not divulge anything about her not being able to divorce him because of the sudden re-appearance of the 'dead' Norris Griffiths; also the real deaths of the two henchmen and the appearance and then similar demise of Sander. The Colombian side had to be kept away from everyone. As well as any reference to the legal papers, which would probably mean the appropriation of the two farms by the council for financial reparations – as well as lifelong prison sentences for murder meted out to them when they found the bodies. His intense assessment of the facts which he could toss in as red herrings were conflicting savagely with those he absolutely must not divulge – and this was giving him a headache – but his mental perambulations were interrupted by a stark question from the detective.

"Do you know who Sid and Nobby worked for?" Marston asked.

Alun sucked in his breath and shook his head, then: "I presumed it was Nathan Grubb," he lied again. "I did meet them once or twice at my property because Nathan was having an affair with my wife and I assumed they were helping him run the farm for Dilys."

"Hmm…. We have reason to believe that her first husband, Norris Griffiths, who died in suspicious circumstances when it was alleged he was embezzling council money – *and* running a prostitution and drugs racket – is still alive."

"I know nothing about that," Alun said emphatically, lying again. "Dilys certainly thought he was dead."

"Hmmm… So why are you in disguise and pretending to be a friend of Sid Prentice?"

Alun went to speak, then stopped: he didn't have a ready answer for that one.

*

When the two girls, Rosa and Maria, had returned to their sun-loungers, Luis moved closer to Leini and enquired, "So what is going on in Wales, then?"

"I was hoping you'd tell me," she replied uncertainly.

"Is that why you come here, then, for find out?" Leini nodded again.

Luis continued: "So… I cannot tell you much, too. Only that Sander seem to decide he not like the heat anymore and him disappeared… and Nicolas-Arturo gone to Wales to find out what happened but we not heard from him since. Nobby and Sid quiet, too. Worse, TV programme – you know, er… "

"*Jonquil's Journals.*"

"Si – this not got to where we are in …"

"Reality?"

"Si – reality. No yet… So no-one know what happened yet. Episode tomorrow, I think – but Colombian TV company no received yet for broadcast."

Thank God for that, thought Leini; *Not much time to send Luis packing, then.* "I know – it's all gone very quiet – and we can't write the TV programme without input from the boys on the ground in Wales," she stated boldly. That was, at least, true – even if it was all due to her and Alun…

There was a pause, then Luis looked at her and said, "It's get too hot here, if we don't keep bribe the police then all finished. And I be in prison for many years – with all others, *if* they still alive… which I now not sure."

"So… do you want out, then?" After a moment, Luis ruefully nodded. "I know nothing when I join here as driver. Is dangerous, now – I know people who want kill Nicolas-Arturo and take over his business…"

Yes, and we have, and I'm one of them, thought Leini. Then: "I might be able to help you," she said.

Luis looked at her quizzically. "How?" he retorted.

"Just trust me," she replied. "Remember, I was with Sander for a while – which is why you recognised me at the airport, of course – so I know a lot of what was going on. But that's why I'm here – to find out what's happened to *him*, Nicolas-Arturo and… well, Nobby and Sid, too. The trail has gone dead in Wales…" She shuddered slightly as she felt the impact of that statement: *dead in Wales*. That was all down to her and Alun – but Luis must never know that. So she quickly asked, "Is there an office, where Sander and Nicolas-Arturo worked?"

At that question, Luis looked at her more critically, then nodded, as if weighing up why he should tell her. Would she not have known that from when she was here last? Of course there was an office; this was a multi-million peso industry – although most of the dirty work was farmed out to agents and dealers in Bogotá, as the boss wanted to keep his home clean. Eventually, though, he asked: "Why you want to know?"

"Because I think you and I have similar objectives," she said archly.

*

"I could also ask you why *you're* disguised as Nobby Bowles," Alun ventured as a parry to Marston's question. Marston looked as confused as Alun had been when asked why he was purporting to be Sid Prentice.

"Because I was hoping the staff would be more open if they recognised one of Nathan's associates."

"Same here," Alun burst back, relieved at being able to use the same answer. "In fact, I think we're both trying to find out the same information," he added – although from a different perspective, he noted to himself.

"Tell me what you know," Marston probed.

Alun told him all he could without any reference to his knowing Nathan, Sander, or Norris Griffiths; nor his and Leini's use of the TV programme as a confirmation of what was going on in Wales for the benefit of the Colombian connection – especially as it was only recently he had realised he was part of that same intrigue when Leini had come clean regarding her involvement.

"Looks as if we've drawn a blank, then," Marston said resignedly at the end. "But what's happened to Nathan Grubb, your ex-wife and the two boys I still know not." Alun was not going to enlighten him, so informed the detective that he would try to find a manager to run the farm for its produce. Marston looked askew at him: "Why? What's so important about this Nathan Grubb's farm to you?"

Alun had to think quickly: "Because… out of respect for my wife, who really liked Grubb and wanted to help him make a success of it… I owe her that… and because if she had married him then I would have been due a share of its proceeds if sold. So I have an interest, albeit a distant one."

"That's very noble of you," said Marston with a hint of sarcasm.

"Well – yes; *and* I don't want to see all those beautiful crops go to waste – it would be ecological vandalism if we did…" Marston just looked at him, trying to work him out but then gave up and said, "Well, if you hear anything, let me know."

"Certainly. And if I come across any rumours about Norris

Griffiths then I'll be in touch, too." He did not mean this, of course; what he now knew about Norris Griffiths — thanks to the papers in the farmhouse loft — was the central part of his and Leini's plan.

"Thanks." And the decidedly unenlightened and increasingly morose detective left.

Alun was pleased his storyline prowess had enabled him to add some useless facts and avoid the important, incriminating ones; he hadn't told Marston anything that the man didn't know already — and that still remained precious little.

CHAPTER 40

L eini was facing Luis in Norris's – aka Nicolas-Arturo Garros, to Luis – office. She had carefully copied many of Norris's very relevant and indicting legal papers which they had hidden in their London flat and which she now had with her; she carefully told Luis that she could help him if he helped her, which would ultimately keep the police away from the estate and secure his future; without stating it too obviously, she also intimated that he could be the new Sander if he wanted. As long, of course, as he didn't ever come back, she added darkly. Luis looked at her quizzically, sensing she knew more than she was disclosing. So Leini elaborated: *if* that was the case, of course... But then it would be in a much safer environment – and he might even get to travel to Wales if he wanted to in the future. At this, his expression changed again: she suddenly wondered if she had said too much and he might twig at what she was getting at... but after she added it would be worth a lot of easy money for him, he dispelled his apparent doubts and smiled a big, glintingly golden smile. Also, sensing that she needed to see some more files and work things out, he left the office and went for a drink with the girls. After all, she did not seem to need any help from him: she even knew Nicolas-Arturo's computer passwords – how, he could not possibly fathom. Then he drove some product down to the dealers and did not return until well after the sun had set.

So when he did, she had a plan for him – an offer which she felt he could not refuse...

*

With the organic centre now devoid of people, Alun went into the office, eventually found the keys and, having worked out to which doors and windows they belonged, locked up the buildings as best he could; then he drove back to the farmhouse. He would return to the shop early next morning and only hoped that Leini had managed to find from Luis an unknown associate of Sid and Nobby who was privy to what was going on and could be bribed not to spill any beans – without being told why his friends were now no longer in charge. He looked at his encrypted messaging app and saw that she had, indeed, found someone not far from him who Nobby and Sid occasionally asked to run the farm or the organic centre when they were on manoeuvres. His name was Gethin – and he would turn out to be very helpful indeed...

*

Leini's hunch regarding Luis had been met with relief and approval: he would keep his position and – because Leini would be in control of things "until either Nicolas-Arturo or Sander returned" – he would not be primarily responsible for keeping the drug dealers supplied. Likewise, Maria and Rosa were given more of a free rein to leave the mansion should they want to – and she even promised them a car so they could escape from time to time. The only caveat was that they said nothing and never mentioned who they worked for or where they lived: most importantly, they must never bring anyone back. After all, Nicolas-Arturo and Sander wouldn't approve of that when they came back, would they? Yet while she wondered how long it would take them all to realise that they never would, she felt she had bought enough time to organise all the things she had to do...

The deal for Luis was that he had to use his contacts to introduce her to local counterfeiters and corrupt lawyers: she did not tell him why yet, but she needed them to change the names on the legal papers that had for so long lain in Dilys' attic without Alun's knowledge. Also, just as importantly, to create new passports and identity cards for her and Alun so that bank details could be changed and their new wealth diverted from Norris Griffiths' accounts into their own. Although Luis was wary, he agreed readily enough when Leini offered him a big one-off amount and raised his pay.

She had been in touch with Alun every day and he had, by now, met Gethin, who had been glad of the work and was delighted to become the new manager of Nathan's farm. He was also offered free residency there in virtual perpetuity – provided that he maintained it well and agreed to it still belonging to Nathan's estate... which would remain a secret to him as Alun and Leini were going to keep that for themselves, of course: all it would take was the scheduled re-arrangement of the deeds, which Luis was already sorting out under Leini's tutelage...

Gethin was also tasked with finding a manager for the organic centre, and had quickly introduced Alun to a loyal friend of his called Myrddin – a fellow Celt who shared Gethin's rusty colouring and strong work ethic.

Ten days later, with all the arrangements made, all the documents changed and no major hiccups with dealers, lawyers or the law, Leini informed Luis that she was returning to London and asked him to book her a flight under her new passport name, Isabella Durante. She had had fun choosing a Colombian name for Alun's new identity and eventually came up with Sander Lozano. After all, she had liked that name once... She then got Luis to take her into town to choose some clothes for her change of identity to look the part for her flight to London and their return trip which, she assured them all, would be soon; she wanted them to meet her partner...

So, with their names on the deeds, it was now virtually assured that control of Norris Griffiths' shady empire would forever rest with them.

What they had not bargained for was Gloria Cordobes.

*

When Gloria Cordobes had tweaked the script, she had ensured that Edmund had survived – whereas originally Alun, aka Edmund in the series, had been murdered and so written out – Alun's discreet way of saying he would soon not be back. Jonquil, of course – aka Norris – could not be written out as he was the eponymous star of the show. So if his real death had been implied, it would have caused confusion in Colombia because Jonquil's parallel character was Norris Griffiths – aka Nicolas-Arturo Garros – whom Gloria was still unaware was now dead... But Leini had now learned that some corrupt officers in the Colombian police watched *Jonquil's Journals*, too... So unbeknown to Gloria this time, Leini had tweaked the script back again: they would not now be expecting a change of drug baron.

She was also aware that Sid and Nobby – Zaccheus and Abel – needed to have closure and wrote the following scenes, which would not be seen for several weeks and would give her and Alun some extra time…

Again, thanks to Leini, it was all in the script.

JONQUIL'S JOURNALS:
EPISODE 161. SCENE 6. THE TAVERN. INT. DAY.

	ABEL AND ZACCHEUS – THE FORMER WITH A BROKEN AND BANDAGED ARM, THE LATTER WITH A DIRTY, BLOODY RAG TIED AROUND HIS HEAD – ARE DRINKING ALE. BOTH ARE SUBDUED, FURTIVE AND FEELING SORRY FOR THEMSELVES. THE TAVERN IS NOT BUSY…
ABEL:	I fink we should find another tavern where nobody knows us… What 'appens if that Edmund comes in and sees us?
ZACCHEUS:	We'll follow 'im and smash 'im up.
ABEL:	Unless 'e does it to us first. We wuz lucky before, that that little Jenny come in and distracted 'im.
ZACCHEUS:	Yeah…
	THEY DESPONDENTLY LOOK INTO THEIR ALES. IN THE BACKGROUND, WE SEE JENNY – NOW DRESSED NOT AS A LADY BUT LIKE HER USUAL OCCUPATION - NOTICE THEM AND

SHE HAS A QUICK CHAT WITH DULCE, WHO NODS, AND THEN JENNY LEAVES PURPOSEFULLY. AFTER A MOMENT, DULCE COMES OVER TO THEM.

DULCE: 'Ello, boys... What 'appened to you two, then? (THEY DON'T ANSWER). Oooh... must be somefing naughty, then. (COQUETTISHLY). But I could make you happy... Any takers?

ABEL: We'd love to, Dulcie, but we ain't been paid for a job we did...

DULCE: Or didn't?

ZACCHEUS: What j'ou mean?

DULCE: There's not much that I don't see 'ere. I 'eard you muffed a job for 'is lordship, Jonquil...

ABEL: 'Oo told you that?

DULCE: My little friend, Jenny.

ABEL: The little witch!

DULCE: No... she were only doing what she were told to. Us girls 'ave to take our opportunities when we can... She's upstairs, actually...

ABEL: So?

DULCE: She's always liked you, Abel...

ABEL: But she's betrothed to 'is lordhip Jonquil!

DULCE: Well, yeah... but the knot ain't been tied yet and she needs to keep in practice in case the old boy snuffs it or changes 'is mind... I'm sure she'd love to see you... Tell you what... Sander's not 'ere so we're running the place by ourselves at the moment. So... If you go and 'ave 'er, I'll give you, Zac, a free one.

We're not busy and I'm bored… What d'you say?

THEY LOOK AT EACH OTHER.

ABEL: (HAPPILY). Yeah… all right!

DULCE: Ooh! Lovely! Follow me, boys…

SHE PRANCES OFF – THEY FOLLOW HER UPSTAIRS.

JONQUIL'S JOURNALS:

EPISODE 161. SCENE 7. AN UPSTAIRS ROOM. INT. DAY.

THEY ENTER THE ROOM. THERE IS NO SIGN OF JENNY BUT DULCE STARTS TO UNDRESS FOR ZAC. SHE IS JUST ABOUT TO TAKE OFF HER TOP WHEN SHE LOOKS AT ABEL.

DULCE: 'Ere, Abel… This is private between me and Zac… why don't you wait outside for Jenny? I know she'll be along in a moment. Go on…!

RELUCTANTLY, HE LEAVES THE ROOM. DULCE CONTINUES DIVESTING HER GARMENTS AS ZAC STARTS TO DO THE SAME…

JONQUIL'S JOURNALS:

EPISODE 161. SCENE 8. WIGGINS' PARLOUR. INT. DAY.

EDMUND IS POLISHING SILVER WHEN THE AREA DOOR BURSTS OPEN AND JENNY CALLS TO HIM.

JENNY: Edmund – quick! They're at the tavern!

EDMUND COLLECTS HIS CUDGEL FROM THE PANTRY AND RUSHES OUT WITH HER...

JONQUIL'S JOURNALS:

EPISODE 161. SCENE 9. AN UPSTAIRS ROOM. INT. DAY.

ZAC AND DULCE ARE IN FLAGRANTE DELICTO.

JONQUIL'S JOURNALS:

EPISODE 161. SCENE 10. THE TAVERN. INT. DAY.

JENNY RUSHES IN WITH EDMUND. JENNY GOES STRAIGHT UPSTAIRS BUT EDWARD WAITS A MOMENT, HIS CUDGEL HIDDEN UNDER HIS COAT.

JONQUIL'S JOURNALS:

EPISODE 161. SCENE 11. UPSTAIRS PASSAGEWAY. INT. DAY.

JENNY SEES ABEL WAITING OUTSIDE AND STARTS TO CARESS HIM, THEN OPENS THE DOOR AND PUSHES HIM INTO THE SAME ROOM AS DULCE AND ZAC, WHO CONTINUE LOVEMAKING REGARDLESS. THEN SHE FURTIVELY RETURNS TO THE END OF THE CORRIDOR AND BECKONS EDMUND. SHE DISAPPEARS INTO THE ROOM AS EDMUND APPEARS AND SHE SHUTS THE DOOR. EDMUND LISTENS AT THE DOOR, BRANDISHING HIS CUDGEL.

JONQUIL'S JOURNALS:

EPISODE 161. SCENE 12. AN UPSTAIRS ROOM. INT. DAY.

JENNY JOINS ABEL ON THE SAME BIG BED AND STARTS UNDRESSING HIM. WITH BOTH MEN PRE-OCCUPIED, JENNY WINKS AT DULCE…

DULCE: Ooh!! Lovely! (AND CONTINUES MOLESTING ABEL. THERE ARE THE USUAL SOUNDS OF CARNAL ENDEAVOUR FOR A MOMENT… THEN, REALISING AN OPTIMAL MOMENT, LOUDLY). Ooh, I love a coach and four!

ZACCHEUS: (JAUNTILY). Who's the coach?

SUDDENLY, ON THIS CUE, THE DOOR SPRINGS OPEN AND EDMUND RUSHES IN, BRANDISHING HIS CUDGEL.

EDMUND: I am!

AND BRINGS HIS CUDGEL DOWN ONTO ZAC'S HEAD; THEN, AS HE SLUMPS, EDMUND DOES THE SAME TO ABEL. SUDDENLY, THE GIRLS PUT THEIR CLOTHES BACK ON AND ALL THREE ROLL UP THE BODIES OF ZAC AND ABEL INTO THE BEDCLOTHES. NOTHING IS SAID… THEN THE BODIES ARE PUT UNDER THE BED…

(TO JENNY). Well, done, my poppet… And you, dear Dulcie… Carry on with your work and I'll remove the bodies during the night. Here… (AND HE GIVES EACH OF THEM £10). I must go, before his lordship misses me.

JENNY: I'd better come with you before he misses me, too!

THEY GO. DULCE TIDIES HER
CLOTHING AND STARTS PUTTING SOME
DIFFERENT SHEETS ONTO THE BED…

*

Alun met Leini at the airport but she had not informed him she
would be arriving as her new alias, which caused him some confusion
and embarrassment when a beautiful Latino-looking lady walked up
to him in Arrivals and gave him a big kiss. She had dyed her hair and
– having become suntanned – had a very different look to the blonde
beauty who had recently left him in London.

They quickly went home and made love – Alun relishing the idea
of it being the same woman but with a completely new appearance,
as if she were another conquest. On her way into the flat, she had
noticed two large suitcases already packed in the hallway and was
pleased to see he had been busily preparing for a hasty exit …

After they had exhausted their lust, she showed him the new
documents, his Colombian passport and new citizenship card – his
Cédula de Ciudadanía – all of which had been corroborated on the
documents.

It seemed that nothing could possibly go wrong.

CHAPTER 41

The next morning, Gloria picked up her phone and said that – now they were back – she would like to see Alun and Leini in her office as soon as practical, just to catch up with a few things since their holiday in Mauritius. But the meeting would not be with Jonathan: she had some issues to talk about which would not concern him.

When they arrived in her office, she was surprised that Leini looked tanned whereas Alun appeared to have spent a holiday somewhere cold and sunless like Alaska …

She came straight to the point. "I know what's going on," she stated bluntly. Alun and Leini looked at her blankly.

"About what?" ventured Alun, with a hint of nervousness in his voice.

"Everything."

Alun looked at Gloria uncomprehendingly but with a rising sense of panic.

As there was nothing forthcoming from either him or Leini, Gloria decided to put her cards on the table. "As you know, when I took over here three years ago, Tellurian TV was on a knife-edge. You – Alun – and Jonathan, had already started to save the company with *Jonquil's Journals*, which you created with the previous owner here, Sam Powell, before I arrived. But it wasn't enough to get the company financially back into shape, so – and this must never be repeated or there'll be consequences – " as she gave them a severe look – "I knew someone who was in need of laundering some money. A lot of money. I'd met him when I was a production assistant at a TV company in Bogotà. The fact that it was a Colombian drugs dealer was the unethical bit, but I had fallen in love with him – well, his money, lifestyle – and we became an item. He

246

had not only put money into *that* TV company but also wanted a way of knowing how things were going in his dealings over here, discreetly, without raising any suspicions. So he sent me over here to Tellurian TV to make Sam Powell an offer he couldn't refuse on the condition that he took me on as CEO and that *Jonquil's Journals* became a parody of what was going on here in this country – so he would know over there that things were ticking over OK. So Sam Powell went to live the life of Reilly in Spain. And that's where you came in, Leini. You had met Sander – Nicolas-Arturo's go-between with me here in London and him near Bogotà – at a party here, I think, and he – seeing you were highly intelligent and very beautiful – recommended to Nicolas-Arturo that you were made Jonathan's assistant to ensure that the scripts stayed relevant, informative and on track. Which is why I tasked you with seducing Alun, who would obviously never know about this deal."

Alun suddenly felt a burst of anger and delusion sweep up his body and was about to explode when Leini's hand shot to his crotch and squeezed it tightly, as a sign to keep quiet. But he was still furious – he hated being deceived – as well as the fact that Leini's love was not real but all part of a very dodgy plot. He went to protest, despite Leini's hand crushing his manhood ever more tightly – but Gloria put up her hand to silence him and continued. "Alun, that was the plan – but everything changed when Leini fell in love with *you* – as I had done with Nicolas-Arturo Garros."

"You mean Norris Griffiths," Alun blurted in a slight falsetto, Leini's hand still tightly grasping his nether regions. Gloria nodded, with a hint of a smile. His heart sank. She must know that they had murdered him. But she continued with: "Strangely, he seems to have suddenly disappeared... but I don't care – I started to hate him for all the things he was doing ruining people's lives... except mine, of course, which he improved beyond all belief." She then went quiet, as Leini again squeezed Alun's hand quickly multiple times, as if pleading with him to stay quiet. Gloria, now somewhat subdued by her trusting revelations and perhaps a sense of apprehension, looked down at her desk and continued. "I never knew he was Welsh at the start, of course; by the time I met him, his Spanish was good – although I always wondered why his accent was so very odd." She smiled a distant smile. "Anyway, Leini had by then just started working here and was going out with Sander."

"So you *did* know about us, then?" Leini hazarded; "I thought you said…"

Gloria looked at Leini. "As you and I know, Leini, your affair with Sander was awkward… but none of us expected you to fall for Alun" – Alun felt as if he wanted to hit her for saying that – "but it was good you did as the scripts became subtler – but also more informative."

Alun was puce with rage by now – he was the award-winning scriptwriter who had created the show without much help from Jonathan, who was little more than a passenger as far as originating storylines was concerned. But Gloria was right about one thing: Leini had given the show an edge which it had not had before – improved by his lust and subsequent love for her, so he said nothing.

It was then that Leini spoke, with a tone of finality - as if trying to wrap things up: "So it all worked out well, then… For all of us," and she gave Alun a sweet smile. "We're getting married, too." Alun darted a look at her. "Are we?" he asked, his fury turning to delight. Then: "We haven't talked about that. And we couldn't anyway because Dilys wouldn't divorce me."

"Well, she's dead now, isn't she?" Gloria said to Alun with a curious smile playing about her lips.

"So you *do* know everything, then?"

Gloria nodded. "I would think so," she added, "And of *course* I know what's been going on – I've obviously read all the scripts before anyone else has! And I often change them, too," she stated. "You, Alun, think it's Leini or Jonathan – but often it's me. But by the time you get to see the show a few weeks after it's been written and recorded, you're already creating scripts for several episodes ahead. So you never notice…"

Alun felt deflated again but strangely optimistic: he had never realised what a good team they were – and especially that Gloria knew everything. No wonder Leini seemed to have a direct line to her when necessary. Yet one thing niggled him: she had not mentioned Nobby and Sid, who were presumably part of the same set-up. He was about to ask, when Leini – obviously not wanting anything more divulged or discussed, very pointedly said, "Well, that's a load off all our minds, then." Alun felt she was hedging, so gave her a look but she just mouthed a silent 'Shoosh' as Gloria was looking away to get up.

"So now you know all of the details… let's carry on," said Gloria. "The ratings are up, and – oh, yes: Alun – you'll see that your parallel character, Edmund, will marry Jenny – who, as you know, is Leini!" Alun looked flabbergasted: he had hoped to write that scene soon but had not dared to do so as he had lacked the confidence to ask Leini for her hand. "Really?" he gulped.

Gloria nodded once again and just said: "Of course – it's all in the script!"

*

"She *thinks* she knows everything – but she doesn't," said Leini tersely and sotto voce when they were out of earshot and on their way back to the office. "She doesn't know that Nobby and Sid are no more – if she ever knew of them anyway, or how they disappeared. And she certainly doesn't know anything about Nathan's farm, or where the bodies are… or the legal papers… and absolutely nothing about our future plans." This last point was embellished with a big grin. Alun did not see it, though, being immersed in the things he had only just learned, adding contemptuously, "And she obviously couldn't care two hoots for Norris-Nicolas-Arturo-Griffiths-Garros either."

"Thank goodness for that," Leini concurred, "or things would get very complicated."

"You're right," Alun agreed. "It would make things *very* complicated. But it seems odd that she doesn't know Sander is dead – judging by what she *didn't* say…"

"Oh, he *isn't* dead," Leini shot back lightly with a smile.

"What d'you mean? Of course he is, I – "

She put her finger to her lips, leaned in to him and whispered, "She doesn't know he's dead – she thinks he's still running things from Bogotà. But the point is that *you're* Sander now. Or soon will be."

The penny dropped. "Ah, I see. Blimey, you're a canny one: mind you, I didn't know she didn't know that – Sander not being dead, I mean."

"Of course you didn't. Gloria thinks she's running the show. But she's not – it's me."

Alun stopped in his tracks, stupefied. "What d'you mean, *you?*"

"Well, I mean... *me*. And now you, of course. I just couldn't tell you everything."

"You mean, you've been running me all along?"

She giggled. "Pretty much." Then: "Let's go home and make love – all this has made me feel really randy."

Alun did not refuse. How could he? She almost knew more about him than he did himself – even if he was sure it was *he* who had instigated the plan without telling Leini; but perhaps she had pre-empted him anyway. It didn't matter either way: they were on the same page and it only accentuated what a wonderful individual Leini was... and what a great team they were together. How he loved her.

CHAPTER 42

In Wales, Gethin and Myrddin were quickly restoring the fortunes of both Nathan's farm and his organic produce store, rendering Detective-Inspector Marston's case redundant and the shop's staff able to sell produce again – much to the annoyance of those who were rather enjoying their salaries without the need to do any work. Gethin proved himself a worthy manager and farmer early on – and was far savvier than the man he was supposedly filling in for in Australia.

In Colombia, Luis, Rosa and Maria had been schooled in the minutiae of running the clandestine business via secure satellite social media platforms which Leini had set up before returning to England – and would never have been thought of by an out-of-touch bent ex-council leader such as Norris; as a bonus, *Jonquil's Journals* was now a huge hit in Colombia, too, thanks to Gloria's contacts and marketing – and not just a tool for a corrupt ex-council leader. What Gloria had not realised, though, was that it further advanced the finalisation of Alun and Leini's plan ...

Yet there were still many objectives to navigate: although the doctored legal files had been accepted by the Colombian authorities with little demur – not wanting to risk having such a lucrative business move to any other South American country – several complications were encountered by the Welsh administrations, which demanded many more 'sustifications', as the local dignitary called them. It all seemed too much for them in that, although Alun could be proved the rightful owner of the farm upon the eventually-accepted disappearance of Dilys, the addition of Nathan's farm – because she was his lover but Alun had left her – caused a fog of bureaucratic obfuscation. It was only when Alun inserted another paragraph into the bogus legal deeds, offering Gethin permanent rights of abode at the farm unless Nathan suddenly re-appeared, that they agreed, fitting well into their socialist ideology: whether it was strictly legal or not they cared little – the ghost of Norris lived on: it was also their way of virtue-signalling their supposedly kind, progressive beliefs...

*

JONQUIL'S JOURNALS:

EPISODE 168. SCENE 4. INT. A SMALL CHURCH. DAY.

	A LARGE CROWD OF WELL-DRESSED PEOPLE ARE PRESENT, AS THEY QUIETLY AND HAPPILY LISTEN TO THE WEDDING CEREMONY TAKING PLACE BETWEEN JENNY AND EDMUND BEFORE THEM. WE CUT TO A CLOSE-UP OF THE DRUNKEN, THUNDEROUS-LOOKING FACE OF JONQUIL IN HIS FAMILY PEW, FURIOUS AT WHAT IS GOING ON IN FRONT OF HIM.
VICAR:	I require and charge you both, as ye will answer at the dreadful day of judgement, when the secrets of all hearts shall be disclosed, that if either of you know any impediment why ye may not be lawfully joined together in Matrimony, ye do now confess it. For be ye well assured –
JONQUIL:	(STANDING UP DRUNKENLY – AND WE NOW SEE HE IS CARRYING A HALF-EMPTY BOTTLE OF CLARET). I do! (THE CROWD MURMURS WORRIEDLY). I do! She's mine, the hussy! I pledged her my troth!
VICAR:	Good sir... Sir Bartholomew!... please sit down and be silent! This is the marriage ceremony!
JONQUIL:	But I love her – I gave her my fortune...!
VICAR:	That may be so, Sir – but this is not the time or place to raise an objection! That should

have been at the banns three weeks ago!

JONQUIL: Banns? What banns?

VICAR: Those administered three weeks ago, sir, as I said.

JONQUIL: But I wasn't there – so how did I know?

VICAR: I am afraid it's too late to object – the service has started, sir.

JONQUIL: But I'm a justice of the peace... I... peace... Ohhh... (HE COLLAPSES BACK ONTO HIS PEW). Peace... oh, I think I'm... peaced... (AND COLLAPSES TOTALLY ON THE FLOOR. THERE IS A SMATTERING OF LAUGHTER, WHICH EVENTUALLY GROWS IN VOLUME AND INTENSITY AS JENNY AND EDMUND LOOK ON, LAUGHING).

VICAR: (CLAPPING HIS HANDS FOR SILENCE). Silence, please! This is a house of God! Let us resume... (AND RESUMES THE SERVICE AS CALM DESCENDS ONCE MORE).

VICAR: I require and charge you both, as ye will answer at the dreadful day of judgement, when the secrets of all hearts shall be disclosed, that if either of you know any impediment, why ye may not be lawfully joined together in Matrimony, ye do now confess it. For be ye well assured (CASTING A LOOK BACK AT THE COMATOSE JONQUIL) that so many as are coupled together otherwise than God's Word doth allow are not joined together by God; neither is their Matrimony lawful.

THE WORDS FADE OUT AS WE **MIX TO**: A CLOUDLESS DEEP BLUE SKY...

EPILOGUE

It was a beautiful hot, sunny day with azure skies when Alun and Leini were married at a church in Putney a few months later. This became a media event in itself – even Lottie Brace deigned to turn up: as a previous star of the show, she aimed for the light wherever it shone brightest to address her adoring fans. As for Charlton Horthorne, he was so well inebriated that he had collapsed in his pew before the ring even went on the finger: an example of fact and fantasy eliding perfectly …

*

The magical, mystical mountains majestically stood out in the distance against a deeply azure sky, and the brightly-hued wildlife sang and squawked as they blurred the blue with searing dabs of coruscating colour. The wedding ceremony in their Colombian mansion was being attended by a smattering of local dignitaries and fearful cartel bosses, all of whom had signed a non-aggression clause to attend the wedding of Señora Isabella Durante and a certain Señor Sander Lozano… who looked nothing like the original Sander – which was why Gloria had not been invited…

A day or two later, after the celebrations, Alun and Leini went into the late Norris Griffiths' study and started writing the plotlines for the continuing saga of *Jonquil's Journals,* which Gloria would be expecting back at Tellurian TV. The show had now become a global success thanks to her edict that there was now to be no narrative inhibition – for without the necessity of reflecting events back in Britain, any supposed once-essential connections were now a hostage to fortune and soon written out. The upshot was that the show would now have an unusual global 18th century slant, more deeply reflecting the priorities, events and social attitudes of the time: this made it ever more popular. Indeed, with the exception of the lead character, Bartholomew Jonquil, the others – and the direction the

stories could now go in – would be very different from now on…

Alun and Leini were now rich beyond belief and had managed to semi-legally become two separate couples in two different countries within the same two skins: dual nationality with a difference. And with the farms in Wales, a flat in London and an estate and mansion in Colombia, life was good… as long as the ghosts of those buried in Nathan's farm never rose above the surface…

But for anyone viewing past episodes of *Jonquil's Journals*, it was still… all in the script…

Parallels:

Real life in novel:	In Jonquil's Journals:
Dilys	Mrs Hattie Wiggins
Alun Loyd	Edmund Wiggins
Nathan Grubb	Jonas Orchard
Norris Griffiths	Bartholomew Jonquil
Leini	Jenny – Maid, very young and pretty (and previously whore from London Bridge).
Nobby Bowles and Sid Prentice	Abel Price and Zaccheus
Sander	Sander Montoya
Gethin and Myrddin – Nathan farm managers.	
Maria and Rosa	
Luis – driver and manager in Colombia	

ABOUT THE AUTHOR

Simon worked for many years in broadcast television at London Weekend Television, Sky, Channel 4 and the BBC as a Producer, Director and Writer. His interests are classical music and opera, prog-rock, walking, rugby union and the importance of history and free speech. He now lives in Wiltshire with his wife, Xiaomei.